Laughing as they Chased Us

Laughing as they Chased Us

Sarah Jackman

LONDON • SYDNEY • NEW YORK • TORONTO

First published in Great Britain by Pocket Books, 2005
An imprint of Simon & Schuster UK Ltd
A Viacom company

1 3 5 7 9 10 8 6 4 2

Simon & Schuster UK Ltd
Africa House
64–78 Kingsway
London WC2B 6AH

www.simonsays.co.uk

Simon & Schuster Australia
Sydney

A CIP catalogue record for this book is available from the British Library

ISBN 0-7434-8934-9

EAN 9780743489348

Typeset in Garamond by
Palimpsest Book Production Limited,
Polmont, Stirlingshire
Printed and bound in Great Britain by
Bookmarque Ltd, Croydon, Surrey

To my sister, Claire

acknowledgements

Thanks to Mark Illis, Siri Hansen, Teresa Chris and Rochelle Venables for their encouragement and advice. Special thanks to Dean, family and friends.

contents

1

wake up

Cecillie carries a bowl of coffee, her first cigarette of the day, the lighter and her comb out to the balcony. She places the bowl carefully on the floor, then sits down beside it, shivering at the cold stone on her bare skin as she dangles her legs through the iron railings.

The ashy scent of the coffee wafting up from beside her is tantalizing but it's still too hot to drink. Cecillie's been in France for nearly six weeks now and it's one of the smells she associates with her life here. It drifts out from the cafés and bars into the streets and of course, it's the most important part of her morning ritual. She loves setting the battered enamel coffee pot to bubble away on the stove while she showers. Still wearing her towel, she adds milk and heaps brown sugar into the bowl, whipping up thick foam with the tiny metal whisk she discovered in a drawer in her kitchenette.

The first week in the apartment was full of such discoveries: the wooden contraption which hooks over the balcony rails for drying clothes, the long pillow that's like a huge draught excluder (she's bought a new pillow case and drawn a smiling face on each end with a green felt pen), the metal square on the wall which pulls down to reveal a rather misty but ornate mirror and which snaps back into place once the catch is released. She's fond of these treasures, knowing that these things would never be found in rented rooms anywhere else on the planet but France.

Below, cars are beginning to move up and down the street. She can hear the revvings and grindings and stop-startings: their exhaust fumes are already filtering into the warm air. This is her favourite time to watch the city; as it heaves itself into the business of the day, while she comes to at a more leisurely pace. Cecillie rests her face against the railings, slowly blowing smoke back at the cars.

Through her open French windows, Cecillie can hear the house is waking up too. The water pipes are clattering, old Monsieur Pasquet from over the landing is having his morning cough and her neighbour, Max, is singing along to some schmaltzy French music.

Briefly, Cecillie joins in – la-la-ing along – her voice high and rather tuneless, until she hears the heavy front door bang. She looks down on the brown, bald head streaked with meagre strands of black hair which belongs to the waddling body of her landlord, Monsieur Bayard, on his morning outing to buy bread.

When he crosses the road, he glances up at her balcony and waves. She waves back and laughs. She always laughs when she sees him, she can't help it.

A minute later, the waiter from the café a few doors down passes by. She waves to him, too. He's sweet, always picking out the biggest *pain au chocolat* for her whenever she goes in.

Every day Cecillie waves to lots of people from up on her lookout, but what gives her the biggest kick is when the buzzer goes in her apartment, and she runs out to shout hello, come on up. It's only been Bryony so far, and once Blythe from downstairs when he forgot his key. But she imagines new friends, a lover, loads of people, calling for her and she'll look down on them like Juliet and say: Hi, come on in.

As Monsieur Bayard goes into the *boulangerie*, she sees his dumpy profile for a moment in the doorway. In the evenings he sits with Claude at the back of the baker's, both plumped heavily in their chairs, talking earnestly; table-pounding, world politics stuff. She's seen them there, really getting stuck in with a bottle of Ricard to keep them company. But in the mornings, because Claude's wife is serving – the dragon, Monsieur Bayard calls her – he reappears quickly, with his bread tucked under one armpit and his free hand busy keeping his hair in place. Then – this is the best bit – when he's underneath her balcony, he checks his bread is secure, raises the other arm and performs an elaborate bow. Cecillie, like a queen acknowledging her people, inclines her head and doesn't raise it until she hears the bang of the closing door.

After that, her day can go anywhere. Now that she's finished her afternoons at the college, she has nothing to do the whole day. She thought she'd get bored but she hasn't yet; the weather's been sunny most days and hours slip by without her noticing when she's on the beach. Sometimes, at lunchtime, Cecillie meets Bryony and the boys she au-pairs for, and accompanies them on a walk, other times she explores the city.

This morning, though, is different. She has important matters to attend to. First she must get the bus to the Post Office for her money, then go and buy the moped; her perfect, yellow moped. Soon she'll be able to ride around the city, stopping whenever the mood grabs her. It'll be great. Nothing will be out of her reach.

In the time that Cecillie's been here, she's taken possession of her apartment, of her street, even her landlord. By possession, what she means, quite simply, is that she feels she's made a difference by being here. She's the girl in a bikini on the balcony, she's the new tenant, she's the English neighbour and Bryony's friend. She's all of these things and more.

Now she's ready to take on the city.

Everywhere she goes people are laughing, kissing, shouting. There's an excitement from which she's excluded. She feels it on her skin as she brushes through the crowds; she hears the whispering inside the houses and offices and catches the scent of it mingling with the wafts of coffee and fresh baking. The city's hiding its secrets from her and she so very much wants to uncover them. When she goes out in the day, she watches, when she goes out at night, she waits. She's tense with the anticipation that something is around the corner, that something *big* is going to happen.

She's made one discovery and holds it as her measure for what's to come. She's found out where the best beaches are; the ones that locals flood to in their cars, distancing themselves from the tourists. She plans to lie back and be surrounded by French, not English voices. When she looks up she'll see tanned, serious French skin; not the red, peeling backs of holiday-happy British. Her moped is going to take her there.

Cecillie stubs out her cigarette on the stone, finishes her coffee and combs her hair quickly. As it falls onto her shoulders it looks very blonde against her tan. She admires the deepening colour on her long legs, her flat stomach where the brownest skin forms a narrow circle around her belly button. She spreads her fingers out and looks at the white v's between each one, she raises her feet so she can see the same whiteness between her toes.

She's grateful that the old Cecillie of England is disappearing so quickly, but just as she's thinking that, she remembers that she's been meaning to write to her grandmother. She quickly composes a note in her head. She'll buy a postcard later.

Dear Gran. Today I bought a moped – bright yellow!! From a very fat man who doesn't want it because he fell off – too fat! I've got two English friends here, but I promise I'm still practising my French. I can say lots of words now! You'd be impressed! It's been sunny here for ages and I'm getting very brown!! Will write soon. Miss you. Lots of Love Cecillie XXX.

She stands up and collects everything together. Next door, Max's windows open and his yellowy-white poodle noses its way out. Its claws make a tacking sound on the stone.

'Hello, Dog,' Cecillie calls, but it ignores her and quickly squats down, depositing a small turd on the floor before scampering inside. She gets a whiff of it before she makes it into her apartment. As she's locking the windows, she watches Max come out, glance briefly at the street below before flicking the dog shit over the edge with a rolled-up newspaper.

She checks in her bag for her purse and map and adds her lighter and the packet of cigarettes. She puts on shorts and a T-shirt over her bikini, and trainers without any socks. In the kitchen she washes everything up and leaves it to dry on the metal drainer before taking a last look around the apartment to check that it's all tidy.

She runs down all the stairs and almost into her landlord who's standing in the front hallway.

'Goodbye, dear girl,' he calls after her.

'See you later, Monsieur Bayard,' she shouts from the open door, and waves.

Frédérique's mobile is frantically ringing in her handbag on the passenger seat. She fishes it out. It's the gallery's number.

'I've just had Hervé on the phone,' Fernand tells her without preamble when she answers. 'Giving me hell about you being late.'

'What?'

'He's been expecting you since nine.'

Frédérique is positive that she doesn't have any appointments for this morning but her boss pre-empts the question. 'It's in the diary, I'm looking at it now,' he tells her.

'I'm on my way,' she says, flustered, glancing in the mirrors to assess her chance of doing a u-turn. 'I'll ring him immediately.'

Frédérique bangs the palm of her hand against the steering wheel and resists the urge to swear. She must have forgotten to transpose the day's information into her personal organizer again.

'Be warned. He's not in a good mood – he bit my head off.'

'Hang on,' Frédérique tells Fernand as she noses her car into the next lane so that she can take the first left. She turns sharply into a side street and shoots through a couple of back roads until she's heading in the opposite direction.

'Sweeten him up,' Fernand is saying, as she presses the phone against her ear. 'I get the impression that he's feeling a bit neglected.'

Frédérique notes the gentle criticism and flushes. She's guilty as charged. She believes Hervé's painting has become stale, but she's been avoiding him instead of confronting the issue; for who's to say that it isn't her own flagging interest which is to blame?

When she gets through to Hervé, she apologizes for the delay and quickly checks the clock, weighing up what is a realistic time to arrive, against what will sound acceptable.

'I'll be there in twenty minutes.' She senses the irritation on the other end of the line. 'Probably less,' she puts in quickly. 'I'm bringing the prints,' she tells Hervé, remembering suddenly that she has with her the postcard set of his paintings which arrived from the printers earlier this week. 'And I think you're going to be really pleased,' she adds, knowing this will hook his interest and buy his patience.

The traffic is kind to her until she hits the streets near Fernand's studio where there's double parking everywhere. On the main street, Frédérique joins a queue at the traffic lights. She taps the wheel in irritation.

Ahead, the lights go green and as she drives forward, a car pulls out from the kerb straight in front of her so that she has to slam the brakes on, missing its bumper by centimetres. Her body's flung back against the seat and she sits there, heart pumping, the engine stalled.

A car horn sounds behind her, a few short beeps, then a longer blast when she fails to get moving straight away. Several cars join in the hooter protest, forcing her into action. As she pulls off she notices the space left by the offending car and swerves in, ignoring the gesticulations from the driver behind her as he passes.

She straightens the car up and, exhaling slowly, lets her good luck sink in. She's virtually outside Hervé's place and when she looks at the time, finds that only ten minutes have elapsed since they spoke.

She opens her briefcase and takes out her personal organizer, flicking quickly to today's date. She stares at the appointment written in red, puzzling over her failure to have noticed it; particularly as the rest of the page is blank.

An adrenaline rush from the near miss gives her a sudden high and she comforts herself: So? Nobody's perfect! She's been going through a bad patch but she'll make it up to Fernand, she decides, starting from when she gets back.

'Yes,' she says out loud, firmly.

On the back of her optimism, she finds a pen and begins to note down everything she has to do. She pauses to prioritize the tasks and her elation evaporates as she contemplates the long list with despair. Where to start?

It seems – as always – an impossible mountain to climb. For months now, she's felt as if she's drowning at work. She swallows hard as the familiar panic begins to rise. It's not only her job which she's messing up. Last week she sent her mother a birthday card, not remembering that she'd already posted one. When she went over for a meal with them, she'd endured her father's weak jokes about her forgetfulness throughout the evening and, even worse, her mother's soft-spoken concern.

Frédérique bites on the end of her pen. She tries to pinpoint when it had started to go wrong and settles on the occasion of her thirty-seventh birthday four months ago, which she spent alone, from choice, in her flat, with the answer phone switched on. She had simply wanted the world to pause long enough for her to catch up.

It seems to be a concrete moment, but deceptive. Her breath catches with the force of the revelation but she knows immediately that this was not the first but only another sign of what she persistently refuses to label with the unsatisfactory word 'depression'.

She is closing the organizer when it dawns on her that she hadn't checked her day's schedule over breakfast as she normally would because she'd been at Jacques's place. If she needed further evidence of what a mistake it had been to spend the night with him, this was it. She could kick herself for being so weak.

Before she went round yesterday evening, she had made the decision not to stay unless they had established where their relationship was heading. At several points in the evening, she'd been convinced that such a discussion was imminent but as it transpired – once again – neither of them had broached the subject.

But she hadn't gone home, after all.

Frédérique pulls down the car mirror and looks at her reflection.

Who's she kidding?

She'd been as guilty of forestalling the discussion last night as Jacques had of ignoring it; he'd seemed relaxed and at ease with her company and she'd let herself go along with the mood of the evening. And this morning she's relieved she did, because, if she's honest, she's nowhere near having her head straight about what she wants from Jacques.

If he were to ring this minute, Frédérique thinks, glancing at her mobile, and ask for her opinion on the matter, she would struggle to formulate one. It's not that she's having trouble pinning down her emotions; it's that she can't make herself feel anything at all. If only he would tell her what he thinks, she's sure that would trigger a reaction in her.

She hurriedly switches off the phone, wryly acknowledging her superstition that such thoughts could conjure up a call from him.

Her apathy, she thinks, is appalling.

She locks the car and sets off. Frédérique is aware of the noises accompanying her – the click of her briefcase, the clunk, bleep of her central locking, the tapping of her heels. They mingle with the other sounds in the street; somewhere there's the sound of a machine, whining, stopping, whining, on and on.

She continues walking, stops, turns round and retraces her steps. The wall inside the brasserie she's just passed is always hung with paintings and today something's caught her eye. She peers through the window. In the centre of the wall is a large painting with a blue background. On the left-hand side is a dense patch of vividly coloured figures; on the right two large faces.

She goes in. Two men are settled at one table with coffee and pastries, a mass of papers between them.

Standing in front of the painting, Frédérique wants to laugh. The colours are remarkable; the azure sky, the pollution-grey squares of buildings and the vivacious figures. Street sellers, she can see now – cooking, jostling, singing, laughing, drinking. And then the two faces, almost wooden in contrast. One young and sorrowful, the other old and tired, smiling shyly.

It's definitely by the same artist. She can spot his style even though some of the older paintings are very basic, slapdashed on odd things like flattened oil cans or wood from orange boxes, made into a panel. This is the first time she's seen this artist's work round here, though. Up until now it's only been on street stalls, among tourist tat along the quayside or in the markets. She's been asking around for a name, but nobody wants to say. Their faces shut down. Places where these paintings are, are places where people are reluctant to divulge that sort of information. She hands over her business cards, but she pictures them sliding forgotten into pockets, or dropped to the ground and trampled under foot as soon as she's gone.

A while ago, she bought one of the large pictures which she's hung in her apartment. It's a busy scene like this one, but dominated by a sinister cityscape. The evening sky is aubergine-purple with silvery lights and there are shadowy groups of people down by the docks. In the centre, a man's white, wide face stands out as if he's popped up in front of a camera, or is walking towards you, threatening: 'Here, you! What's going on?'

The better paintings are thematic, like this one. And very simple. It's the simplicity which makes even the rougher, less skilled paintings, effective.

Her greeting of 'Messieurs Dames' as she'd stepped into the brasserie had elicited muttered responses from the men at the table, but no one had appeared from the back. She calls out, 'Bonjour,' in the direction of the kitchen. 'Bonjour.'

A woman dawdles out, wiping her hands. 'Madame,' she says warmly, hurrying once she sees Frédérique's polished leather briefcase propped on the counter. She senses Frédérique means business. 'How can I help?'

Frédérique points. 'I'm interested in the blue painting over there.'

The woman glances briefly. She's a model of efficiency now. 'Number eighteen? Did you want to buy it?'

'How much is it?'

Sometimes the prices in this place are sky high. The artists try it on with the tourists who get carried away with the atmosphere of the quarter, buying up everything in sight as mementos to take back home. It's become worse since the area became more popular – you won't be able to move around here in high season, in a couple of months' time. Sometimes Frédérique is forced to go direct to the artist to negotiate. In fact, she thinks as she waits for the woman to reply, it's hard to get a real find over here these days, not solely because there's a lot of bad work riding on the back of the quarter's reputation, but because the place is always swarming with gallery scouts.

'That one's . . .' The woman tuts and clucks as she consults a tattered piece of paper pinned on the wall behind the counter, covered with crossing outs and scribbles. She locates it and reads out a surprisingly modest figure.

Frédérique doesn't hesitate.

'I'll take it now.'

Frédérique watches as the woman wraps the painting in brown paper, hunts through some drawers under the counter for some tape and then seals the four corners. Frédérique's hand is shaking so much that she makes a mess of her signature on the cheque.

'Can you tell me the artist's name?' she asks as she hands it over. She holds herself tight, hardly daring to hope. The woman consults the list again. It seems to be a long time before she returns to the counter. She speaks confidentially. 'Monsieur Luc Vanier. No address.'

Frédérique leans forward, complicit with this woman who possesses the precious morsels of information about this man, her artist. Luc. Luc Vanier.

'That's all I know, Madame,' the woman tells her, shaking her head. 'Not many of them give an address. They come in, collect any money, spend most of it on drinks and a meal, which, in my opinion, they look like they're in desperate need of, and leave another painting. Come and go. I don't remember this one.'

She seems to notice Frédérique's disappointment because she quickly adds, 'He'll be back soon, Madame, of course, to see if he's sold anything. Don't worry about that.'

'Has anyone else asked about him?' Frédérique asks, suddenly worried that another gallery may have got in first.

'I don't think so.'

'When he does come back,' Frédérique says quickly, 'I wonder, could you give him this, please?' She takes a business card out of her briefcase. 'I'm really interested in this artist. Can you tell him that and ask him to ring me.' She writes 'Frédérique' across the card. 'As soon as possible.'

The woman takes the card, turns it over, once, twice.

Frédérique shuts her case up. 'Please tell him that it's important.'

'Of course, Madame.'

Frédérique watches her pin the card to the list. She says goodbye and walks quickly back to the car to put in the package.

She's taken longer than she said to Hervé, but she knows she can handle any consequences. There's something about the way the painting is lying in her car, waiting for her to get it home, there's something about the way her white, clean card is pinned to the scruffy list next to his name which has given her hope. Luc, she thinks, Luc. She already feels closer to him, feels that finally she's made the breakthrough.

Luc arrives at the graveyard at the back of Sainte Catherine early, as dawn is breaking. He's there to catch the light, to see the sun appear from behind the church and start its long climb up over the city. This week the sunrises have been beautiful. A deep orangey-pink. He's mixed the colour exactly right and it's sitting in his painting room, in a glass jar with the colour ratios written on a piece of card, taped to the top. He thinks happily of it as he makes his way to the front of the church which he plans on sketching.

His bag, slung over one shoulder, pulls a little at the muscles. Inside is a sketchbook, pencils, a flask of coffee prepared the night before, which he imagines, wrongly, he can smell, and a fresh ham baguette which he definitely can until he passes into the short alley formed from one side of the church and a dense line of chestnut trees. Here his nostrils are assailed by the stink of sour piss and alcohol. He holds his breath and walks softly past the heaps of old coats and newspapers that hide the men that sleep under the trees at night. He tries not to disturb them. It's early and they're never in good shape first thing in the morning.

The front steps are covered in rubbish like giant bits of confetti. Coke cans, cartons, paper bags, bits of sandwiches. A woman will clear it all up before the tourists arrive. She'll wake the men too, and get them to move. They always emerge out onto this terrace, swearing, clustered together, shaking and spitting, dragging out bottles and cans from underneath their coats, before setting off on their own particular, special route round the city; returning during the afternoon when the coachloads of tourists are brought in. Rich pickings. Luc's heard that the tourist information bureaux are giving out warnings not to visit Sainte Catherine on foot.

Luc sits on a bench on the terrace facing the church. The sun creeps up. A bold, orange sphere. As it rises above the spire, it bathes everything in a warm glow, tinting the white flowers apricot in the flower bed beside him, making the stone look like pimply, pink flesh. He breathes it in. He can almost taste the sweetness of the peach light.

He pours himself a coffee, stuffs some bread into his mouth and works steadily for several hours until Nou-Nou staggers out from the alley and stands swaying, before spotting Luc.

Nou-Nou hawks deep down in his throat, turning his head away, then spits on the paving, centimetres in front of Luc's feet. Luc resists the urge to move them. It's the kind of reaction Nou-Nou delights in.

'Haven't you finished yet?' Nou-Nou asks, peering over Luc's shoulder. Hot fusty breath drifts past.

'Not yet.'

'I thought you guys basically painted it straight off. All at once. Not this sketching here and little fuckin' paintings there. Or is that only fuckin' geniuses?' He cackles, scratching hard at his crotch.

Luc shrugs but says nothing. He hears the phlegm gathering in Nou-Nou's throat and it makes him want to clear his own.

'Got a fag?' Nou-Nou asks.

Luc lights two, and hands one over, putting the packet into his pocket before Nou-Nou gets his hands on it. Nou-Nou, unpredictable at best, can turn nasty. Luc tries to keep two steps ahead of him, but doesn't always succeed. He let Luc sketch him for smokes and vodka more than a couple of months ago and Luc's still paying for it. He regrets the relationship of giver and receiver that has stuck ever since, especially as, if he's honest, he doesn't actually like Nou-Nou.

'Tomorrow,' says Nou-Nou loudly, moving to stand in front of Luc. He inflates his chest in preparation for a grand announcement. 'Tomorrow I'm leaving. I'm leaving this shit-hole behind.' The last word ends in a flurry of coughing, but Luc knows what he said. It's what they all say, all the time.

Luc nods. 'Good for you.'

He can understand that the men would want to get away, but he could never leave. If, or when, this church is left to rot along with the rest of the quarter, he wants to be here, to see it and to paint it so that others will know what's been lost.

Nou-Nou's asking him for some money, pulling at his arm. He hasn't been listening.

'Fuck you,' he says, flicking away his cigarette butt. 'You know I haven't got any.'

Nou-Nou tries to grab at his sketchbook but Luc's too quick for him. He pushes him away.

'Piss off,' he tells him and Nou-Nou does, with a stream of abuse which he carries across the terrace back into the alley where he sets off shouting from the others.

The caretaker's here. She emerges from inside with a broom and plastic bag. Luc flicks back to the sketch he was working on. He looks at it, but his concentration has gone. He packs up his belongings and walks over to the church. The woman nods to him as he climbs the steps.

He hears the thump-thud as the heavy doors swing closed behind him. The church is divided in two by the light. Around Luc it's dark and his skin prickles with cold, but ahead above the altar, the east windows throw the new day's light to the floor as far as the pulpit. He walks down the aisle. His trainers squeak on the stone floor, the sound piercing the hollow silence.

At the altar, among the lumps of cold, molten wax, are two stumps of candles, their flames still flickering, almost invisible in the light. He puts a coin in the box and takes a candle out. He lights it from one of the candles and, placing it with the others, he thanks the city for his life.

Luc pities the tourists who never experience the quietness of the vast space without the whispers, the footsteps, the breathing of others around them, without the sensation of knowing that there's no one else here. But he wouldn't give up these moments for anything. He likes to keep them for himself.

He hears the rustle of the rubbish bag as the caretaker comes in and turns to leave. He calls to the woman, 'Merci, Madame.'

He stands on the top step and looks around. In the few minutes he's been inside, the day has really arrived. He smiles, stretches and adjusts the bag on his shoulder. He looks up. No clouds. He'll go into the city centre before the heat gets a real grip, check out his sales and pick up the paint he needs. Then he'll head down to the blue café where there'll be a breeze, coming off the river.

Blythe, lying in shorts on top of his bed, feels his eyes finally close in a sleep that threatens to be deep. 'Not now,' he moans, trying to drag himself out, lurching from unconscious to conscious. Not fucking now he thinks, when I've got to be awake. He finished late at the bar and thought he'd grab a few hours' sleep before Bryony arrived but he's been dreaming vividly, and the twitching of his hands as he mixed dream cocktails and juggled dream bottles kept waking him up. Sleep pours into his brain.

He wakes momentarily, when his body spasms to a sensation of falling, before drifting off again. The muffled sounds of the building sift through his struggling brain. Someone running down the stairs, music playing – Cecillie's, he guesses – and a rhythmic thumping, irritatingly off beat with the music, which he realizes as he forces himself to sit up, is his own heart pounding.

His bed in the corner is never touched by the sun, but the air in the room is stuffy and he's sweating even half-naked. He'll get dressed, he decides, before Bryony arrives and they'll go out, straight away; go and sit outside a bar or even go down to the beach, if it's hot enough. It's a crime to stay indoors; they should chill out in the sun, get pissed. Great.

He gets up, splashes his face with freezing water over the sink, grimaces into the small mirror above it, sniffs at his armpits and splashes under them, too. As he's drying himself, he looks out of the window. He opens it wide and shoves a rolled-up magazine in the gap to stop it banging closed.

Another fuck-off hot day. It's only June but it seems to have been like this for weeks. This thought fills him with a sharp happiness as it always does when he thinks how lucky he is to have escaped rainy, miserable England. Bryony laughs at him whenever he says that, telling him he's got his feelings about

England out of proportion. One day she even turned up with a newspaper showing the weather from capital cities around the world. It said London sunny, 27 degrees.

'See,' she'd argued. 'There's good weather there too.'

He'd had to agree just to be nice but in his heart he knows it's different. It was only one fucking day, for a start off, but it goes deeper than that. People there have a different agenda, it's like they don't want to enjoy themselves, it's like they can never be really happy. He can't believe how long it took him before he realized that he didn't have to be the same. Sometimes he can't understand why everybody else hasn't come to the same conclusion. By rights there should be hardly anyone left over there except maybe old people. Why places like this aren't teeming with Brits, he doesn't know.

What he really struggles to believe is that Bryony wants to go back. She's been here for ten months and still seems to consider it a temporary arrangement. Of all the luck, he sometimes jokes, he finally escaped the UK only to meet an English girl who actually misses the bloody place.

Bryony hasn't said it straight out, but it's there under everything she does; the phone calls to her parents, the long letters to her friends. She loves the kids she looks after but life back in England is pulling her, stronger and stronger. She's due to return at the end of September, to university. Four months, she says, but he can hear the sigh in her voice. Four whole months.

And what's he supposed to do for these four months? He'd never intended to stay this long in the first place. He ended up here with some of the others after the skiing season had finished but they're all long gone now. He's meant to be travelling, for god's sake, not settling down. Although it is kind of cool here, he admits. The great weather helps big time, of course.

Bryony isn't worried. 'It'll work out,' she always says when he tries to talk. And he presumes that somehow it will, though he can't imagine how.

Blythe looks longingly at his bed. Bryony won't be happy if she finds him asleep when she arrives. It's her day off and she won't understand why he's so tired. She doesn't know what it's like not to be able to sleep for hours and hours, sometimes days and then for it to suddenly come on you like an invasion. How can she understand when she falls asleep anywhere, any time, curled up with her arm over her eyes? When she sees sleeping as easy, a comfort. He envies her that. Sleep for him is a battle that he rarely feels he's won.

He's getting an erection from picturing Bryony on his bed. Jesus, surely she's late. He looks at his watch again. Any time now. Blythe's eyes water from a yawn which stretches his mouth wide. He rubs his jaw which is aching.

The front door bangs closed and he listens out for the sound of Bryony coming up to the door. Then he hears her voice. For Christ's sake, she's been caught by Monsieur Bayard. Irritation rushes through him. He's here like a jerk with a huge stiffy while she's having a nice little chinwag with Monsieur B. He's about to get his arse across the room and call her in when there's a quick tap-tapping and Bryony appears.

'Hi!' she says.

'Hi,' he replies, and he feels as he always does when she comes into his room – shy, stupid, as if they don't really know each other. It always surprises him that she never notices.

He watches her now, so casual, so unaware. She puts her bag

down on the floor, unties her hair, shakes it so that it swooshes in the air; then bunches it in one hand. One, two, three quick movements and it's a little knot, with sprouting ends, at the back of her head.

His prick twitches as she comes up to him and gives him a kiss. Only a little kiss on his cheek, but with her so close, he feels the pulsing warmth of her body, as if she's brought the heat of the day inside with her. She moves away but he grabs her to him and kisses her properly, quite hard. He picks her up and lays her down on the bed and starts to take off her clothes.

2

bloody lovely

Cecillie stands half-in, half-out of the phone kiosk, waiting for her grandmother to answer, keeping an eye out for buses. She hasn't got a lot of time, but after thinking about her earlier, she'd suddenly needed to hear her gran's voice.

A bus comes into view but it's for the wrong part of the city. She watches its journey down the road. The way these long jointed autobuses move reminds her of Chinese carnival dragons; the body gracefully gliding behind the swaying head, as they weave along the roads, curving through the narrow streets and then travelling fast along the glossy wide boulevards in a perfect straight line.

'Gran? Gran?' she repeats. 'It's Cecillie.' She presses the receiver to her ear and listens hard.

'Sweetheart, how are you?'

Cecillie feels a spurt of panic at the frailty of her grandmother's voice. But the next moment the line is clearer, as if she's stepped closer to the phone. Relief and love tumble inside Cecillie as she listens.

'This is a nice surprise, sweetheart.'

'It's a quick call; it gobbles money at this time.'

'I got your letter, dear. I liked the picture of your landlord.'

Cecillie's excitement bubbles up. 'He's a sweetie. He's been so friendly, everyone's really friendly.'

'Have you seen Cassandra, lately?' her gran asks.

'Not since I finished at the college,' Cecillie confesses.

Cecillie groans inside. She's asked this every time she phones. She knows better than to mention that she hasn't replied to a note that her grandmother's friend left over a week ago inviting her for a meal. This would be classed as terribly bad mannered – probably criminal – and Cecillie hates letting her grandmother down. She wishes she wasn't expected to be constantly in touch with Cassandra just because she sorted out the apartment and French course for her. It's not that Cecillie doesn't like the woman – she does, although she's old and rather stuffy. It's just that whenever Cecillie visits, Cassandra bombards her with suggestions and ideas and possible contacts that she's supposed to follow up. It's very kind and Cecillie doesn't want to be ungrateful but she'd prefer to find out things her own way, to strike out on her own. Cecillie's sure that she has very, very different ideas to Cassandra on what life in France is about.

'I'll probably see her this week,' Cecillie reassures her.

'Pass on my best wishes, please.'

'I will.'

'I can speak French pretty well, now,' Cecillie says. She's not as good as Bryony and Blythe, of course, but she can make herself understood most times. Especially since she's enlisted Monsieur Bayard to help; he's taken the task very seriously and carefully corrects her pronunciation as well as her words.

'My landlord's helping me.'

'Well done, sweetheart, I'm so glad you're enjoying yourself.'

The bus that Cecillie wants appears at the top of the street. She can let it pass and wait for the next but her money's almost gone already and she hasn't got any more.

'Oh no, I've got to go.'

'Keep in touch, Cecillie.'

'I will. Are you OK?'

'I'm fine.'

'And, um . . . Mum and Dad?'

'They're fine, too. I'll give them your love.'

'Yeah, OK. Got to go, got to go.'

'Bye, sweetheart, take care.'

'Love you,' Cecillie says into the phone, desperate to prolong the connection. The phone makes her grandmother's presence tantalizingly real; Cecillie badly wants a hug. The telephone is flashing for more money and she looks into her empty purse, even though she knows there's nothing there.

'I love you too, sweetheart. Be good.'

The dial tone cuts in and Cecillie stands dazed for a moment before shoving the receiver down and running to the bus.

It starts off as she makes her way to stand at the rear door, her usual viewing spot. But she doesn't see anything; instead she's concentrating on keeping back the tears as she replays in her mind the conversation with her grandmother. She always feels homesick after she's spoken to her, but it passes. She'll phone more often, she decides. Time, she thinks guiltily, will not be rushing by for her grandmother like it has been for Cecillie. It will have gone slowly alone in her sitting room every day in front of the fourteen-inch television screen, with the sound up so loud it nearly knocks your head off.

And after all, if it hadn't been for Gran, Cecillie wouldn't be here.

Cecillie had loved that moment, *loved* it, when Gran had suddenly clattered down her knife and fork over Sunday dinner, cutting through her father's silent hostility, cutting short her mother's shrill version of the mad, bad world that Cecillie had called up by tentatively suggesting once again that she might travel.

Her mother was in the middle of her 'nowhere is safe these days, I couldn't bear it if anything happened' monologue, when her grandmother had brought to an end in two seconds what Cecillie had been trying to break through for years.

She said, 'Enough is enough, Marion. You have to let the girl live her life.'

On the bus, there's one of those strange moments when all conversations pause at once, and Cecillie hears the echo of the sweet silence in the dining room when she saw her gran wink at her and knew that at last she was on her way out of that house.

Cecillie listens to the black rubber joint of the bus pleating and expanding like a giant wheezing concertina before the passengers' voices resume; they rise and fall in time to the rolling and rocking of the bus. The hiss, clunk, ting of the bus as it progresses along the route is familiar accompaniment to Cecillie's view of the buildings, the sky, the rushing crowds. She's learnt a lot about the city, this way. When she gets back to her apartment in the evenings, she settles down by the open window to study her map in the evening light, carefully marking in black any new bus routes she's taken.

But it isn't enough.

Now, she pulls the map from her bag, unfolds it, sees with pleasure a growing mesh of lines, but with greater excitement the large areas where only an odd line strays or which are completely free of black ink. In her bag is the yellow felt pen she bought this morning in preparation for the new journeys. The moped will take her buzzing down the back alleys, cruising along the coast tracks. Deeper in, further out. She pictures the buttercup-coloured lines mingling with the black, then heading off away, to the outskirts of the city, the criss-crossing of many lines to and from the beach higher up the coast.

The bus slows and stops at the neck of the dead end only a few metres from where it usually terminates. She peers through the window to see what the hold-up is. Nothing.

Ahead are the tall buildings on the perimeter of the cul-de-sac. It's one of Cecillie's favourite spots. From here, their uniform sand colour makes them look as if they've been hewn out of an immense piece of unbroken stone decorated with row upon row of white painted shutters. Set against this bland background is a riot of colour from the awnings of the cafés and bars; and in the centre the cool bulk of the wide chestnut trees throws shade out on the left. Cecillie glances round the bus impatiently.

The doors at the front swish open and two stiffly uniformed ticket inspectors climb on board. In the second Cecillie thinks she has to get out, she hears the click of the doors being locked automatically. Oh, shit. She's seen these guys in action before. Everyone's trapped until the ticket inspectors have worked their way up the bus, like automata. She's in trouble. She knows very well that she has only some small change and a stick of chewing gum in her purse and no ticket. What bad luck.

She watches the hard, tanned faces of the officers as they move efficiently up the aisle. They bark out words, nodding so quickly it looks as though their heads might snap off their necks. She wishes they would.

She might get away with it if one of them takes a fancy to her and lets her off for being a foreigner. As they come nearer, Cecillie leans against a pole and closes her eyes.

'Ticket, Mademoiselle?'

Cecillie opens her eyes to meet those of an inspector. He's young, susceptible. She smiles, shrugs, pouts a little. He repeats his request.

She shrugs and holds out her palm where the golden-brown coins rest, and smiles up at him. She puts her all into the smile, her face aching with the effort. 'Can I pay, please?' she asks him in English.

The inspector looks steadily at Cecillie and when he grins, she's sure she's home and dry. But the second inspector appears behind him. He's older – obviously the senior – with a neat moustache and perfect almond-shaped eyes which skim over her breasts outlined under her T-shirt.

'English,' the younger one tells him and walks away.

'No pay,' the inspector says in careful English, 'you stay on the bus and we get a policeman. You understand?'

She gets the point. This guy has his flies sewn up nice and tight. He joins his colleague further up the bus. She looks at their arses; plump, smug arses. No one else gets done, everyone else has been good boys and girls she thinks bitterly, and regrets for a moment using the last of her money to call her grandmother. Only for a second. She doesn't allow herself any longer than that. It's her own fault so she'll just have to pay the fine on her credit card and lump it. She consoles herself with making up rude names for the inspectors.

The bus restarts and is soon sliding into the parking bay. The doors at the front open and the passengers line up to get off. The younger conductor stands next to her and takes out a pad. The slimeball starts asking for her details.

'I'll pay by credit card,' she interrupts him, in French.

He looks surprised but says, 'I still need to know your name.'

She repeats it twice, but he can't understand what she's saying. His arm keeps getting knocked by the passengers as they file past. He slips the pad back in his pocket and moves closer to Cecillie, who's pressed right up near the door. She can feel the heat from him and smell the iron odour of his sweat. She sighs. This has really fucked up her day.

'We'll wait for these,' he tells her, indicating the people queuing to board.

It's a long line of faces which are staring at her. When the doors open, Cecillie manages to shuffle back a bit from Slimeball. An old, very wrinkled woman tuts, and mutters something in French directed at Cecillie that she doesn't understand. Cecillie sticks out her tongue. It sets the woman off again, louder this time. Somebody laughs.

She spots a good-looking guy on the pavement. He points at Cecillie then himself and mouths something to her which she can't make out. She shrugs to show she hasn't understood. He smiles as he comes up the steps and stops opposite Cecillie. She's about to say hello when she's pushed out of the bus – so hard that she almost falls – but she's immediately steadied by a hand on her waist.

The man shouts 'Run!' and she's being dragged along by the

hand until she's running side by side with him down one length of the cul-de-sac.

Someone is chasing them. Cecillie hears the slap slap on concrete of black polished shoes in pursuit. She doesn't dare look around but then realizes that there's no way out ahead. She pictures them having to run round the horseshoe-shaped road back towards the bus where they'll be caught. She glances back. The youngest inspector is closing in. He shouts, 'Stop, stop.'

They continue running, the stranger leading now, shouting for people to move out of their way; some cheer and others whistle and clap as they pass through. He dodges skilfully past some tables while Cecillie stumbles and knocks over a chair. Perhaps he lives here, Cecillie thinks, hopefully: she doesn't think she can go on much longer. She's finding it hard to keep up. She's gasping like mad. Too many fags, she thinks. It's a long time since she's done anything this energetic. Not since school and not very much then. She tries to concentrate on the stranger in front, noticing how his jeans pocket is half hanging off, the thick, metal strap of his watch, his hair which is wet at the ends from sweat. She drops back. Her calves are aching, her heart's thumping, her chest hurts each time she breathes in. Her bag bangs repeatedly against her hip, making a tiny point of pain. She tries to rearrange it but feels her rhythm falter, flag. Then she sees the gap between two buildings. A black sliver of shadow on the stone.

They run into blackness and a strong sewage smell. The alley is so narrow that Cecillie can sense the coarse wall centimetres from her skin. She can't see a thing and has to slow right down. She stumbles on the uneven ground and scrapes her knuckles as she puts a hand out. Behind them she hears the angry shout of the inspector as he stops at the entrance.

'Salauds!' His voice echoes thinly.

'Bastard yourself!' Cecillie shouts back, her voice echoing too, the sound falling around her. She hears her rescuer's laughter and it sets off her own. Her body is buzzing with adrenaline.

Her eyes have adjusted to the dark and she jogs along. She can make out the form of her accomplice ahead: a luminous patch on his rucksack bobs and dances in front of her.

They emerge into narrow streets. The light here is dim. A few metres ahead is a large brick building with an open wooden door through which the man disappears, but Cecillie has to stop. She hangs forward, trying to relieve the pain in her chest and throat. All she can hear is the blood pounding in her ears and her rasping breath. It's a minute before she can stand upright. She looks around.

Untouched by the sun's brighter rays, the stone here looks darker, as if damp. Like sand wet from the sea. Metal shutters bar windows and doorways. There are piles of rubbish sacks, newspapers and boxes outside most of the buildings. The smell of sewage is strong and the air still. It's a bit creepy. The streets are completely silent and deserted but she has the feeling she's being watched. She walks towards the building and stands in the entrance. It's a huge empty warehouse. There's no sign of the man.

Cecillie feels as if she's run into a completely different world. An abandoned, secret world. She shivers and decides to head back. Her confidence in the stranger is fading as quickly as an awareness of the dodgy situation she's in grows.

'Over here!' The call startles her.

She half trots, half runs towards him, her legs heavy.

'I didn't mean to leave you behind,' the man says as she reaches him. 'Are you OK?'

'Yes, thanks,' she replies.

They come out onto the warehouse forecourt, a few metres from the river. Cecillie's amazed. She didn't know you could get this close. A container ship towers above them as it crawls along the water. Cecillie feels tiny compared to its bulk. The noise of the engines is incredible.

There's a low brick wall fronting the river bank which she leans against. The man sits on it, a short distance away.

There's a strong smell of the sea, of fish and of burning – an oily, coaly smell, coming she assumes from all the motors, and also from a huge pot of what she guesses is tar, which is smoking away on one of the long barges moving alongside the ship.

They must be in the middle of the docks. In the distance, to the right, tall cranes poke into the blue sky like long, thin ladders; in both directions along the bank are huge pieces of rusting machinery, obviously disused. The whole neighbourhood looks derelict. All the buildings have windows that are either broken or boarded up.

Then she notices a few chairs and tables set outside a tiny blue painted building squashed between the warehouses. It's a café. The name is too faded to read, but there's a stand with a new-looking sign advertising Poulain hot chocolate. It's a funny place for a café; Cecillie can't imagine it getting many customers – there aren't any other shops or houses in sight.

Once the ship finally moves away, it's warmer, as the sun's revealed. In the quiet, Cecillie's ears buzz gently with the aftereffects of the engine, as if she's just come out of a club. On the other side of the river is the city centre: the cathedral and the *mairie* are very clear but because they're in the distance, they're like toy buildings, models of the real thing. Cecillie's finding it hard to orientate herself.

'Shall we go in?'

Close up, the café walls glisten and shine with watery dapplings from the reflections of the sun and the river. The large window holds the miniature image of the city centre she was just looking at – like a postcard photograph.

'It's beautiful,' Cecillie says, quietly.

Inside, the walls have also been painted a chalky blue, deeper than the weathered front of the building. It's shabby and smells of chocolate and damp. Cecillie breathes it in; it's like the river has seeped inside. She loves it, she loves it already. She can imagine spending hours here, doing nothing, chatting, looking at the view. This, she knows, is what she's been waiting for.

They have their pick of the place as there's no one else in. Cecillie selects the table in the window. The waiter raises his hand in acknowledgement as her companion shouts across for two coffees.

He's even better looking than Cecillie first thought, with open features, clear brown skin, and deep blue eyes. The skin around his eyes as he smiles at her is a network of crinkles and lines, making what could be a too-perfect, plastic model's face, human. He's lovely, Cecillie catches herself thinking, he's bloody lovely.

The waiter places two coffees carefully in front of them. On her saucer there's a wrapped chocolate.

The two men shake hands warmly.

'This is Maurice, the patron and a good friend. Also the best hot chocolate maker in town.'

Maurice laughs, shakes Cecillie's hand quickly before returning to the bar.

'And I'm Luc.'

'I'm Cecillie.'

'You're English?' he asks.

She nods.

'You have a beautiful name. Almost French. Except that you say it flatly. In an English way.'

Cecillie wants to tell him how it's spelt but she hasn't got a clue how to pronounce the alphabet. Instead she takes out a thick black pen from her bag and writes on the Formica table top – Cecillie.

'Like that.' She moves to rub it off but Luc stops her hand.

'Leave it for now,' he tells her.

Cecillie watches him select and unwrap two cubes of sugar, balancing both on the spoon before lowering them slowly into the coffee. He has slim hands with long supple-looking fingers. She's only seen those sorts of hands on women, and the male music teacher at school. They're covered in paint. Scarlet, violet, bottle green in smears and blobs. As he stirs his coffee, the joints of his fingers break the smooth surface of the colours and the paint cracks and flakes. She remembers now feeling the strange dryness, the crumbs in his hand when they were running away from the bus. The front of his clothes are covered in the same coloured spots.

'Thanks for helping me. Do you do it often?' Cecillie cringes at her question. To cover her embarrassment she fiddles with the chocolate.

'Pulling women from buses you mean?' he asks her. He takes the chocolate from her, unwraps it and offers it back. Cecillie blushes. She plucks it from his fingers and puts it in her mouth. She chews self-consciously as he studies her.

'To tell the truth . . .' he says. 'I liked your face.'

Cecillie blushes harder; her hand strays to her chin, her worst feature. She's not pretty, she knows that, but her tan suits her, brings out the colour of her eyes. Put together – her slim, brown body, her blonde hair, her green eyes, her vigorous health – she knows that she's more attractive than she's ever been. She's been pleased with these changes, taken them on board gratefully. But her face, alone, she doesn't feel bears scrutiny, and certainly not compared to his.

'Also I hate to see those bastards catch anyone.'

'Well, thanks,' says Cecillie. It isn't an adequate response but it's the best she can do – she is so embarrassed. Luckily Luc doesn't seem to notice. He fishes around in his rucksack which he's hung on the back of his chair and retrieves a small white card.

'Would you excuse me for a moment?' he asks. 'I have a phone call to make.'

He walks to the furthest end of the bar, where Maurice pulls a telephone out from under the counter. Luc places the card in front of him and picks up the receiver. She hears Maurice laugh at something he says before he dials. When he starts talking, Luc hunches over the phone. Maurice disappears into a room behind the bar.

Cecillie goes over to the jukebox, leaning on it, as she studies the selection. There's French stuff mainly, but some old English records too. The Beatles and Rolling Stones. Luc looks up, smiles at her and waves her to him. He's holding out a coin for the machine. She takes it and chooses 'Jumping Jack Flash'. The music fills the café. Luc grins, puts a hand over one ear and carries on talking.

Cecillie is suddenly aware of Maurice behind her. She smells him first; cocoa and alcohol. Not on his breath, but from his clothes, a sickly overpowering smell. She turns round and steps back. Her bottom is pressed uncomfortably against the edge of the jukebox. She shifts a little to the side. Maurice has watery, slightly protruding eyes, in a leathery, crinkled face. His neck protrudes at such an angle out of his shirt that he's not standing as close as Cecillie first thought. He reminds her of an animal of some sort. A tortoise suddenly comes into her mind and she has to stop herself smiling because Maurice has a very serious expression on his face.

'Luc,' he says, nodding over to the bar. Cecillie glances over, looks back at Maurice. 'Luc is a good man.'

'Yes.'

'Do you like my little café?' he asks revealing stubby, brown-tinged teeth.

'It's great,' Cecillie says quickly.

Maurice's expression lightens suddenly. 'It used to be popular,' he tells her. 'Workers unloading the ships. Do you understand?'

Cecillie thinks so. She nods.

'They closed down this dock and moved all the ships further up the river with new machines.'

'I'm sorry,' she says.

'No need, my English lady. I need the rest. Do you understand, my English lady?' Before she can reply, Maurice reaches for her hand, presses it gently then lets it go. He talks slowly, carefully. 'You're the first lady he's brought here.' Cecillie's heart jumps and she reddens again. 'I hope he'll bring you again.'

'I hope so too,' she says, but Maurice turns away before she's finished speaking. He's back behind the bar just as Luc's replacing the receiver. Weird, Cecillie thinks. The whole morning's been weird. Like a dream. She can't imagine Bryony and Blythe even beginning to believe her when she tells them. But she's really here in this strange place, and she loves it. She doesn't ever want to leave it and what's more, she thinks, as Luc's walking over to her, she's found the best-looking bloke in the city.

'Great news! A gallery's interested in my paintings.'

'You're an artist?'

'Yes.'

She laughs. 'I thought you painted houses and things.'

'A decorator,' he says looking down at his clothes. 'I'm a mess.'

'No, you're . . .' She stops herself quickly. She was going to say how great he looks. And now that he's turned out not to be the decorator she thought he was, he seems even more cool. But she can't say any of that because if she does, she might as well just come right out and tell him that she fancies him – loads. She's got to play it right so that she doesn't put him off. She very much wants this not to be the last time she sees him. She wants this to be the start. But she can't say that, so she says nothing.

She's aware of their bodies. She wonders if Luc is too. They're about the same height, they are both slim. She would like to step forward and feel how their two similar bodies fit together.

She's distracted by the sight of the big-faced clock behind the counter. It's nearly half past eleven and she'll have to go soon. But she doesn't want to leave. Somehow she knows that this is her big chance and she's not sure yet how well she's secured it.

The record has finished. Maurice is chinking bottles as he slides them out of crates and onto the counter. Luc calls over to Maurice for cokes and they sit down again.

'I haven't got any money for the drinks,' she tells him. 'I was on my way to get some when . . .'

He interrupts her. 'It's on me.'

'Thanks. Next time, I'll pay.' She kicks herself for saying that, but Luc doesn't seem to have noticed her slip-up.

'You're on holiday?' he asks her.

'Not exactly. I'm staying here for a while.'

'With your family?' he asks.

'My parents live in England. I've got a studio apartment, in a big house.'

Maurice brings their drinks, removes the old cups.

'So where's your apartment?' he asks.

Cecillie tries to appear casual as she tells him the name of her street but her heart is thumping.

'I know it. You're in the quarter next to us.'

'Next to you?'

'This café is called La Frontière because it borders the two quarters. Maurice's little joke. Nobody knows it by that name though; we call it the blue café.'

'Then that's what I'll call it!'

Luc laughs and then draws an imaginary line on the table with his finger. 'Right now you're sitting in the quarter where

I live, which we ran through, but two steps to the right when you go out, you'll be in the next one – yours.' He dots a spot on the table for emphasis.

Cecillie scrabbles in her bag, takes out her map. She unfolds it and places it on the table.

'I saw the quarters marked on the map,' she says. 'But I never thought they were important. There's no difference between them, is there?' She follows the pale pink lines which denote the quarters' boundaries and finds the spot where the café is, where they are, and places her finger on it.

Luc tut-tuts. 'How long have you been here?'

'About six weeks.'

'OK. A quick tour.' He gestures towards his forehead. 'For the moment – in our heads and on the map.' His finger moves across the map. 'I'll speak slowly,' he tells her.

'OK.'

'My quarter – this one here – is very poor. There's the port with the quays and a lot of immigrants. Foreigners. We also have this – the most beautiful building in the city: a church called Sainte Catherine. Then there's the quarter at the north point of the city.' His finger swoops round to the top. 'That's for the rich people. They have more space, bigger houses, but it's less interesting. Your quarter's not bad – mostly houses – squashed between this one and the artists' quarter, which is the only one that crosses both sides of the river.'

I must follow this, Cecillie thinks as she listens. Their eyes briefly meet; they both look away, down at the map. I must remember it all.

'That's the industrial part of the city – factories, lots of new, small houses, and then of course there's the city centre – office workers, shop owners, you know? There are two other quarters that have grown up from the suburbs, here and here. That one has the new big sports stadium that's just opened – it's been in all the papers.'

'I love it all,' Cecillie says. 'What I've seen so far, I love it all.'

'But my quarter is the best, you were going to say?' He grins at her and she hedges, not wanting to say the wrong thing. 'Maybe . . .' and he laughs.

It's no good, Cecillie has to leave. She slowly folds the map and pushes it into her bag.

'I have to get to the Central Post Office.'

He's standing before she's finished speaking. 'I'll take you. There's a short cut.'

They go back the way they came except that they take a flight of stairs into an underground car park. Bleak light here shows up the squat bodies of lines of cars. They walk past one which has been burnt out; the shell sits in the middle of bits of melted seats and charred carpets. It stinks of piss. There are two free spaces either side of it.

'You shouldn't come this way on your own,' Luc says once they've come back up onto the streets.

'I'm not scared.' She isn't. It's no big deal.

'I can tell,' he says. 'But . . .' He stops her, holds onto her arm. 'Promise you won't come this way on your own? I don't want you to get lost, Cecillie and end up somewhere dangerous.'

'How do you know it so well?'

'I've lived here all my life.'

At the end of the street are some wide stone steps going up. At the top there's a kind of plateau where the wall of windows at the back of the Post Office dazzle her with reflected sun. She hears Luc shouting behind her. She turns around. He's stopped at the top of the steps, his hand shielding his eyes.

'What? What did you say?'

'What number? What number house?'

'Four.'

'OK. Four. OK.'

Cecillie knows what that means. She wants to shout, Yes! Yes! Yes! but she carries on walking, determined not to look back again until she reaches the Post Office. But halfway across, she allows herself a final look. It's too bright to see if Luc's still there but she has a feeling he is; watching her. So she waves and goes inside.

3

something more

Frédérique showers, mists her body in perfume, layers it in silk underwear, a long sea-green wool dress and a silk scarf. She eases her feet into green high-heeled shoes and in front of the mirror passes her hands over her breasts, her thighs and bottom. The dress is looser on her, she notices since she last wore it; but that's no bad thing. She can stand to lose a couple of kilos. She turns in front of the mirror. There are no underwear lines, no hanging threads or stray hairs; apart from a final coat of lipstick, she's ready to go.

She hasn't spent this long getting ready for ages. She's taken the time tonight because she wants to look sexy for Jacques.

In a room of strangers, Frédérique has always believed she could pick out any woman Jacques would find attractive, any woman he wouldn't entertain. He likes a classic look, nothing too idiosyncratic, but it's the small touches that clinch the deal for him. Armed with this knowledge, she's wearing a new scarf; she's had her hair cut neat today in its closely cropped style – she left work a little bit early to fit in an appointment – and she's put on her pearl earrings; the ones Jacques likes.

Frédérique kisses the excess of her lipstick off on a tissue and looks closely in the mirror. Her eyes are still shadowed underneath, but the drawn, sallow skin she'd begun to think was her age catching up with her has fleshed out a little, been touched by a gentle glow. All in all, she doesn't look too bad.

Earlier today Jacques had phoned her.

'I missed you this morning,' he told her, in a soft tone. 'It wasn't the same without you.'

She'd answered lightly, remarking how she'd had to settle for a croissant on the run rather than the leisurely breakfast that he indulges her with. Jacques had laughed and made a comment about bribing her to share another with him.

'I won't need to be bribed,' she replied, in response to his flirting.

Just recalling this makes her feel turned on. Tonight, she's no intention of coming home. She says out loud, 'Naughty woman,' and laughs at herself.

As she comes out of the apartment block, into the air, she's happy. Her mood lasts. She drives through the park on the way into the centre of the city and the colours of the flowers and trees seem fresh and beautiful, like they do after a sudden cooling shower, even though it's hot and the ground dry.

At the end of the call, Jacques had said, 'We should talk.'

'I've been thinking that too,' Frédérique had replied slowly.

'Then let's do so,' he said. 'Tonight.'

Listening hard, she had known from his tone of voice, and the way he'd said goodbye that there was nothing to be worried about.

How different life feels to only a few weeks ago. At last she feels alive! She had been scared to hope, she realizes now, and so she'd kept all her feelings pressed down, not daring to let them breathe.

First Luc, and now this. How can it get any better?

Once out of the park, Frédérique takes a longer, but less busy, route into the city. It's a straight smooth road, where she can savour the speed of her car. She turns her music up loud and breathes in the hot air of the suburbs through the open window.

As she approaches the city centre, she succumbs to an uncertainty that bubbles up and the nearer she gets to Jacques's bar, the less confident she feels. There is a chance, she thinks, that she's misread their conversation.

Frédérique knows she's probably being silly but, by the time she's parking in front of Jacques's bar, she's decided to book a taxi to take her home at twelve thirty. With that safety net in place, she feels less vulnerable. She can always cancel it later, she tells herself.

She stands for a moment looking up at the bar. It's conspicuous among the other sand-coloured buildings, with its white-painted facade and the black metal staircase which runs up and down the whole of the building, outside and in.

There's a light on in Jacques's apartment at the top and Frédérique wonders if that means he's back. He'd suggested she meet him downstairs in the bar as there was a chance he might be delayed and, after hesitating a moment, she decides to stick to that arrangement.

The bar is quiet, just a few stragglers who have stayed on from after work. Frédérique sits down at the counter. Behind it is the tall English barman that she's seen a few times before. He's wearing a scarlet T-shirt which clashes with his red hair.

Frédérique smiles at him as he hands over her drink. His sharp blue eyes flick quickly to her right and she turns to see Jacques, who has entered the room.

He's wearing a very formal grey suit, with a slate-blue tie. His black, wiry hair is sleeked down so that it ripples in shiny waves across his head. He looks extremely self-assured, almost arrogant. If you didn't know he owned the bar, you might guess he did; or was at least someone of importance here.

She's always found him attractive, she thinks and though she blushes at admitting the thought, she can't resist giving him a teasing look and a little wave as he starts his way over.

Jacques touches Frédérique's cheek, briefly, with the flat of one hand, with what she takes to be a sign of approval, before he kisses her.

'You're looking good, Fred.'

He guides her in front of him, into the small anteroom to the main restaurant. There's one table set out with two places. There are candles and flowers. They've eaten here before but only on special occasions. Is that what this evening's to be about, she wonders, but doesn't ask. She limits herself to remarking, 'It looks lovely.'

A waitress brings the food to the table, but Jacques immediately dismisses her. It's paella stuffed with mussels and crab. Their favourite dish. Jacques serves some to Frédérique.

'OK, tell me.'

'Is it that obvious?'

There had been no place in their earlier phone call for her news about Luc and she's glad now because she wants to see Jacques's reaction.

'That you want to tell me something? I'm afraid it is.'

She laughs. 'I'm an open book to you.'

She waits until he's served himself and they've begun to eat. 'Come on Fred, out with it.'

'I've met him.'

'You have?'

'Yes. Mmm, this is delicious.'

'Met who?'

'You know who.' She watches his face; it's a complete blank. His eyes search hers. She's waiting for him to understand.

'What are we talking about here? The man of your dreams?'

'Kind of.'

'Oh?'

'Don't look so surprised. You remember. This artist I told you about a couple of weeks ago, that I've been trying to get hold of for ages. He phoned up and came over to the gallery yesterday with his work. I wasn't disappointed – his work is good and what's more, he's young, he's good-looking. You'd approve – he's superbly marketable!'

'I see.'

Luc was younger than she'd imagined from his phone call: the sing-song city accent now so little heard, so out of fashion, had led her to expect someone older. These days most young people have the neutral, flatter accent like her own, but he couldn't have been more than twenty-five; tall, slim with brown, floppy hair wearing scruffy jeans and a T-shirt.

He noticed her approaching and smiled. He had nice eyes, though rather wide-spaced. An attractive young man, she thought.

She introduced herself and apologized for being late.

'Luc Vanier,' he said, although it was obvious she knew who he was.

'Have you had a chance to look around? Do you like anything?'

'Sure, some.' He didn't seem keen to elaborate, so she took him straight to her office to get down to business. He sat in one of the armchairs with his legs stretched out while she unzipped his art case. Her hands were shaking.

She cracks a mussel, then another one.

'I was so excited, I was so nervous,' she tells Jacques. 'I began to think what if the work he's brought is rubbish, what will I do then? I almost didn't dare to look. He must have thought I was mad, taking so long before opening his portfolio.'

She pauses, drinks some wine. 'Jacques, they are good. Better than I'd hoped for. Better than anything I've seen in a long, long time. I mean there are some dreadful pieces of course and he needs more control, but overall . . .'

For a few moments she'd forgotten about Luc; the paintings absorbed her – they seemed familiar, but startling too. A pink and orange blaze of a church, a sludge-brown river with precarious white yachts. And people, a lot of people: dockers, street sellers, office workers, tourists even. All the people of the city.

'I really like what you're doing.'

He sprang up, eagerly, grinning wildly. 'You do?'

She nodded.

He laughed and stood, jigging up and down in front of her. 'That's great,' he said. 'That's cool.'

It makes a nice change to deal with someone so fresh, she was thinking when, at that precise moment, it sank in that she was on to something. She found herself laughing too. 'I've picked out five I'd like to propose putting in the gallery. What do you think?'

He came over to the table to consider the ones she'd selected. He took a while as if he was trying to see them for the first time, like Frédérique.

'Sainte Catherine is a beautiful building,' he said. 'I could paint it for ever.'

'I'm ashamed to say that I've lived here all my life and I've never been there,' Frédérique told him.

He studied her and she felt pressed to continue. 'You find that surprising?'

'Yes,' he told her and added, 'you should go.'

'I will now.'

'We take the standard cut,' she told him to fill the silence that followed. 'We also like you to sign a contract with us. Nothing too drastic,' she added hurriedly, noting a sign of what she and Fernand refer to as the artist's compromised-integrity look. 'I'll give you some paperwork to look at over the next few days before we draw up the final agreement.'

Frédérique prepared a receipt invoice while Luc packed away the remaining paintings. She gave him the paperwork which he pushed inside the case.

'Come on,' she said. 'I'll show you around.'

As they came out of the office and walked across the stairwell, someone called out to Luc from the bottom of the stairs. A blonde girl wearing shorts and a very tight top with tiny straps. Her hair hung down in strands and the sun, from the window behind her, made it white-gold.

* * *

'Ah,' says Jacques, looking up. 'This is more like it. The young virile artist and his beautiful muse.' He licks some oil off his lips, making them shine even more.

'Jacques! You look positively rapacious,' Frédérique admonishes. 'Anyway, she's not beautiful; she's got a rather horsey face. But she's striking – very blonde and tanned.' Frédérique laughs. 'I felt quite dowdy next to her.'

'I can't believe that. Not my elegant, sophisticated Frédérique.'

'Don't make fun, I'm serious. She looked so fit, so young. They both did.'

'Unformed you mean?' he says mock-distastefully. 'How tedious.'

'You're just trying to make me feel better.' Frédérique raises her glass to him. 'And I appreciate it.'

They're sitting among the debris of a well-enjoyed meal. Jacques pours the last of the wine into Frédérique's glass.

Jacques sits back in his chair, looks at her, and says nothing. Frédérique doesn't know what to make of his expression.

'This Luc sounds too wonderful for words.'

She rushes in, interrupting him. 'He's talented, definitely. I'd love you to see the paintings, Jacques.'

She reaches over the table and touches his hand. She wants him to share this discovery. Her mind sweeps on, imagining him being as impressed with the paintings as she is.

'You know I don't like any of this raw ethnic art,' he says after a minute.

'It's not like that! The colours are so vibrant, so animated and he's from this city, one of our very own.'

'What about the girl?' he asks, sitting forward.

'I didn't like her very much,' Frédérique says.

'Why not?' Jacques raises a questioning eyebrow.

'I don't know, just a feeling. Although I can see why Luc would be interested in her. She's streetwise, she's attractive . . .'

'What did you say? Golden. A golden, English girl, hmmm. Unusual.' He strokes his chin, parodying thought.

Frédérique shakes her finger at him. 'She was obviously desperately in love with him. Big moony eyes. He was just as bad. You know the type. So pleased with themselves as if they're the only ones who matter.'

'It does sound dreadful.'

'It was.'

The girl had waited at the bottom of the stairs for them to come down. Luc kissed her hello in a manner which left Frédérique in no doubt that she was his girlfriend. She was tall, as tall as Luc. Everything about her was long, but pared down, sleek, like an athlete. Her top left nothing to the imagination; she had very tiny breasts and deep grooves between her collar bones.

'I like your place,' the girl said with an accent Frédérique immediately placed as English. 'I expect everything costs thousands, though.'

The girl smiled, showing big strong teeth.

'People are willing to pay for good art. And the artists of course, need to live. Your boyfriend would agree with me on that, I'm sure,' Frédérique replied as the girl grinned at her expectantly. Frédérique didn't like the way she'd responded. She sounded old and serious, a bit stuck up.

'There are different ways of living,' said the girl. 'And art displayed like this,' she gestured, as she circled the floor like a dance, flipping her body round, her hair flicking out, taking in what Frédérique could only assume was the whole gallery, 'is for the rich.'

What annoyed Frédérique more than what the girl said – she is used after all these years, to ignorance over art – was that whenever the girl spoke, she looked at Luc. As if she couldn't take her eyes off him, as if she was expecting his approval. And he was as bad.

'Your girlfriend . . .' Frédérique started to say to Luc as they both watched her make her way down to the end of the room and stand considering a painting. Sideways on, she could have been just another angular young woman, until she turned her head towards them and her face blazed with life.

'Cecillie, you were saying?' Luc interrupted her thoughts. 'You were going to say something about Cecillie?'

'Oh, yes – Cecillie – seems to have rather a romantic view about art.'

'It's not just art,' he replied, intent on watching Cecillie. 'It's everything.'

Frédérique was, she realized with some irritation, superfluous. They were plainly, openly obsessed with themselves, creating their own world and playing their parts. And, as they stood grinning at each other from opposite ends of the room, she rather resented this taking place in an environment that she'd always considered to be her domain, so she said goodbye and left them to it, going back to her office. There, she picked up Luc's paintings and the next minute laid them down again before wandering to the window.

Luc and Cecillie were outside sitting on a moped, Cecillie at the front. Frédérique was going to turn away, but instead she moved to the side and continued to watch as Luc lifted Cecillie's hair up from her neck and kissed her there, pressing his face against her as if he was breathing her in. Then he let her hair fall back down, as he passed his hands over her shoulders, down her arms and then to cover the tiny breasts for a moment, before travelling down her body and stopping at her waist. Cecillie turned her head to speak to him, as she started the engine, so that Frédérique saw her face once again, a private, closed-down face, before they put on their helmets and drove off.

Frédérique doesn't tell Jacques how she watched the lovers. She's a little ashamed of it. She wonders now, as she follows Jacques up to his apartment, where the couple were going, how they spent the rest of the day. She imagines them driving around, or wandering through the city, hand in hand, aimless. Or perhaps they spent it making love. She has an unexpected vision of their two young bodies romping around in a paint-strewn, messy apartment. The picture is so vivid in her mind, that entering Jacques's flat, with its neat, clean whiteness, is a startling contrast. But as she settles on the settee, she's relieved to be here. She's visited enough artists' homes to know that you daren't sit down in half of them for fear of ruining your clothes.

Frédérique has the drowsy head of a well-dined and slightly drunk person. She kicks off her shoes and tucks her feet up off the floor, her dress exposing her knees. She doesn't bother to pull it down. She's feeling amorous and wants Jacques to know so. She watches him select a bottle of wine and open it. He looks as freshly dressed as at the start of the evening. He starts to loosen his tie, as if he's heard her thoughts, and clears his throat, as if he's about to make an announcement. Suddenly, she doesn't feel brave enough for the conversation she knows is coming.

'I think I've made a real discovery,' Frédérique says, to delay the moment. 'Fernand's not so convinced but I know there's something special about this artist. You know how wonderful that feels?'

'I can guess so from looking at you,' Jacques says, putting the wine and two glasses down on the coffee table in front of her.

'I've not been much company, have I, these last few months?' Frédérique asks, uncomfortable with the memory this conjures up of the bleak, black mood that she's endured until this week. 'What would I do without you?' she asks him, as she does every now and then, half-joking, half-serious.

He hovers in the middle of the room. It unnerves her a little.

'But the tide has turned!' she blurts out. 'I mean . . .'

'The tide has turned,' he repeats. 'But what has turned it for you?'

She doesn't need to think about her answer. 'Luc, I've found Luc,' she tells him. 'And . . .'

'And?' he prompts, but she shakes her head, dumbly. She can't take the first step, she just can't. It's a pivotal moment; the atmosphere has subtly changed, become agitated. She feels inadequate, prays for Jacques to rescue her. Rescue them. He doesn't speak or take his eyes off her.

'Why don't you come and sit next to me?' she suggests.

He does, first removing his tie and throwing it onto the chair behind him. When he's settled, she slides her feet under his leg. It's warm.

'I've heard enough about this Luc,' he says, at last. 'I want to talk about us.'

Frédérique waits for him to continue but instead he takes a long drink and stays silent. The room is beginning a slow whirl; Jacques's features seem to be duplicating themselves at an alarming rate. She attempts to refocus, concentrating on his mouth, which looks set, his forehead which is creased.

'Things have changed, between us, wouldn't you agree?' he asks her in a low tone.

She nods.

He looks relieved and talks quickly. 'I hoped we were thinking along the same lines, but I didn't know.' He puffs out a sigh. 'I hadn't realized until these last few months how much you meant to me. I even look forward to seeing you when you're miserable,' he jokes, and Frédérique laughs, but it sounds unnatural. She hadn't thought she'd be this nervous.

'I know what you're going to say,' she interposes. 'We've got to make a decision; we're at that point, when a decision is required.'

'So.' He stops suddenly. He looks fierce. She feels his hand warm on her ankle, circling it, holding it tight. 'Will you marry me, Frédérique?'

Jacques's face is jarred into focus. Her heart hammers in her chest. Jacques slides his hand up Frédérique's leg, takes her hand. She stares at him. Finally she says, 'This is a . . .' She hesitates; she was going to use the word shock and changes it to 'surprise.'

'It is?'

She speaks gently. 'Isn't it jumping the gun, Jacques? I mean not so long ago we were only friends, and to rush straight to marriage, aren't we . . . ?'

She leaves her question hanging and Jacques takes a moment before he replies. 'Why not?' he asks her. Then he's talking in a rush. 'I'd been thinking like you but then I realized – why delay things? What about children? I know you want them and you're running out of time.'

She flinches. 'I'd hate you to be offering me marriage because this is my last chance,' she says stiffly.

'I'm sorry, I'm being clumsy. It's what we both want and need, isn't it? So why wait?'

She recognizes a truth in his words. She understands what he's trying to say; only she hasn't been able to rationalize her thoughts before. She looks at his hand, looks at his face. A husband. She likes the sound of that. Someone with whom she can rest and be calm; a centre from which she can go on with the rest of her life. She sees it very clearly. The ideas of settling down, of having children, *important* things, haven't been options for a long time; she's had to push aside those desires, but now they come rushing back as possibilities. Jacques is one step ahead of her, that's all.

'It does make sense,' she says. 'Logically.'

'Don't say that. It's not just that,' he insists. 'It's the whole thing. We sleep together, for god's sake, Frédérique. Doesn't that mean anything to you?'

She flushes. 'Of course,' she tells him. 'I've never vocalized it before.'

He takes her hand. 'I wouldn't ask if I didn't think it was completely right.' He kisses her fingers gently. 'Why have you gone quiet? Are you saying no?' He looks crushed.

She feels affection for him mushroom inside her. 'I'm not saying no.'

'Are you saying yes, then?'

She suddenly understands that she can make him happy and she feels powerful and generous all at once. 'I'm saying yes.'

She sees the relief on his face and laughs. Her husband, father to her children. She tests the words in her head, but cannot hold the picture. It doesn't matter – it will come.

'Yes, yes, Jacques, I'd be happy to marry you.'

They sit in silence for a moment. Frédérique's trying to absorb everything; she knows from his face that Jacques is feeling the same; a mixture of terror and excitement about their decision.

Jacques delves under the settee and retrieves a box which he hands her. 'I didn't get you a ring,' he says tightly, betraying that he's still on edge. 'I'd like us to choose that together, but I wanted to give you something to mark the occasion.'

Inside the box is a delicate, gold necklace.

'This is perfect.'

He helps her put it on. She feels his warm fingers touching the back of her neck. He'll be doing this for her in years to come. A familiar ritual, the original moment no longer spoken about, but acknowledged, relived each time.

'You can move in here,' he says, whispering into her ear. 'It's closer to the gallery and, of course, I have no option.'

'Oh.' She turns a little, talks over her shoulder. 'I hadn't thought about that.'

She goes to his bedroom to look at the necklace in the mirror. She's a little unkempt and flushed. She sees the telephone on the bedside table and is tempted to ring someone, anyone, to share the news. She'll call her mother first; that'll get the word going round to friends and family, she thinks, and smiles.

There'll be wedding arrangements and all sorts to deal with she realizes, and she doesn't feel scared one bit. She feels part of the world again.

The intercom buzzer sounds and she hurries out. 'I ordered a taxi.'

Jacques comes up to her. 'But you're going to stay, aren't you, Frédérique?'

His eyes are dark and he's got a very sexy look about him. Her body immediately responds. She half-smiles and stretches, flirting, not answering him.

'Stay,' he says, angling her against the door. 'We've got something to celebrate.' He starts to kiss her. 'Say the word and I'll pay the taxi off.'

She kisses him back. But then he kisses her harder, forcing his tongue into her mouth, hungrily, searching. It feels pointed and demanding. A serious tongue. She's not prepared for it. She wants to push him away, but instead holds herself stiffly, aware all the time of the door handle pressing into her back, Jacques's knee hard against her thigh.

'I think I'd better go,' she thinks she says, but Jacques doesn't seem to hear. He's holding her tight, breathing hard as he kisses her on the neck. His lips leave cold, wet patches on her skin, making her shiver with revulsion.

'Fred, Fred, you'll stay now, won't you?'

She pushes him away, frantically, letting out a short scream, like a yelp. Jacques stands in front of her; they're centimetres apart, not touching, not speaking. Frédérique doesn't know where the scream came from, and she feels stupid and tearful.

She turns abruptly, opens the door and starts to run down the stairs. The heels of her shoes clang against the metal; the noise fills her body, pounds into her head. Behind her, Jacques calls out her name. She stumbles and closes her eyes, expecting to fall but instead she's caught, slowed and steadied by an arm around her and she opens her eyes to the scarlet T-shirt of the English barman.

'Are you OK?' His face bent over her is concerned. She can't speak because she thinks that if she does she'll start to cry, but she's crying anyway, tears are pouring down her face.

She hears Jacques from behind say, 'I'll take care of her now, thank you.'

Frédérique shakes her head, silently asking the barman to stay. He pulls her in towards him until her face is flattened against his warm T-shirt.

Close behind her, Jacques speaks; someone touches her hair, briefly.

'Frédérique, why don't you come upstairs?'

'I want to go home,' she sobs.

'You can't go like this. Come back up.'

'Noooo.'

'She doesn't want to.'

She feels the barman's words rumble out of him.

'She doesn't know what she wants. She's upset.'

'I'll take her down for a taxi.'

'I suggest you go back to the bar and mind your own business.'

'I'll find her a taxi first.'

'No!'

'It's all right.' Frédérique feels as if she's emerging from a dream as she steps away from the barman, noticing the black and brown marks left on his T-shirt by her ruined make-up.

'I'm fine,' she says.

The man swears and then she's being pressed against another body. This time the familiar contours of Jacques. She holds on.

'I don't know what I was doing,' she tells him, crying again. 'It all seemed too much.'

'Listen,' he says, stroking her hair. 'I'm sorry.'

'It's not because I've changed my mind.' She pulls away from him, so that she can look him in the face. 'You do know that, don't you?'

He holds onto her waist, and kisses her softly on her cheek. 'I'll get this taxi dealt with and you go up and make us a good, strong coffee and we can talk.'

4

where you come from

When Luc wakes up, his first thought, as it has been since the day he met her, is of Cecillie. He pictures her, not naked underneath him, or on top, rocking their bodies together, nothing directly to do with sex, although he loves her body with its familiar bumps and ridges of flesh, its moles and freckles and the sheen of her skin. That comes later in the day, when he's almost knocked over by a wave of longing for her. No, the first morning picture is Cecillie scooting up on her moped, taking off her helmet and shaking her hair free. He feels that that is Cecillie at her most Cecillie-ness. Completely Cecillie.

He holds this image in his mind for a second and then he's out of bed, dragging on shorts and T-shirt, stepping into his flip-flops and shuffling into the kitchen, switching on the lights as he goes. Every evening he sets out the coffee equipment so that there's nothing more to do than fill the pan with water, turn on the stove and fetch the paper bag with his breakfast pastries that Bernard from upstairs will have left him outside his front door. Usually he opens the door just a crack; enough to grab the packet without allowing himself even a glimpse of the outside world. He knows from experience that this would prove too great a distraction. This morning, though, he risks a look. Cecillie's coming later to take them to the beach and he can't resist checking for clouds. The sky is clear and he closes the door, smiling, happy. It's going to be a good day.

But not so for work. The sneaky look, that precipitate glance has him wandering back to the bedroom where he stands contemplating the mess. There's a strong smell of garlic which he traces to a plate with the remains of yesterday's meal, on the other side of the bed. With unerring accuracy the sheet he flung aside as he got up has landed on it, and the white cotton is smeared with vivid orange-red streaks of tomato sauce. Luc strips the bed, his mind re-shuffling his schedule to include an unforeseen trip to the launderette. He bundles the bed linen into a carrier bag, picks up the plates, and proceeds to pile on the cups, a glass and cutlery that are distributed around the room. He takes it all, a rattling balancing act, with the bag rustling against his legs, into the kitchen where he dumps everything on the table. He ignores the closed door of his painting room as he passes through the hall. Adrenaline's beginning to work his heart but he has to feel it in his gut before it's worthwhile going in there. He runs some hot water into the sink and for a while is absorbed by the rhythm of collecting, washing, stacking, wiping until the kitchen is as clean as it's ever going to be. He quickly eats two *pains au chocolat* standing up as he waits for the water to boil and then takes the full coffee jug, a cup and the last pastry into the painting room, holding his body tight in anticipation, his stomach signalling the familiar mixture of nerves and excitement.

He puts everything down and then goes over to open the

window, letting in the sounds of children playing, the clanking of the cranes in the distance; and the sulphurous odour of the drains outside. He stares at the stained grey plaster of the building opposite, screws up his eyes and pretends to sweep colours across it, first blocking in shapes of buildings, then populating the streets between them with shoppers hustling through the city parade, their faces slack and vacant. His mind settles into the semi-hypnotic state which precedes concentration. He feels the slow release of pleasure at being about to start work.

Away from the window, he's greeted with the rich syrup aroma of paint which reminds him of what Cecillie said the first time she saw this room.

He'd been dreading her initial reaction to it – so much that he'd delayed bringing her to his place for days, always suggesting they meet at her apartment, a bar or the blue café. He'd been constantly aware of them circling it, evading it by taking side routes, and roundabout ways. In fact, each time he was at Cecillie's, the treacherous spot on her map glared at him; free from the yellow and black lines that she painstakingly filled in over the rest of the city.

He was horrified to think of her wandering around, as others had before her, picking up his brushes, shuffling through his sketch pads. He'd exposed himself before to this casual ignorance of the significance and importance of the room and he knew that if she didn't understand, then cold would clamp down on his heart and it would all be over. He'd dreaded it being over.

But what she'd said as she'd followed him in, with an exclamation of surprise, was that it was like the end of the tunnel.

And she was right. The rest of the apartment is cave-like – dark and damp – but in his painting room, it's light all day.

She had stood where he's standing now, slowly taking in the table, the pots, the glasses, jars, brushes, paintings, the splotched and splashed walls, paper, and books. And he had held his breath.

She turned to him, the light from the window falling on her; she'd looked dazzled and dazzling. 'This smells like you,' she said, inhaling deeply. 'This room is where you come from.'

They made love here then; the first of many times so that he likes to think that, as he works, he can always detect the note of their blended scent.

He paints steadily for nearly three hours until he can no longer focus. He shrugs his shoulders up and down to release the tense muscles and paces around the room, bending and stretching his legs.

His body is constantly hot and hungry; hungry for sex, for food, for sleep, for exercise, for Cecillie. It's burning up food inside him quicker than he can put it in, more than he can afford to buy. Maurice has taken pity on him and whenever he goes into the blue café, he gets extra large servings for the same price he paid before. But he also feels incredibly well – tight and strong and bursting with energy.

Before Cecillie, he would have painted non-stop for hours, without eating or resting, swigging water from a bottle until the evening when he staggered off in a daze to the blue café to drink and eat. He looks back with interest, almost amazement, that he could have lived for so long on his own – closed in, as he now sees it – and not gone mad. He hadn't had sex for months, nearly a year? He can't remember. Now he can't get enough. When he's with Cecillie he wants to touch her, hold her, enter her, wrap himself around her. And if he can't touch her, he wants to look at her. He loves the way her skin tone changes to reflect the different light of the day: she's butter-coloured in the bright of the afternoon sun, darker, and harder like the shell of a chestnut as the evening comes.

She absorbs him when he's with her and haunts him when she's not there. He's on the brink of being obsessed. He finds the idea of having found someone who can bring him to that pitch incredibly exciting. He doesn't fear tipping over the edge, because he knows he's in control by the way he's able to ration his thoughts of Cecillie, saving them up as rewards for work done well, savouring the time he spends with her.

It's a good job too because he's got a lot to do if he's going to get everything ready for his exhibition. The scale of the project seems to be spiralling and this concerns him sometimes. Frédérique left a message for him a few days ago, confirming the date of the opening party. He's painted 1 AUGUST in giant black letters on the wall so that if his attention is slipping, he only has to see that to knuckle down. As long as he maintains the perfect balance between work and play that he's attained, everything will be great. He meets Cecillie for lunch, or for dinner, or like today he takes the afternoon and evening off, because in the spaces when he does paint, like this morning, he packs so much energy into it that he achieves a greater fluency than he ever has before.

He studies what he's been doing. It's a painting of the ancient oak tree, the single remainder of the old central park where he spent a lot of his childhood playing. Now the tree is dwarfed, cramped by the silver-grey office blocks which surround it, marooned in the tiny circle of sour brown earth that it's allowed. Ranks of office workers with blank, featureless faces file past the tree, not seeing it, not touching it. It's a sad and angry painting – like a lot of his paintings – except that one male worker is gazing upwards where, among the tree's branches, which are fighting towards the sky, a flock of tiny birds has settled. Within the empty oval of his face there seems to Luc to be a mildness of expression and he's concerned that he's made it too easy for people to focus on that sweet moment which the rushed worker has chanced to witness, and to ignore the outrage that the man should feel; that Luc thinks more people should feel about what's happening to their city.

It's not the first time this softening has crept into one of his paintings and the idea that his own happiness may be knocking off some of the hard edges, and blinding him to harsher realities, nags at him.

He begins to pack away his equipment, sticking brushes into glasses of cleaning fluid and folding away the plastic sheet covering the sketches he was working from. He rushes a little because he's remembered the bed linen needs washing and there's only an hour before he expects Cecillie.

She's waiting outside his place when he gets back from the launderette. He sees her from the top of the street, sitting on the pavement next to the moped, smoking a cigarette in the sun. He gets quite close before she springs up to meet him. He can feel the dry heat from her skin as he holds her.

'You're hot,' he tells her as he takes in her smoky, starchy scent.

'So are you.'

'I've been to the launderette.' He shakes the bag of washing.

'We need to cool off.' She laughs and pulls away from him. 'Let's get going.'

She gets on the moped, starting it easily. 'Come on,' she shouts.

He opens the front door, flings the bag of sheets inside, and locks it.

On the moped behind Cecillie he looks down at her backside, admiring how it sits neatly, roundly on the seat. Out of the traffic, as the bike moves faster, he presses against her spiny body. With his hands around her waist, he feels her muscles tighten, relax, tauten, twisting with the movement of the bike she handles so easily. He enjoys the cool air blowing up around them, with the centre of warmth where their bodies meet.

Later, on the beach, Cecillie's wet stomach and breasts, as she drops her body onto his, shock his skin. Behind her the sun is full in the sky and it filters through her dangling hair, casting dappled shade on his face.

They're lying in a small indent at the foot of a dune. Almost pure-white powdery sand surrounds them; ahead is a blue streak of sea. They've been swimming and now they're resting. They are both good swimmers which pleases them; they take it as further evidence of their fitting together.

Today they have raced and dived, grasping each other in the water, playful like children. They have floated on their backs feeling the sun hot on their faces. Cecillie swam back to fetch her shades to put on, and Luc, twisting his head to watch her could see through the sun spots on his eyes the city, always there. Quiet, serene almost. The warmth of the sun, the sense of well being, is like a blessing from the city. Beneficent.

'What are you thinking about?'

'The city.'

'Have you never, ever, really left it?'

'Only once. When I was young.'

Not so young – fourteen, in fact. His mother had still been alive then, and he had gone to see his father, who had left when he was eight and moved north. Up until then, they had communicated only by letter, occasionally by phone, although the crackling space had made things difficult. A strain. Each time, his father had insisted that Luc visit to meet his other family – his half-brothers and sister. And Luc had always said yeah, great and thought no more of it.

On his fourteenth birthday, as a surprise, Luc's mother announced that she'd arranged for him to go there for the summer holidays. The children were seven, four and a baby, and they lived in a whirl of noise in a small farm cottage in Brittany. His father's new wife laughed like a donkey, the noise resounded around the rooms, knocking into the cries, screams and wailings of the various siblings. He had been urged to hold, feed and walk these children, and to play and play. He'd had a suspicion he'd only been invited as an extra pair of hands because he saw little of his father who was at work most days, and who sat in dazed silence once the children had gone to bed.

His father became briefly animated at the start of the evening meal when he pronounced to the table how lucky he felt, how honoured to have his whole family around him, to live in a beautiful place, to be in love with his wonderful wife. He asked everyone to reflect on their good fortune, and be grateful. They all bowed their heads, as if they were saying grace, and stared at their dinner plates until the clatter of his father's knife against his plate meant that they could eat.

This litany didn't inspire gratitude in Luc; in fact he felt quite the opposite. He was dreadfully homesick with a pure and savage longing to be back with his mother, in the quiet house, with the city noises outside. In Brittany the countryside's dense silence was sinister; it frightened him. He felt trapped, claustrophobic. He kept getting lost. Each time he went out on his own, he couldn't find his way back. He couldn't distinguish landmarks as he could at home where there was always something unique about a street. The trees and fields all looked the same, the paths cut through long corn and meadows were of confusing uniformity, stretching for unknown kilometre after unknown kilometre; the crack of a twig nearby him in the opaque, dank wood was menacing – a prowler, a killer; the steamy hot breath and huge rasping tongue of the cows, which his cousins patted and fed like pets, made him shudder.

His half-brothers were like a different species. The hedges, the woods, the long grass were an adventure, a comfort and a game to them. Part of themselves.

He arrived back in the city one evening. The train was met by his mother who quietly kissed him hello and told him, as they hugged, that she'd missed him dreadfully. He'd felt stunned with relief and love for her and this love flowed out into the busy streets, across the hot, noisy, dirty, smelly city leaving inside him a clear sense of pride and belonging.

Afterwards, he had such vivid pictures of the city, that he could only think of expressing them by colour. He'd always been good at art. He was one of those children, the envy of others, that easily copied a picture, drew a face; someone who instinctively knew which colours would mix well, complement, or be extremes. Suddenly it was something which he needed to do. And that was how he began.

Cecillie shakes her hair around so that it hisses against his skin, briefly touching, skimming his face.

'You're lucky,' she says, rolling off him. A hip bone fleetingly presses into his flesh. She searches for the cigarettes, lights two and passes him one. 'My childhood was permanently dark. The curtains had to be kept closed for my mother.'

'She was ill?' he asks softly, surprised by the sharp tone of her voice. He brushes the hair that's trapped in the corner of her mouth, passing his hand over her cheek.

'Not physically, well, not exactly,' Cecillie says. She stares out at the sea and talks in a strange, flat tone. 'I had a sister, who was killed. She was ten, I was eight. We'd been playing outside the house with friends. I came in to get a drink and she got run over while I was in the kitchen.'

He can't see her face but she has the air of someone in a trance. He wants to touch her but has the feeling that to disturb her would be damaging, like waking a sleepwalker.

'I remember hearing the brakes and the screaming and my mum running out and someone stopping me in the garden; they wouldn't let me follow her.' She takes a long drag. 'Mum was ill afterwards and stayed indoors and she wanted me to stay with her, didn't want me out of her sight.' She looks at him. 'Even when I was old enough, I was hardly ever allowed out on my own, without there being a huge fuss. My mum or dad drove me and picked me up from everywhere.'

'That must have been hard.'

'I hated it. But I couldn't fight it. It wasn't worth all the tears, and Mum would get ill. Really ill. I used to go and stay with my grandma and she'd let me go out, go to parties, be normal. They never knew that.'

'But they let you come here?'

'They didn't want me to, of course. That was where Gran came in.'

He knows that Cecillie's grandmother, and her friend, Cassandra, had made all the arrangements in France for Cecillie, and he also knows that her grandmother transfers money every month to Cecillie. A lot of money by his standards; enough for Cecillie to live on comfortably. She's always been open about it, never hidden the fact, but she'd never hinted at any of the reasons for it. He's sure that Blythe and Bryony don't know either, otherwise Blythe would be less ready with his sarcastic comments on the subject.

'I didn't want to come here either, you know?' Cecillie tells him. 'Australia was my dream, but they wouldn't hear of it. My mum practically had a heart attack at the thought.'

Cecillie wags a finger at Luc, mimics a woman's high-pitched voice: 'My only one, my precious child at the mercy of drugs, drink, rape, murder . . .'

She continues. 'I didn't have great hopes for France. It didn't sound exactly adventurous; especially with Cassandra sorting everything. But I was so desperate to get away, I'd have agreed to anything and I couldn't throw it back in Gran's face, could I?'

'I'm glad you had to compromise,' he says after a moment, touching her shoulder.

'So am I,' says Cecillie, leaning in for a kiss. 'I was surprised how much I loved it, as soon as I got here.'

* * *

As the day begins to cool, they drive to the tourist bay to use the showers on the beach. They dance with their T-shirts still on under the tall metal shower which pounds out freezing cold beads of water. Cecillie laughs at the pinking tourists filing by, clutching their beach goods – towels, bags, books, balls and children. She waves to some and calls out in English, words Luc doesn't understand. He doesn't care. He's happy just looking at her. The evening light throws shadows across her body, deepening the hollows of her collarbone, paring the flesh on her legs and arms to golden, fragile stalks. He holds her against him, reassuring himself with the strength he feels in her thin body and the hot kisses she plants on his neck.

Their T-shirts slap icily around them in the wind as they head back towards the city. The lights are beginning to come on and every quarter becomes equally beautiful with the patterns of the lines and curves of white, red, gold blanketed in black. A twinkling fairy-tale prettiness. The journey back seems so much longer. He can't wait to get Cecillie home. He wants her desperately and he leans against her, his hands searching out, wandering over her body.

'You'll make me crash.'

'Keep concentrating,' he tells her. His hands have found her breasts, and are rubbing and pulling her nipples through the cloth.

She groans, leans back against him then sits up, sharply. 'Stop Luc, please, or I will crash, really.' They both laugh as he moves his hands away, but the desire stays within him, in abeyance.

As they get closer to the city, the breeze lessens, the air warms, until they're back in the streets with the dense, sultry night and their clothes completely dry.

They make love slowly, lingeringly, half-sleepy with the pleasant tiredness of a day spent outdoors. The bedroom is cool, the walls have kept out all the heat; the clean, unaired sheets which he threw hastily across the bed feel damp. But their bodies are hot. Luc watches little beads of sweat pop out of Cecillie's skin like tiny, silvery pearls of mercury. They glide across her body and he gathers some up with his tongue, tasting the saltiness of them. His cock is moving inside the slippery space of her. They hold each other tight, rocking together until he has to let go, feeling her body trembling in response.

He wakes up to the gentle rush and sigh of Cecillie's breathing, like the sound of the sea swishing up against the shore. He lies still, trying to match the pattern of his breathing to hers. He's read somewhere that copying the sounds of someone sleeping beside you tricks your mind and lulls your body back into unconsciousness. But instead he feels his cock harden, his breath begins to speed; he tries to pace it again, but he can't. He reaches out to Cecillie but she sighs and turns on her side away from him so that his hand slips across her buttocks which quiver under his touch. He's now wide awake with an intense, useless erection.

He gets up, goes into the painting room and looks out of the window. High, high up is the moon, small but outrageously fat and white with a blurry-grey halo of light around it. He opens the window and stands in front of it, his legs wide apart, his arms held up, letting the draught soothe the aching parts of him. He is so grateful for this.

And then it comes to him. He wants to paint her. He wants to create something from this heat, the trickling hair, the bone, the skin, the salt, the air, the sea, the burning sun. He shuts the door, pulls a large blue-painted canvas into the centre of the room, gathers brushes and paints, and starts to work.

Luc's shivering breaks the flow of his painting. But it's finished, for now. He's been oblivious to time, to the increasing light in the room, to everything except the feel and look of Cecillie that he'd absorbed from yesterday. In front of him is the result. He thinks it's wonderful. It, Cecillie, glows at him.

He lights a cigarette and smokes by the window. The breeze is sharp on his skin and he hunts around for something to wear. The only thing to hand is the old T-shirt he's been using for a cloth. It's stiff with paint but he pulls it on, coloured dust swarming around him. When he's finished his cigarette he turns back to look at the painting.

A shock of shame runs through him. It isn't love shining out but lust. How can Cecillie be this to him, no more than a stark body for sex? He closes his eyes to steady his shaking.

Opening them again, he realizes, with a rush of relief, that he was mistaken. It is love after all, sex too, but the white harshness of passion, pure passion and he feels himself falling in love with Cecillie all over again. It's the most intimate, the most revealing and the most painful painting that he's ever done.

Still shaken, he goes to the bedroom. Cecillie's lying across the bed, face down, her limbs seem everywhere, a leg on one side, an arm on the other, her strong back in a diagonal across the bed. He pulls on his shorts and goes out of the house, closing the door quietly behind him.

His skin loosens up from the warmer air. He starts to run. He runs and runs, his heart pumping with the sudden effort. There are a few people around. As he approaches them, he calls out softly 'coming through', dodging into the road, springing back onto the pavement. Down one alley, across another, anticipating the broken gate, avoiding the café tables across the pavement, taking the short cuts. He knows the way so well. Then the narrow streets open up, the concrete becomes grey paving stones and he's arrived. Just in time to see the plastic bags being dragged inside the heavy door. He runs up the steps and pushes in.

'Bonjour, Madame.'

'Bonjour, Monsieur.' Her voice is calm, as if she's been expecting him. He walks quickly down the aisle, lights a candle, closes his eyes and stays for a minute. Then he's striding down out of the church, running down the steps, running and running again. He stops at the baker's at the bottom of his street to buy some *tartes aux pommes*; Cecillie's favourite.

When he gets back, Cecillie's still asleep in the same position. He undresses and lies down beside her. He falls asleep immediately.

'Luc.' Cecillie is kneeling on the mattress shaking him awake. He instinctively reaches out for her, his hand touching her arm, finding its way up to her breasts.

She whispers in his ear as her hand slides under the sheets and takes hold of his cock, already stirring. 'Frédérique's here.'

'Shit!'

She laughs as he scrambles up, then retreats from the room as he grabs his painted T-shirt to throw at her. He'd forgotten his meeting with Frédérique.

The women are in the kitchen. He hears their voices before he opens the door. When he goes in, they both stop talking.

Cecillie's leaning against the sink, in only her vest-top and bikini bottoms. Her long legs look longer from that angle, her hair is mussed.

Frédérique is neatly dressed and fully made up. She's perched on a chair, her stockinged legs crossed at the ankles, a cup of coffee untouched on the table. She looks relieved to see him. He stoops to kiss her hello without taking his eyes off Cecillie. She grins at him and he notices she's eating one of the *tartes aux pommes* he bought earlier.

'Sorry,' he says to Frédérique. 'I forgot.'

'Don't worry. We can arrange another time if you'd prefer to?'

'Yummy,' Cecillie says, kissing him on the cheek as he reaches past her to pour himself a coffee.

'No, it's OK,' he says to Frédérique as he turns round and stands next to Cecillie. 'I'll swig this and then we'll go.'

'Fine.' Frédérique glances around the kitchen and down at the floor. She can't look at them. Luc pities anyone faced with this unsubtle display: Cecillie practically naked, himself feverish with love and sex. He tries to think of something to say to lessen her discomfort, but is distracted by the trickle of longer blonde hairs that run up the inside of Cecillie's thighs, and his desire to run his hands across the soft prickle of them. Nothing else seems important. He could almost forget that Frédérique is here and sink his teeth into Cecillie and surrender. He has to tear himself away. He gulps the coffee down.

'Ready?'

He sees Frédérique out of the kitchen into the hallway, then returns to Cecillie. She's tucking into another *tarte aux pommes*. She licks away flakes of pastry from around her mouth. Her fat, pink tongue.

'Has she been in my painting room?' he whispers.

'Of course not. Not with me to guard it.' She bares her teeth and snarls like a dog. Pastry crumbs scatter on her chest.

'Don't you go in, either. Promise?'

'Are you hiding something from me?'

'Something *for* you. Promise?'

She nods.

He licks some of the crumbs from her chest, then takes a bite out of the pastry.

'Heyyyy,' she complains.

'Don't go far from here,' he mutters, holding onto her. 'I won't be long. Wait here until I get back, I haven't finished with you yet.'

In the restaurant, Luc and Frédérique sit opposite each other.

'You look tired.'

'I was up all night painting.' He regrets saying that immediately. He's learning to keep some things to himself, hidden away from Frédérique's insatiable interest.

But today she seems preoccupied and simply warns him, 'Don't wear yourself out,' as she orders two coffees and some croissants from the waiter.

'I'm not sure it's suitable for the exhibition, the painting I was doing last night. I don't think it will be. I don't know . . .' He stops speaking abruptly, telling himself to keep quiet from now on in case he says something really stupid. The painting's too fresh in his mind and it's making him feel off-balance, as though he's been pulled out of a deep sleep and had to start acting immediately. His body's operating on auto while his mind is fuzzily trying to catch up.

Frédérique takes out her personal organizer from her briefcase, places it on the table and adds a pen neatly on top. She still won't look him in the eye. 'Don't you think it's good enough? Do you want me to have a look at it? To be honest, I'm not sure we'll have time to pick and choose. I'm afraid we're on a pretty tight schedule. You need –' she flicks through the pages as if she's got all his paintings listed there '– at the last count, four more pieces, maybe three at a push. That's a lot in five weeks.'

'I'll have to think. It may be too personal.'

Frédérique's eyes widen but she doesn't ask for a further explanation. He's glad, because it's too early to discuss the painting. She presses the organizer flat at the diary section. Luc can read today's date. She scribbles a quick note in illegible handwriting.

He feels his warm happiness from earlier failing, being dragged into a black hole. The restaurant is oppressively quiet, only a few tables are occupied. He's impatient to get back to his work; to contemplate the portrait again after a break from it, perhaps work a little more on it today if it feels right. He doesn't want to be sitting here. He finds this aspect of the exhibition tedious; he'd prefer minimum involvement. He's sure that Frédérique knows what she's doing and, besides, what's there to discuss? He'll paint, he'll produce some paintings, Frédérique'll hang the results up along with some of his older ones and hopefully, please, someone will buy some of them. And then he'll be able to buy as much food as he likes. He's starving, he realizes. He can't wait for the croissants.

'Do you think . . .' Frédérique begins, finally looking in his direction. 'Do you think there's any chance that you won't be ready? We are pushing this through in much less time than usual, after all.'

Even at his most pessimistic times, he's never considered that possibility, but now with this black tiredness filling him, he wants to lay his head on the table and say Yes. Please go away. I'll never do it in a thousand years. Instead, he yawns and says, testing her, 'It's a possibility.'

'Large or small?' Her eyes are fixed on his, intent now. It's his turn to look away.

'I don't know.'

They sit in silence. Luc's mind is blank. The waiter brings their order. The croissants smell delicious. He begins to salivate in anticipation but doesn't want to appear greedy so attends to his coffee first. He balances two sugar cubes on his spoon and lowers them into his coffee; he stirs them in and then takes another cube; he needs the energy. He's about to take one of the pastries when he notices Frédérique's hand is shaking. He almost makes a flippant remark about it but, alerted, he takes note of other uncharacteristic flaws – the nail varnish on a couple of fingers is chipped, there's a tuft of hair sticking out above her right ear, there's a tiny grease stain on her shirt – which looks rather creased – and the lipstick on her top lip is smudged.

It is possible that Luc's previous perception of Frédérique being immaculately presented could have been unsound, especially if he'd never examined her like this before, but paying attention to detail is what he's good at. He doesn't miss much, sometimes to Cecillie's annoyance.

No, there's something about these imperfections, and Frédérique's tense distraction, which tells him that something's wrong and he suddenly feels guilty for being awkward earlier. She evidently doesn't want to be here this morning any more than he does. But as he watches her, he feels irritated; she should, after all, be making more of an effort.

'Look,' he says, 'I want this exhibition more than anything. I'm getting a bit jumpy but you'll have all the paintings. There are five more weeks and I've finished one new one and I've been preparing a second. If I do decide to put this one in, that's three of them. And the fourth one – we'll see.'

His hand stretches out to the croissants. His fingers are just touching the warm pastry when Frédérique speaks.

'Don't worry about me,' she says, out of the blue. Her voice is too bright, quavering. It makes him draw his hand back.

'But it would be, it would be . . .' she continues and he sees, with horror, her eyes fill with tears. 'It would be the worst situation . . .' She fumbles around the table, finds her serviette and dabs at her eyes. 'Please excuse me. I feel so awful. I'm sorry.'

Luc watches, helpless, as she struggles to compose herself again. The restaurant is quiet, which seems to amplify the sound of Frédérique's crying. He wants her to stop, but he doesn't know how to make her stop. It's as if the black hole has changed its mind and is now spewing all the energy back out at him, but twisted and distorted. He feels the pressure physically, like ice in his head, freezing all thoughts, all sense. He's useless at this kind of thing. He never knows what to say or do. Frédérique continues dabbing and sniffing as she tries to compose herself. Luc feels like the worst kind of spectator. He touches her arm.

'What's wrong?' he asks Frédérique gently. He feels an idiot. His voice sounds sickly false. 'Is there anything I can do?'

She shakes her head but puts the serviette down. 'You know Jacques's asked me to marry him?'

'No, I didn't,' he tells her. The news doesn't surprise him; when he first saw them together they came across as an established serious couple.

'He asked me around the same time as I met you. I said yes.'

'Well that's great, Frédérique. Congratulations,' he says tentatively.

'Since then,' she pauses. 'I've changed my mind.'

'Oh.'

'It makes it all rather awkward.'

'Awkward?'

'With the exhibition.'

So that's what's wrong. He'll deal with the disappointment later. 'You don't want to go ahead with the exhibition at Jacques's bar. That's OK, we can change venues. We'll postpone it, hold it somewhere else. It'll give us more time too,' he adds.

'There wouldn't be a somewhere else,' she tells him. 'It's only because of Jacques that it's going ahead in the first place. He's covering a big percentage of the costs; the gallery wouldn't countenance such a high-risk show on an unknown artist.'

He bridles at this assessment of his artistic status. 'But why is he involved in the first place? You don't usually hold shows there do you? And I get the impression he doesn't even like my work.'

'Because of me, of course.'

'I'm sorry?'

'It's a present,' she laughs bitterly. 'An engagement present.'

'Fuck. I can't believe this. What you're saying is because you've called off getting married, the exhibition will be off, too.'

'The exhibition won't be off. I haven't told Jacques anything. I'm waiting until after the exhibition,' she adds flatly. Luc must have looked puzzled because she rushes on. 'What else can I do? He's spent too much money already, he's gone way over the top sending invitations to all sorts of people. All the leaflets, posters, price lists; everything's printed, the press know. Dates are fixed. There's my reputation and the gallery's and yours too. None of us can afford it to be off, Luc. I can't risk telling him.'

'Then why did you tell me?'

She looks startled, then flushes. 'You're right, I shouldn't be burdening you with my problems. I should never have brought this up.'

'It's OK,' he tells her, which is a lie.

'I've been going over it in my head so much and had no one to talk to.'

Luc shrugs. 'I'm sorry I couldn't be more help.'

They sit in silence for a moment. Luc's curious and can't resist asking, 'Can you really let him spend all that money and then ditch him?'

'I know it seems like a really horrible thing to do,' she says almost in a whisper. 'But what other way is there?'

'When are you going to tell him?'

'Afterwards.' She picks bleakly at the corner of a page. 'Soon afterwards.' She places her handbag on her knee and produces a pair of sunglasses. She wipes the lenses slowly with a tissue, blows her nose and then puts the glasses on. In a second she's transformed to a more cool, collected Frédérique, just a little wobbly around the edges. Luc finds it disconcerting not being able to see her eyes.

'Maybe you'll feel differently afterwards.'

'I keep telling myself the same thing. But I don't really believe it. In my head, Jacques is what I want, but in my heart . . .'

'That's a shame,' he butts in, then hesitates. He doesn't want to upset her again, so he continues cautiously. 'You two do seem quite suited?'

'But there should be more to it than that, shouldn't there?' she responds quickly.

'What do you mean?'

'Love, I mean love.' She blushes again. 'Don't you think?' she asks him.

'Well,' he says, quickly, 'I can't really say, you know, I don't know the whole situation . . .'

'What do you think about love, Luc?'

'It's important, I guess; it's one of the most important things in our lives.'

She nods. 'I do have good reasons, you know,' she says.

'I'm sure you do.'

He can't tell whether she's looking at him and he certainly can't carry on gazing into the black of her sunglasses. He looks away, fiddles with his empty coffee cup, wiping a streak of coffee across the white china. The croissants have gone cold now but he would still eat them all if he could. It seems such a shame to waste them. He wonders whether he should suggest that they leave now, or whether he ought to keep Frédérique company for a while longer. He thinks of Cecillie waiting for him at his place, lovely, happy Cecillie and aches to be back with her.

'Doesn't everyone feel like this?' he asks, with forced enthusiasm. 'Have second thoughts and everything? It's a big step.' He's waving his hands around excessively as if that will help. Where's he picked all this crap up from?

'I think you're referring to wedding nerves. That's near the time of the wedding, which we're not. Near, I mean,' she says, with a frail smile.

'Oh.'

A tear appears from behind Frédérique's shades, runs down her cheek. She wipes it away. 'Excuse me.' She heads off towards the toilets.

He considers leaving while she's away. That way, he reasons to himself, she won't have to face him again and they can meet up when she's feeling better. Or he can stay and eat all the croissants before she returns, put the plate under his chair and pretend the waiter cleared it.

Frédérique reappears before he has time to act on either thought. She's washed her face and removed her sunglasses. This is the first time that he's seen her without any make-up. She looks pink and watery from all the crying, but nicer somehow, more approachable.

'Listen,' she says, without sitting down. 'I've not been very professional and I apologize.'

She picks up all her belongings. 'Please, concentrate on your work, that's all you should be concerned with, I'll sort out the rest. You'll get your show, Luc. I promise.'

She shakes his hand and turns to leave. 'Thanks for being so understanding. I appreciate it.'

5

the love bit

Blythe, standing outside the leisure centre clutching his carrier bag of swimming things, feels like the biggest prick on earth. Bryony's late. Why is she always late? He's sure she must do it to wind him up. He hung around reception so long it wouldn't have surprised him if they'd called security. He's walked along the street and back a dozen times. Now he's leaning against the glass walls of the building, trying to look casual but really he's supporting himself. His legs are totally shot, his head aches, his eyes are burning. The sun, bouncing off the glass behind him, is making him sweaty. His T-shirt is sticking to his back, his boxers under his shorts are damp around his balls. Drops of water trickle down his spine into his arse-crack. He sticks his hand down the back of his shorts to wipe away the tickling sweat until he realizes he can be seen from inside the building, scratching his arse.

He can't handle this waiting. He needs to lie down, to cool off. He's only had a couple of hours' sleep this morning and it shows. He's got rotten armpits and stale smoker's breath. He's fucking filthy. And he's gagging with thirst.

Last night was heavy. Fridays are always popular and it was one of the busiest he's known. The bar was packed and hot, the music was thumping. It was a great atmosphere. Blythe didn't have time to think behind the tiny counter where he bent and stretched, opening this bottle here, mixing that cocktail there, chopping – lemon, pineapple, orange, sticking cherries onto sticks; dodging Michel and Sandrine – he was glad it was those two, they're both good, quick and they aren't fazed when it gets crazy. Between them there were only seven glasses broken, Blythe only did the one. He likes it when it all goes right. He likes it when his moves become so mechanical that he works without thinking. Moving forwards, backwards, twist, turn. Forwards, backwards, twist, turn. The faster it is, the more you have to switch your mind off and let your arms, hands, feet react on their own, working to the thunk of the heavy bottle in your hand, the snap-hiss of the beer bottle top, the twist of the lid on the shaker. As soon as you become aware of what you're doing that's the point when you're likely to trip up or hesitate, or get covered in grenadine or coconut liqueur – he's done that before now. He likes the way he glides from the bar to the till, prides himself on remembering all the prices, gets annoyed with the others if their fingers hesitate over the buttons, not sure what to punch in. Most of all he likes taking time out to juggle the glasses, one two three, sending a glass in a spinning arc in front of him, with the appreciative applause from his punters. It's a show, and he gets paid for doing it, but he's good, he knows. He's the best fucking barman there!

But it's knackering. As the night went on the lights over the bar seemed to dazzle and transform the faces into manic masks; a blur of eyes and teeth. Perfume saturated his nostrils, leaving a metallic taint in his mouth which he can taste now, coating the inside of his mouth. He leans his head back against the glass and closes his eyes.

Immediately Jacques's face pops into his head. Last night he was with that woman who looks like Bryony again. It was the first time he'd seen them together since that awkward evening a few weeks ago when he got caught up in their shit.

After the bar closed, Blythe had sat in the kitchen as usual with a small cup of coffee left over from the pot on the stove. The stewed caffeine made him feel spaced out, gave his vision an exaggerated clarity. He watched as Bernadette, the cleaner mopped the floors, wiped the tiling on the walls, sloshed the water in a big metal bucket that clanged and clattered as she pushed it around.

Blythe always takes the time to chill out after the hustle of the evening, particularly after a frantic evening like last night. He enjoys listening to Bernadette's chirpy family stories, to the rhythmic sound of the flap flap of the mop and the swish of the cloth against the background silence of the building.

'Did you see the woman who was here with Jacques tonight?' he had asked her.

Bernadette stopped mopping, straightened up and stood with her hands supporting her back.

She shrugged. 'What's she like?'

'Small, short dark hair.' He pressed his hands to his head, to describe the way the woman's hair clings to her skull.

'Oh, Frédérique.' Bernadette smiled broadly. 'She's a lovely woman. Always has a chat.'

'His girlfriend?'

'No. Though –' Bernadette lowered her voice '– she's been

staying the night, you know.' She hissed the last part of the sentence. 'In the same bed. I've seen when I'm cleaning.'

'More than friends then?'

Bernadette picked up the bucket. 'Maybe. All I can say is they've known each other for years.'

'They had an argument the other night. She was crying.'

'Lovers' tiff, perhaps,' she said and winked.

Blythe got up, took the bucket off Bernadette, poured the dirty water down the sink, and turned on the cold tap. He swirled some clean water around the bottom of the bucket, before emptying it and handing it back. He turned the tap on full for a minute to flush the sink clean while Bernadette put the cleaning equipment away.

'I got caught up in the whole scene and Jacques had a go at me later about it.'

'Nobody likes their private business on show,' Bernadette told him and patted his arm. 'Especially not to staff.'

Blythe left when Bernadette locked up. The sky was lightening. Down by the river it was dawn-cold. A wind whipped up from the sea along the bank where there was no shelter and the cool air hit him full in the face. It was refreshing. He continued walking along the river then doubled back into the city centre where the music from the late-night clubs vibrated a beat through the pavement. He was still too buzzing and hyper to go back to his place and sleep. If he walked for a while, he figured, he'd come down enough to sleep. He didn't notice how far he was going or where.

It was about six when he arrived back at the house. Cecillie and Luc were sitting on her balcony. They were watching the sunrise. The sensible option would have been to leave them to it and go straight to bed, but he didn't. He sat with them, drinking more coffee, some lager, smoking fags and later a bit of grass until he'd been so out of it that the next thing he knew he was lying on his bed, being woken up by some shit-awful noise, outside his door.

He opened it to a mad scene of Monsieur Bayard and Max the Pratt from upstairs who was holding his dog in his arms. It was the dog making the noise, howling its fucking heart out, and Monsieur B was shouting at Max who was shouting back.

They looked at Blythe, the dog stopped howling, directed its beady eyes at him and growled. Monsieur Bayard, his round face anxious, drew Blythe out of his room and appealed to him.

'I was asleep, Monsieur B,' Blythe moaned.

'Please, tell him. Everyone's been complaining. Tell him it's not right.'

'I don't know what you're talking about.'

'The pissing.'

'The pissing? What pissing?' For a moment, Blythe thought he'd misunderstood the language.

'His dog pissing on the stairs, stinking the whole building out. Tell him. It's not right.'

Blythe looked at Max. He was red in the face and sweat was trickling down the sides of his head. The dog was licking the sweat off Max's face. Jesus, that guy was creepy.

Blythe sighed. How did he manage to get himself caught up in stuff all the time? He must have a label on him saying ALL SHITE STICK HERE.

'It stinks!' Monsieur Bayard shouted, waving his arms around. He looked so funny that Blythe struggled to keep a straight face.

'Listen mate,' he said sternly to Max, 'You're upsetting our good landlord here, so control your dog, all right?'

Max carried the dog upstairs. Its eyes were closed. The dog was fucking asleep. He fucking envied that dog for that.

'It's not him,' Max suddenly shouted from above, setting the dog off barking. 'It's you. You dirty English hooligan.'

Blythe sniffed a couple of times. He couldn't detect anything, he never had noticed anything. Monsieur Bayard was shaking his head, arms folded. 'I have so much trouble with that man.'

Blythe went back into his room and closed the door. Sleep. But when he looked at his watch it was time to go and meet Bryony.

Now he thinks how he could have gone back to bed after all, as she's obviously not coming. It's happened before when one of the boys gets sick and she isn't able to get in touch with him in time.

Then he sees the three of them approaching, Bryony in the middle with a boy holding each hand. They take up the whole pavement, oblivious to everyone else having to walk slowly behind them, or step out into the road to get past. She's hurrying them along by swinging their arms. One, two, one, two. The smallest boy has to trot beside her to keep up. As they get closer, he hears their high voices, the squeaky pitch which ends each sentence like a question. He walks to meet them and the boys shyly hold back. He feels like a giant. He squats down.

'Salut, Fabien, Patrice.'

They peep out from behind Bryony. Big brown eyes. She prompts them.

'Good morning, Blythe. How are you?' they say in English.

'They've been practising the whole way here,' Bryony tells him.

'Good morning, Fabien. Good morning, Patrice. I'm very well, thank you. How are you?' He puts on a posh voice and shakes their hands in turn. Both boys giggle and hide again.

Blythe stands up. Bryony's brown eyes are watching him too. He steps back quickly after they kiss hello. He doesn't want her to know how bad he smells.

'I'm sorry we're late,' says Bryony, in French so that the boys understand. 'We couldn't find Fabien's swimming trunks, could we, Fabien?'

There are more giggles from Fabien.

'It doesn't matter. You're all here now.'

Bryony touches his hand briefly before she's scooting off after the boys who are running ahead. Blythe has to hurry to catch them up.

In the pool, Blythe looks down at his white chest and stomach, even paler in the artificial light; he feels flabby – it's amazing how quickly his body has lost its tone. Although it's hardly surprising. One minute he was skiing every day and now he doesn't do any sport and he drinks way too much. His legs, distorted by the moving water, look shrivelled and milky. They remind him of how, as a child he'd cried in the hospital when his newly mended arm was revealed from plaster cast. It was like a big white worm with flaking skin. Bryony has tanned lightly but as he looks down the front of her swimming costume, he can see a paler curve at the top of her breasts where he knows the skin is white. He finds this view so attractive he has to force himself to look away. The boys are nut-brown. They bounce up and down in the water splashing each other.

The compulsory black rubber swimming cap issued at the pool side is a bastard to get on. The boys are beside themselves with laughter as Blythe clowns around, stretching and pulling and rolling his eyes.

The cap grips his head like a vice, making his eyes bulge out. Some of his hair above each ear has escaped. No matter how he tries to tuck it in, he can't control it. And the cap stinks, like a massive fucking condom. He knows he must look insane. Bryony sweeps a practical, un-judging eye over him. She looks pretty with her hair all pulled away – her eyes look bigger; her head is so small that she had to have a children's size. The boys have their own thinner, more stylish caps in bright green and blue.

In the water, the boys forget their shyness. Blythe is assaulted with a barrage of attacks. They dive through his legs, they grab his arms, his ankles. He gets hold of one of them; a firm, squirming, slippery body. Like the rubber cap that he couldn't handle, it twists away from him, creating a tiny tidal wave which hits his stomach.

He feels like a piece of equipment, being wheeled around to be used as it suits them. Hands grip, loosen, feet touch, push off from his body. He stands either with the top part of his body out of the water, freezing cold, legs apart; or he crouches down, arms held out, aching, legs going numb – but at least he's warm – while they race a circuit around him. Such excitement, such planning and organizing to do the same thing over and over again, with only slight variations.

Bryony swims past every now and then, calling out words of encouragement. Blythe isn't sure if they're for him or the boys.

They want to test who can hold their breath the longest. He

gets the impression from the nudges and sniggers that they know he'll do badly at this. They swim to a deeper part of the pool. Blythe dives down after the boys, opens his eyes under water.

The boys look huge, dangling in front of him, noses held, eyes wide. Then they drop like brown pebbles and sit on the bottom, looking up at him, as if they are relaxing on a settee watching some weird television programme: which he realizes is him.

He forces himself deeper towards them, kicking hard. He's going to get hold of the little buggers and tickle them out of the water. He swims nearer, circles them, then moves in, but they shuffle back on their bottoms away from him and he's out of air. He blows out bubbles which dance in front of him, then he's pushing upwards panicking that he won't make it, his lungs are stretched to bursting. He surfaces in a froth, gasping for breath, his face burning with effort. Seconds later two tiny sleek hats bob to the top, together.

'We win, we win.'

Blythe hauls himself to the side of the pool and clings on. Beached, like a great white whale. He can't stop coughing, his eyes are streaming and his head is pounding furiously. The boys grip onto his arms. 'Blythe, Blythe.'

'Where's Bryony?' Blythe asks them, between gasps.

'There she is, there she is.' The boys are pointing but Blythe can't focus. He scans the pool but all he can see is a mass of seething bodies, then he spots a familiar face. It's Bryony. Blythe knows it must be Bryony but with the black cap on she looks the absolute spit of the woman from the bar, so that he half expects Jacques to rise out of the water in front of him like some sea demon, fierce and ready to attack.

Blythe lays his face against the cool tiles and closes his eyes.

He wishes he'd never been there that night. Jacques has always been a bit full of himself for Blythe's taste, swanning around, like the Big I Am, too good to help out, even when the bar is really busy, but he doesn't want there to be any bad feeling where he works. He needs the job, for god's sake, if nothing else.

He regrets what happened afterwards more than anything. Blythe had struggled up from the cellar with a crate of beer and Jacques was waiting for him. Jacques did a quick check that no one else was around and said softly, 'I suggest you mind your own business next time.' His lips were so tight he could barely let the words out.

'I was looking out for the woman – she was upset.' Blythe adjusted the crate in his arms. It was heavy.

'You were mistaken.'

'I suppose she was crying with happiness, was she?' Blythe said when it would have been much wiser to keep his mouth shut.

Jacques's face burned with anger and Blythe thought he was in for a punching. He wanted to get back to the bar. They were fast running out of beer in there and the others would be wondering where the fuck he was. He didn't want them thinking he'd been for a sly fag break. But Jacques was blocking the way.

He lost his grip on the crate for a second; it rattled and dropped a fraction before he secured it again. It scared the shit out of both of them but at least it broke the tension. Jacques headed off upstairs.

'Arsehole,' Blythe said under his breath then kicked himself when he heard Jacques's steps pause. But Jacques didn't respond so Blythe doesn't know if he even heard him. All things considered, he's lucky still to have his job intact, never mind all parts of his anatomy.

'Is Bryony your girlfriend?' asks one of the boys.

'What?'

'Is Bryony your girlfriend?'

'Yes,' he replies. 'Yes she is.'

'Do you love her?' the little boy asks. 'Do you love her?' he asks again and again, his voice getting shrill with excitement until he's shouting, and Blythe has to put a hand out, to touch the boy's arm.

'Quiet, Fabien, calm down.'

'But do you?' the boy implores and Blythe looks at Bryony, who is now definitely Bryony, waving away. Suddenly, the idea of it being Bryony with Jacques that night and not Frédérique, makes him want to throw up. He holds on to the side of the pool and clamps his teeth together, clenches his fists and swallows hard. Perhaps, he thinks, he does love her, perhaps this is what love is. And he knows with certainty as he's thinking these words that that is exactly what love is.

'Yes,' he mutters to the boy, through his teeth. 'Yes, of course I do.'

The boys shriek and launch themselves, with a loud splash, towards Bryony. He feels faint and hangs onto the side.

Bryony fastens herself onto his back, winds her legs around him, slides her arms around his waist. She feels lighter, less substantial in the water. He can't feel the mould of her, the weight of her breasts, the round of her stomach. It's as if she isn't quite there and suddenly he needs to feel her properly so he turns round and hugs her to him.

'Are you OK?'

He nods. 'Fucked, that's all.'

'Was it busy last night?'

'Busy as shit.'

They watch the boys chasing each other, popping up and down in the water.

'They really like you, you know. They were so excited this morning, I could hardly control them. Then we had tears, too.'

'I think they're great. Even if they do think I'm one big joke.'

'They don't.'

Blythe isn't always completely comfortable with the boys. He's conscious of waiting for them to say something that will embarrass him or show him up. Perhaps point out his slight roll of stomach, the spot on his chin, with the innocent truthfulness kids have. Jesus, he's so thick. What does he imagine they'll say? My papa's dick is much bigger than yours in voices so loud that everyone will turn and look and laugh, including Bryony? It's not as if she isn't aware by now of all that's a bit dubious about him. And she's still with him, isn't she?

But an embarrassing moment does come up when they're sitting in a full café devouring hot chocolate and toasted cheese sandwiches. Blythe's sitting opposite Bryony and feeling much better. He's wolfed down two sandwiches and his stomach feels settled for the first time since last night, his headache is clearing and he at last feels clean. Bryony's looking adorable. She hasn't dried her hair very well and the wet ends have soaked the front of her T-shirt, making it completely see-through over one breast. He can see her nipple hard with cold. It makes him feel horny.

'*He* said you're his girlfriend.'

'Who's "he", Patrice? I've told you before.'

'Blythe, Blythe, Blythe,' chants Patrice.

'*Blythe* said he loves you,' Fabien says as if he's disgusted by the idea. Blythe can't believe what he's hearing.

'Yuckee!' pipes Patrice, rolling his eyes.

'Well, *I* think that's nice,' Bryony says to Fabien, cutting his sandwich in two for him, but looking quizzically at Blythe. He wonders whether she expects him to speak. Bryony keeps talking to the boy but doesn't take her eyes off Blythe. 'I love him too. Now, eat up your sandwich.'

He hadn't ever imagined telling someone he loves them for the first time through a third party, and kids to boot. When he'd said yes, earlier, he'd had to think about it, had to weigh up what he felt before he spoke, but now it seems like he was only waiting for the final piece to lock in with the other fragments in his brain and make the whole thing real. Of course he loves her, how could he not? And if Bryony means it too, if she hasn't said it just to shut the boys up, he wonders how love can have sneaked up on them both, without them noticing.

'Do you have sex?' Fabien asks very loudly and this time the café falls silent as everyone pricks up their ears. Blythe, almost choking on a mouthful, finds himself blushing, then blushes some more because of it. Are such little boys supposed to know about sex? Surely at their age it's all football and action men, isn't it? He looks at Bryony who seems unperturbed. She sorts out a napkin to wipe off Fabien's hands.

'You know that's really none of your business,' she says softly. 'That's mine and Blythe's business. OK?'

'OK.'

'Yuckee!' says Patrice.

Bryony goes off to find the toilet, the boys go to stroke a dog a couple of tables along and Blythe is left sitting on his own, stunned, but with a flurry of happiness inside him.

He walks them back to their house. It's a rather grand, but shabby house near the centre of the city. It's solid with the air of a family home, a parent's house, and that's why Blythe doesn't like it.

He doesn't know how Bryony can stand not having her own place. Or how she can be so at ease in a stranger's home. He watches her opening the fridge to get juice out for the boys, opening the kitchen window, looking through the mail which she picked up in the hallway; as if she belongs here.

But he always forgets that she enjoys being part of a family. Her own family is huge and very close. She has a stack of letters filling a box in her bedroom; not just from her mum or dad, or from the two sisters and brother, but cousins, grandparents and an uncle who sends her money every now and then. Besides a few birthday cards, Blythe's had one letter from his mum since he's been here, telling him his granddad had died, and he doesn't even know where that letter is. He thinks he may have thrown it away. He phoned his mum back. He's not very good at writing.

What he finds hardest about Bryony's job is that he can't pop and see her, he can't surprise her, take her out on the off chance. And she can't come to him either. Their meetings, their time together has to be planned, timetabled in. Like now, what he really wants to do is take her back to his room, kiss her, make love to her, talk to her. Ask her about the love bit. Particularly ask her about that.

They stand in the hall, saying goodbye. Bryony keeps glancing behind her, to see what the boys are doing.

He asked her once. 'Do you have to be so perfect, so responsible?' He knew what her answer was before she said it but he'd pressed on, making a joke of it. 'Can't you get up late a couple of times?' he asked her. 'Forget to pick up the boys once in a while, stay with me overnight without telling anyone? Then it won't be such a shock for Henri and Sophie when they get the next au pair who spends half the time clubbing and the rest recovering from a hangover.' Bryony had laughed. 'It doesn't feel like a job,' she'd said. 'And I can't let the boys down.'

Patrice comes down the hall towards them, holding something behind his back. It's a packet of biscuits. Blythe can see why Bryony cares so much for them. They are cute and funny and they love her. Their little hands are always touching her, tugging at her, attracting her attention. It's like massive flirting of the most innocent kind.

'Just one each,' Bryony says, calling after the rapidly disappearing child. 'And make sure it is only one – I've counted them so I'll know.' She turns back to Blythe with her face still held in a stern expression which makes him smile.

'Did you mean that?'

She looks puzzled. 'That's just an old trick,' she tells him.

He blushes and shakes his head. 'I meant about you saying that you love me.' This is not the time or place, but it seems important to him to establish the truth before he leaves her today.

'Of course.'

'You weren't just saying it?'

'How about you? I only have the boys' word for it,' she says, teasing him.

'Yeah, yeah, I know.' He shrugs.

'Why don't you stay? We'll be able to talk while the boys play.'

Blythe looks at his watch, shakes his head. He's on the afternoon shift. 'I'll be late for work.'

'Have dinner with us later then? Sophie and Henri would love to see you. They're always asking about you.'

'I don't know.' He's not keen on these family meals but he doesn't want to disappoint Bryony.

'We could go for a drink afterwards,' she says, pressing close to him.

He holds her tighter. 'Oh well, in that case.'

Bryony kisses him a chemically, cocoa-y kiss that makes his blood sing.

'I do love you,' she says.

'I love you too.'

Not far from the house he stops and lights a cigarette. When he blows the smoke clear from his face, it's like seeing a fucking ghost.

It's Frédérique from the bar for real this time walking across the road in front of him. He follows her. She's a classy piece. Expensive clothes, shoes, briefcase. Everything about her is expensive, like out of a fucking magazine, including the new car she's getting into. Nice legs too.

Oh Jesus, he thinks, he made a mistake the other night, that's for sure. What a piece to mark his card with Jacques for. This woman wouldn't have any trouble taking care of herself. She's just Jacques's type.

She swings the car slowly round. It's heading towards him and she accelerates so quickly, the tyres squealing, that he has to step quickly back onto the pavement, dropping his cigarette. She drives straight past him. Blythe sees her face clearly. She does resemble Bryony, but with a harder edge; older too. She doesn't even notice him.

6

shouldn't be here

Frédérique parks her car and remains seated, her hands on the steering wheel, staring down the street at Cecillie's moped which is propped up on the kerb a couple of hundred metres away. She scans the buildings, the dirty-cream stone, the balcony railings. At the end of the street a big ball of sun is going down in a cloudless sky. Today's been unexpectedly hot even for July, and the evening air is so heavy that when Frédérique left the air-conditioned gallery, her body didn't have time to acclimatize. She'd started sweating the minute she'd stepped outside. And now with the engine off, she can feel the heat building up. The damp back of her dress unsticks from the seat as she sits forward to start the car and she's relieved to feel the cool air being pumped around her feet, then her face. Ahead the yellow moped glows in the evening sunlight, looking as if it's about to combust.

She has a pretty good hunch that Luc's with Cecillie. She's just come from his place and he wasn't there. She knocked hard several times, but knew while she was doing it that it was pointless. It felt empty.

She presses play for the CD and music fills the car. She leans back, her head falling against the headrest, and closes her eyes. The music is too intrusive to think clearly. She sits forward and switches it off. The sun has reddened to a crimson which is leaching into the sky, dyeing it purple, lilac, pink.

It was the conversation with Fernand as they were leaving the gallery this evening that had brought Frédérique to her senses. He'd followed her out, locking the doors behind them, and they'd chatted for a few minutes next to her car.

'I'm worried about you,' he said suddenly, placing a hand on her arm.

'I'm fine,' she replied quickly, but Fernand persisted.

'You seemed so happy recently, you know. As if things were looking up for you, with your young man . . .'

'Luc?' she'd asked, startled.

'I meant Jacques.' He winked at her. Then he laughed before she had time to respond. 'But now you've brought up Luc, what's happening with him? How's his work going?'

'OK,' she told him.

'Are his new pieces up to scratch?'

She hesitated. 'I haven't seen them,' she confessed, blushing. Her heart bumped with the sudden knowledge that she'd done something wrong.

'Why ever not?'

She mumbled half-heartedly that she'd been busy.

'But it's important, Frédérique. It's not like you to neglect that.'

'I was trying not to smother him. As there's so little time, I thought he could do with being left in peace.'

Fernand had given her a quick hug. He must have noticed

her distress because he played down his original comment, saying, 'I'm sure it'll be fine. But I'd check it out all the same, if I were you.'

'You're right.'

'You know what these artists are like, they forget they're supposed to be painting and start screwing all day. Especially these young ones.'

She had turned away to hide her face. The idea of Luc and Cecillie together, screwing, fucking, making love had been shocking but the realization that she'd put the whole exhibition at risk was worse.

Frédérique finds a tissue in the glove box and wipes her face.

She's been so concerned with trying not to give Luc any reason to suspect that her interest in him has become personal, that she's completely failed to handle the whole thing professionally. There are only two weeks before the show and what if Luc hasn't been working, like Fernand suggested? The gallery – but Jacques especially – has invested a lot in Luc and Frédérique should have been making sure that he delivered the goods.

Frédérique's stomach burns at the thought of letting Jacques down. It's going to be bad enough for him afterwards.

They couldn't stay at the beach. Everyone was feeling too frail from last night's hangovers to cope with the sun beating down. They came back to Cecillie's apartment to eat and cool off.

On the floor are bowls empty of the couscous and salad that Cecillie made, and two bottles of vodka, with a whole bloody sack of oranges that Luc bought. They've already finished one of the bottles and started on the next. Hair of the dog.

Blythe's memory of parts of the previous night is hazy. He clearly remembers Bryony turning up late, with her big straw bag because the bag, he knew, signified that she would be staying the night, and his anger over her lateness dissolved. The rest of the evening is a blur of drink, laughing and mucking around.

He tests himself to see if there any remnants of that happiness left. He gets a slight buzz when he thinks of Bryony sleeping with him last night and with the prospect of another night together at the end of today, but it's still not enough to shake off feeling down. He can't understand why he's like this. He wants to enjoy himself, he wants to have a good time. It's not often, after all, that Bryony's French family go away for a couple of days and they get to spend this much time together.

Perhaps the plain fact is that he overdid it last night and he's paying for it today; his hands are clammy, his face is burning and his stomach is churning, which are pretty good indicators, after all.

But he didn't have any more than the others. Certainly not Luc, who seemed intent on getting really out of it. At one point, Luc had fallen over and Cecillie and Bryony had tried to pick him up with a lot of giggling and a few failed attempts. Blythe was too pissed to help at all. Today Luc has bruises on his knees and a cut on his hand. So, it wasn't only Blythe in a state, but even so the others seem to have settled back into drinking without any difficulty, the same easy way.

He feels detached, like some kind of spectator. He wants to

join in, achieve the nice, fuzzy brain like last night or at least drink himself into oblivion if he can't. But the more he drinks, the more sober he seems to be getting. The more distant.

He looks at Cecillie and Luc. They're lying flat on their backs. Their thin bodies are stretched out side by side and their hands lie, fingers laced together, on Luc's bare, brown stomach. He's only wearing shorts, Cecillie her tiny bikini. They're all bones. Their skin is shiny where it's pulled taut across ribs, hips and knees. You can't help looking at them. Everyone does. Like when they all go out together, people can't keep their eyes off those two.

He thinks they've fallen asleep until he notices that their fingers are moving over and over each other, twining untwining, stroking, pressing. He wants to disturb them, break their spell. The whole world population could get blown up around them, he thinks, annoyed, and these two wouldn't bloody notice. Probably wouldn't care either.

He has Bryony to blame, he remembers with a twitch of irritation, for suggesting coming back with them. He would have preferred to go somewhere on their own. He'd had a sudden urge to walk in the pine wood near the beach, with its fresh bitter-sweet scent. He'd suggested it to Bryony but she dismissed the idea.

'Come on, it'll be a laugh,' she told him. 'All of us.'

But she was wrong. He couldn't feel less like laughing. He tells himself that he's being a pain, a real fucking jerk, and takes a look at Bryony to see if she's noticed how fucking bored and cramped he is. She's sucking the remains of an orange quarter which she's just squeezed into her drink. She smiles at him and her lips glisten. She does know that he's not feeling right. He can tell by the way she stares at him, like her eyes have forgotten how to blink.

'Pass me a cigarette, Luc,' he says so that he has an excuse to turn away.

Luc is nearest the one remaining cigarette packet. His free hand fumbles on the floor beside him, grabs it and throws the packet across. Blythe could have reached out and got it himself, without too much effort and Luc looks questioningly at him. Ignoring him, Blythe takes out two of the five remaining cigarettes. He lights them both and then sits up, leans across and puts one in Luc's mouth.

'You two can share this one. I need a whole one.'

'You're so generous, Blythe,' Cecillie mumbles in English. 'Aren't you going to go and buy some more?'

'Later. Maybe.'

'It's your turn.'

'You smoked most of these. I haven't got a rich granny-kins to be able to afford to pay for that kind of habit.'

Cecillie raises her head and looks across Luc's chest, eyes narrowed, at Blythe, then at Bryony. Then she shrugs like a French girl and says, 'Fuck off you miserable old shit.' before lying back down again.

The cigarette passes between them to and fro, to and fro, smoke curls along their bodies before it's pulled out towards the open windows. It gathers in a cloud in front of Blythe and from behind it, he studies Bryony who's sitting with her legs tucked up against her chest, her eyes fixed on Cecillie and Luc.

'This is like a fucking porno film,' Blythe says. And everyone laughs except him.

He gets up and goes out onto the balcony. Outside the air is still; heavy with fumes and dust.

It shouldn't make him angry to see Cecillie and Luc looking so happy together, but it does. That's the truth. It makes him fucking mad. He's jealous, he knows it and he's not proud of it, but at least he's honest. With himself, anyway, he's not sure he'd have the balls to admit it to anyone else. Although he suspects that Bryony's caught on. It's always needled him, how they're so wrapped up in each other, but these last few days it's been much worse. It's because they have it all. They've got a future together, while he and Bryony have theirs ticking furiously away.

He flicks the cigarette end out across the street and looks at the red sky.

Bryony's faith that everything will sort itself out like some bleeding miracle astounds him. They're now halfway through July and they're no nearer a decision. She's been avoiding talking about it, and he hasn't pressed her because he doesn't want to upset her, but ever since that day at the pool when they said they loved each other, he's felt an urgency to get things settled. It's doing his head in.

He needs decisions. The way he sees it there are three options. That's what he'll say if Bryony asks. Or rather *when* Bryony asks because, surely, he thinks tapping on his pockets vainly for another cigarette, surely she's going to have to start asking the questions soon. So, he'll offer her the three options: travel together, return to England together or Bryony goes back and he carries on travelling. He'll say that but all the time he knows that really there's only one option.

He can't. He just cannot go back to England. Not yet. That

is out. He's got nothing to go back to. And he wants to return to the mountains in the winter; it was special there, plus he's virtually been promised work for the whole season.

The idea of trying to keep a relationship, their relationship going when they're miles apart is not only unsatisfactory but also unrealistic. He can't even write letters.

So that leaves the one. Bryony has to agree to travel with him, otherwise it's finished. Over.

He hopes, he really, really hopes that she'll see it the same way. In good moments he's sure she will, he has no doubts about it, but on bad days . . . He shrugs his shoulders which are stiff and aching. He supposes that this is what today's all about. A bad day. And that's when he's convinced that Bryony will decide to go back.

How do other people manage, he wonders, having always to think about another person? Knowing that everything you do affects them; that it's much harder to make someone happy than it is to piss them off, to hurt them. Is that why so many relationships fuck up? It gets too exhausting, always having to bear someone else in mind.

He looks inside. It looks dark in there from out here. He sees Bryony's white hand, waving to him. He gives her a quick wave back and then turns round to face the street. If only they could both fall asleep and wake up with the memory of the last few months wiped clear, then he could walk away. But his stomach hurts with the idea of not having known her, his mouth is dry with nerves about telling her that unless she doesn't go back to England then it must be over.

He goes back in. Bryony and Cecillie are sitting together. Huddled on the floor like they're plotting something. Luc must have gone for a piss. He hears Cecillie say, 'Here he is.' And sees her touch Bryony's hand as if she's comforting her. Cecillie's interfering again, he thinks angrily, as Luc reappears, and Cecillie stands up.

'Anyone for coffee?' she asks, diverting Luc to the kitchenette. 'You can help me.'

Blythe pours himself a large glass of vodka and drinks half of it in one go without adding any orange juice. His eyes smart. He stretches his legs out so that his feet are lost underneath Bryony's skirt, which is puffed around her. He can feel the warmth of her skin against his as their bare legs touch, wind together, radiating heat. She turns her face, flushed with alcohol, towards him.

'What were you and Cec talking about just now?'

'Girlie stuff – you know.'

'About us?' he asks, searching her face for signs of strength for what they are going to have to go through, but all he sees is the same Bryony. He wants to throw himself at her feet, bury his face in her skirt and say to her sort it out, sort it out.

'What about us?'

Blythe ignores her question. 'Come over here,' he says.

'I can't stand up,' Bryony says solemnly. 'I feel dizzy.'

'Crawl here then, so I can kiss you.'

She crawls over and he does kiss her, and she kisses him back, her tongue seeking his, her hands moving down his chest to where, surprisingly, his prick is pushing at his shorts. She rubs and squeezes it gently and then stops when he throws his head back, opening his eyes wide. The vodka's kicked in and the room's begun to spin.

Behind the screen Cecillie and Luc laugh loudly.

'Jesus, they're probably having sex in there,' he says.

'Don't listen if you don't like it,' Bryony whispers. But the only other sound from the kitchen is something metal dropping on the floor.

Suddenly Bryony grabs his hand and holds it down in the folds of her skirt. 'What will we do Blythe?'

His heart lurches. It's starting, the whole thing is starting. He looks at her; she pushes some hair out of her eyes and looks intently at him.

'Well,' he says slowly, 'I guess there are three options.'

He tells her each one, as he planned, but without telling her how he feels about any of them. He tries to moderate his intonation so as, he hopes, not to give a clue for his own preference, but his voice sounds hollow. Bryony sits there silent; he's too drunk to be able to judge her expression.

'What do you think?' he says, being forced to ask for a response. When, eventually, it comes, he doesn't want to see it. She's crying.

There's a knock at the door. Cecillie opens it. Monsieur Bayard shambles into the room, his eyes blinking, smiling like an idiot, greeting the girls who immediately begin pandering to him. Monsieur Bayard is loving it. He lets himself be led by Cecillie to a spot on the floor, while Bryony provides him with a cushion. Cecillie presents him with a glass of vodka, into which she squeezes some orange juice and fishes out the pips with a spoon. Luc appears with the coffee pot.

Blythe looks at Monsieur B. The girls think he's really cute and encourage him. Not that he needs much encouragement, he's always popping up around the building. Like a fucking meerkat. Blythe can barely make a trip to the shit-house without him appearing en route, eager for a chat.

'You are lovely people,' Monsieur B says, settling his big arse. 'You are the best tenants that I have ever had.'

He throws the vodka down his throat and smacks his leg with his hand. Blythe isn't wholly convinced by this eccentric Frenchman act. He suspects the man of aspiring to wangling his way inside the girls' knickers. Blythe's forever warning Bryony not to be on her own with him.

Bryony gets annoyed when he says this. She tells him that he always thinks the worst of everyone and he tells her that he's learnt it the hard way. Last time she'd said, sharply, 'Come on Blythe, lighten up.'

Everyone's just sitting, staring at Monsieur B, waiting for him to perform.

'My old bones,' he says adjusting his bottom on the cushion to sit more comfortably. 'My old bones.'

Frédérique's about to get out of the car when the English barman who works for Jacques emerges onto the balcony of one of the apartments. She automatically sinks low in her seat to try and keep out of his view and then realizes how suspicious that looks, how ridiculous. She should have jumped out and shouted up to him. As it is, now she'll have to stay put until he goes in and pray he doesn't spot her.

He looks out across the houses and then goes back in after a few minutes. Frédérique's relieved but she feels sordid. For a moment she's tempted to drive off but she can't bear the thought of a night of not knowing. Now that she's here she might just as well get on with it. It can't get any worse, she tells herself.

Her phone rings. The noise startles her and she rushes to

pick it up from the passenger seat, her heart opening out in anticipation of seeing Luc's name, but of course it isn't Luc at all and her mouth dries immediately at the sight of 'Jacques' showing on the screen.

'Hello?'

'Jacques,' she manages to say.

'Frédérique, darling, how are you?'

'I'm fine.'

'I'm not going to chat. I rang to see if you're coming over this evening?'

'No, Katrin can't work tonight so it'll be tomorrow.'

'Who said anything about work? How about dinner?' he asks and, before Frédérique replies, adds, 'Just the two of us. We don't seem to have had much time alone recently.'

She sighs. She should go over. It's true that it's been a while since they spent time with each other but that's because of how she's been manoeuvring it. It's cowardly behaviour, admittedly, but she can't trust herself alone with Jacques at the moment. It had seemed the perfect solution: they needed extra help, Katrin from the gallery needed extra money plus she wanted to gain more experience in setting up exhibitions – and Frédérique had a chaperone. She had known it wouldn't last, that at some point Jacques would notice.

But she can't face seeing Jacques tonight and so she says, 'I'd love to, but I've got a lot of paperwork to catch up on.'

'If I'd have known how little I'd get to see you by suggesting this exhibition, I'd have kept quiet.' He's flirting with her and she responds in the same vein.

'Now you know what a tough life this art business is,' she tells him. 'You never believed me before.'

'Where are you now?'

She's in the middle of telling him that she's trying to find Luc, before she realizes she's made a mistake.

'It's nothing to worry about,' she reassures him. 'But Fernand suggested I try and see him.'

'What about?'

'I need to check on what Luc's been doing.'

Jacques's confusion is palpable.

'Why the urgency? Hasn't he been keeping you up to date?'

She's hot, hot and her head feels heavy and full. She presses the button, the window buzzes down a fraction. Even hotter air comes in.

'He's left a couple of messages saying things are going well but I need to see for myself where he's got to, we've not got long before it opens and we need to make sure . . .'

Jacques's voice has an edge to it. 'He knows there's a lot riding on this, I take it?'

'Yes, of course he does. It's not his fault. I should have followed it up before, but I didn't, but I am now,' she says firmly. She's desperate for Jacques not to pursue an explanation of why she didn't.

'Are you on your way to his apartment?'

'I've tried there. I'm at his girlfriend's.'

'And he's not there?'

'I don't know yet. I'm outside. In the car.'

'Are you sure it can't wait?'

'Unfortunately not. But I'll see you tomorrow.'

'I'm looking forward to it already.'

'Me too.'

Frédérique stands in front of the building. It has a wide front door made from dark wood and inlaid green glass. She checks the name plates on the entrance buzzers. The second one from the top says, simply, Cecillie.

Frédérique stares at it, then tries to remove it. After a few attempts she catches the end and slides the card out of the holder. The writing is childish: both 'i's' are topped with properly formed circles. Frédérique tries the door. It's shut. She steps back and looks up at the balcony where Blythe had appeared. She can hear music and people talking and laughing.

She's startled when the door opens but it's an old man who teeters in the doorway, holding it – at some considerable effort – open for her. She shoves Cecillie's name card into her handbag and rushes in. She stands in the cool darkness of the hallway before she heads up the stairs. As she gets to the top of them, women's high laughter explodes around her. It's coming from the apartment on the right. She stands in the middle of the landing. There's more shouting and, in the midst of it, ringing clear and strong is Luc's voice. He's trying to say something but he gets drowned out.

Behind her come slow footsteps on the stairs and Frédérique scans around for somewhere to go. The door to the room opposite the stairs is open slightly and, assuming it to be the bathroom, she slips inside. She peers out at the old man who let her in, visible now as he heaves himself up the last step. Frédérique hears his wheezy breath above her own nervous breathing. When he finally makes it into the apartment on the left, she closes the bathroom door and turns round. She freezes. She isn't in the bathroom at all; she's in the hall of another apartment and, at the end of it, hanging in front of the shuttered windows, is the body of a man.

* * *

There's a scream, a scream which none of them take in at first, their eyes blankly fixed on each other's for perhaps only seconds, as the scream becomes more piercing and louder. The door is flung open and Frédérique stands there, white-faced, shaking. Her mouth is working, opening, closing but she's not speaking. Blythe has never seen anyone look so terrified. Nobody moves.

'What do you want?' Cecillie suddenly shouts, stepping forward. 'What are you doing here?'

Then Frédérique launches herself at Luc and starts to cry, a kind of sobbing wail so loud that Luc has to shout above it. 'What's wrong?' he asks Frédérique, shaking her. 'What's wrong?'

'What's wrong is I never invited her here,' Cecillie shouts. 'This is my place,' she says, pulling at Frédérique's arm. 'You shouldn't be here.'

'Leave her, Cecillie. Let me talk to her.'

'He's dead,' Frédérique says, her voice quieter now, muffled into Luc's T-shirt. 'He's dead.'

'Who's dead?' Luc asks. 'Who's dead?'

'The man next door, he's hanged himself.'

Blythe feels Bryony press against him, her hand seeks his. He squeezes it. Luc looks puzzled, and Blythe shrugs his reply: he's no idea what Frédérique's talking about. The woman's mad, he thinks, she's lost it.

'My god, Max!' Monsieur Bayard says suddenly and rushes out. Blythe follows him. Monsieur B turns round before he goes into Max's apartment. 'Stay there,' he tells him. 'There's no point in us all having a look, if it's true.'

Others from the house are beginning to emerge from their apartments, to creep up the stairs to where the action is. The old couple from Cecillie's floor hover in their doorway, with expectant faces. Monsieur Bayard reappears. He looks shaken and wipes his face with his shirt sleeve. 'He's dead for sure.'

'Who?' Blythe hears someone asking. 'Who's dead?

'Max,' Monsieur Bayard says loudly, as if he is making an announcement to an audience. 'Max has killed himself. He's hanged himself. Now, will somebody call the services?'

'The police are already here,' someone shouts from downstairs.

The old man from across the landing comes forward, shakily. 'I phoned them when I heard a girl screaming. I thought someone was being murdered!'

'She found the body,' Monsieur Bayard says, patting his arm, gently. 'She's a little upset.'

Two policemen run up the stairs, pushing through the people.

'Everyone go back inside,' one of them shouts, but nobody takes any notice. A call comes from the floor below.

'They want to speak to the woman that found him.'

'I'll go and tell her,' Blythe says.

Frédérique's face emerges from Luc's T-shirt. She doesn't look at Blythe, only at Luc. 'Will you come with me?'

'He's busy,' Cecillie says.

Luc disentangles himself from Frédérique, and steps towards Cecillie to kiss her goodbye. Blythe hears him whisper, 'I have to, Cec. I can't let her go on her own.'

'Sure,' Cecillie replies, and shrugs, but she looks as if she's going to start crying too. God, that's all I need, Blythe thinks. She'll set Bryony off as well.

'I'll be back soon.'

Blythe follows Luc and Frédérique out. He watches how

Frédérique clings to him, hides her head as they push through the people crowding the stairs. Blythe waits as various uniformed people go to and from the apartment, until finally the body's brought out and there's nothing left to see.

Cecillie is storming around, tidying up, swigging vodka from the bottle. Bryony is on the bed. Blythe sits down beside her and she cuddles up against him.

'Did you see the body?' she asks him.

'Only for a moment.' He had watched the stretcher go by as if it was a film. It didn't seem real. 'Just the feet really, sticking out from under a blanket. With his socks on. Poor old tosser. Great big feet with bright white socks on.'

'What was he like, Cecillie?' Bryony asks.

'Strange. He only liked his dog.'

'Where's his dog then?' Bryony asks.

'It died,' Blythe says. 'A few weeks ago.'

'I didn't know,' says Cecillie. 'I thought I hadn't seen it around.'

'Oh no. That's really sad. Isn't that sad?'

'I'm trying to feel sad,' Cecillie says, joining them on the bed, 'but I guess it hasn't hit me yet.' She hands the bottle to Blythe who swigs some down and passes it on to Bryony. 'What I'm really pissed off about is Frédérique coming round here. You'd think she owns us.'

'Stay, Luc,' Frédérique says as soon as he's closed the door behind them. 'For a coffee?' She moves to go to the kitchen.

'No. Thanks.'

She stops and looks at him. 'Please?'

He shakes his head. 'You ought to go and rest, get some sleep.'

But she doesn't want to lie down although she feels exhausted. Even though there's a pain behind her left eye which sends shooting colours across her vision every time she moves her head.

'I don't think I'll be able to.'

She walks into the living room and sits on the settee. Luc follows her and stands in the doorway. She wonders if he's waiting for her to invite him in and gestures with her hand to the other settee. He sits on the arm of it.

'As soon as I close my eyes I know his face is going to come back.' She hears her voice rising with the panic. 'It's there waiting. I've been pushing it away all the time but as soon as I close my eyes that will be it.'

Luc slides down onto the seat. 'Is there someone you could ring? To spend the night with you so you don't have to be alone.'

Neither of them has mentioned Jacques, though he is the obvious choice of course.

'You've been great Luc, a real help. I feel a complete idiot.'

He murmurs disagreement. He looks incredibly healthy, she thinks as she watches him. 'There's no one I want to be here.'

It's a lie, there are two people. Jacques because he would know exactly what to do. He would soon be busy – running a bath, playing soft music, laying out towels, fixing something to eat. She could close her eyes, she's sure, if Jacques were here. But it isn't possible. It would be unfair to use Jacques like that. She has forfeited the right to their old friendship.

And Luc, the other person, doesn't know what would help

her, doesn't even know where anything is, she realizes, watching his eyes dart around her living room, taking it all in. He won't be staying. She won't be falling asleep in his arms.

She must, though, have dropped off for a few minutes because suddenly Luc's standing in front of her holding a bowl.

'Here,' he says, sitting down beside her. 'Drink this.'

She takes the bowl. Hot chocolate. She thinks of all the cupboard-opening this would have entailed – chocolate, sugar, cup, fridge, the fiddling around with someone else's stove, finding the milk pan.

'You're an angel,' she says and begins to cry.

'Don't, Frédérique. That's enough.'

In the taxi, she couldn't stop crying, she couldn't stop herself repeating to him over and over the questions the police had asked, and her failure to reply, her failure to have noticed in greater detail the scene that she'd discovered. She couldn't even remember the clothes the man had been wearing, except that she'd had the impression of black. All she was certain of was the long black figure dangling in front of her and a thick purple-blue face with popping eyes. She knows his name now, the hanging man. Max. It makes things better and worse.

Luc had held her in the taxi, but here her tears won't be enough to make him do that again. In her apartment, gestures and words take on a different meaning. He isn't comfortable on his own here; he's probably concerned about what Cecillie would think.

'I've never seen anyone dead before,' she tells Luc now, wiping her tears away with her hand. 'I thought people were supposed to look peaceful and calm. Not like that. This man looked like he had *struggled.*' She takes a deep breath and forces herself to be calmer. 'I suppose it's not the nicest way to go, is it?'

'No.'

They sit in silence until Luc eventually says, 'So, when do you want to come and see my work?'

She'd forgotten she'd explained to him why she was at Cecillie's. 'Whenever it suits you. The sooner the better, I guess.'

'I suppose I should have brought them over,' he says sheepishly. 'I never thought about it.'

'Not at all. That's for me to arrange.'

He takes some cushions from behind him and puts them beside her. 'Come on, lie down.'

She finishes her drink, sinks onto the cushions and, kicking off her shoes, pulls her feet up under her. Luc disappears and returns a moment later, half carrying, half dragging her duvet. He helps her tuck it around her. She hadn't realized she felt so cold.

He sits down opposite her, his hands pressing his knees. 'How about tomorrow afternoon?' Luc asks her and it takes her a second to realize what he's talking about. 'If you think you'll feel OK?'

She looks at him, nods. 'That will be fine. I'm looking forward to seeing what you've done.'

'I think you'll like them,' he tells her, his face brightening. 'I'm pretty happy with how it's been going.'

'That's good,' she says. Then out of nowhere, she tells him. 'I love you.'

She watches him recoil from her, his face flush but she

doesn't stop. 'I'm in love with you, I can't stop thinking about you. But you knew that, didn't you?'

He stands up and walks around the room. 'No,' he tells her. 'I had no idea.'

His honesty stings. Every day Frédérique has prepared herself as if it will be the day that she sees Luc. That's meant dressing simply but with great care, that's meant her body being in a constant state of nervous excitement, that's meant her mind going over and over again what she'll say, how she'll behave, how she'll feel when they kiss hello, anticipating that lovely fleeting moment when she feels him close to her; that's meant wondering whether there'll be an opportunity to reach out and touch his hand as they're talking.

Every evening she's played back an old message he left on her answer phone which she hasn't wiped. She knows it off by heart: 'Hello Frédérique, this is Luc. Thanks for your note. Everything's going fine. No problems at all. I'll see you soon. *À bientôt.*' It's short, but it's friendly and informal. She's listened to it over and over again; studying it at first for any giveaway signs of tenderness, with hopeful longing. Lately though, the more she'd listened to it, the more she'd strained to hear something else in his voice as she replayed the message. Perhaps a coldness or an offhandedness which she'd previously missed. She'd huddled over the answer phone – click, rewind, play, click, rewind, play. Repeatedly until she forced herself to stop after what? Twenty, maybe thirty times. She wouldn't dare count. Her behaviour, she knew, was ridiculous.

And now he's here and she's a complete mess and she's just told him what she'd vowed never to tell him and he hadn't even suspected it. She can't believe how repulsed he looks.

He sits down again. Leans forward. 'This is crazy, Fred, you've had a shock . . .'

'And now it's your turn,' she says. He doesn't disagree.

She keeps talking as if explaining will take his horrified expression away.

'I've offended you.'

'No! Not at all,' he says. 'I'm flattered but . . .'

They look at each other without speaking.

'I expect you get this all the time.'

He tries to make a joke of her comment, grinning sheepishly. 'Women falling in love with me? Yeah, on a daily basis.'

With a sudden clarity, Frédérique thinks, how clumsy he is in his attempts to handle the situation; how young. Jacques would have the assurance, the confidence to alleviate her discomfort, her feeling of stupidity. She's angry with Luc which is unjustified but real.

'You think it's infatuation? It's inconvenient, but she'll get over it.'

He shrugs. 'I wouldn't like to say. I guess I don't know you very well.'

'Well, I don't *want* to feel like this.' She hears her voice shaking and under the duvet she clenches her hands, her nails bite into the palms. 'I'm a nervous wreck. Do you think I'd let an *infatuation* do this to me? I don't want to love you. I wanted to marry Jacques.'

'That's because of me? You're saying that's because of me?' He shakes his head slowly as if he can't believe what he's hearing. It incenses Frédérique.

'Yes,' she says savagely. 'Of course it's because of you.'

'I don't know why you're behaving like it's my fault.' He

speaks harshly, then more calmly he tells her, 'I don't want you to love me, I only want you to like my work.'

He stands up quickly as if he's about to go. He stops and looks down at her. She pulls the duvet up further around her neck. She'd put it over her face if she dared, she doesn't want him to be able to see a single bit of her.

His gentle tone surprises her. 'It seems a waste, Frédérique,' he says.

'What?'

'You and Jacques you seem, you know, right for each other.'

'I don't think I ever loved him,' she says, quietly.

'And you know, you and me, even if there wasn't Cecillie, we'd never get it together.'

'Why not?'

'We're from two different worlds.'

'We're from the same city,' she says quickly.

'Different parts of it.'

'We've got the city in common. You won't leave it and neither will I,' she says, challenging him to deny it. 'I'll always be here.'

'Cecillie's not going anywhere either,' he tells her and he can't hide the pleasure he gets from saying those words. 'You can be sure of that.'

After he's gone she lies there, stricken. Luc will be on his way back to Cecillie. In a short while they'll be talking about what's happened. They'll be discussing her, probably laughing about her. And why not? It is ridiculous: she's thirteen years older than him, she's engaged to someone else, he's in love with someone else.

She remembers Cecillie's shrill voice: 'What are you doing

here?' and the vicious plucking fingers on her arm. 'You shouldn't be here, you shouldn't be here.'

Then the hanging man's face bursts into her mind. Her stomach heaves. She throws herself off the settee and into the bathroom, falling against the sink where she retches up the cocoa. The mixture of chocolate and vomit is overpowering, revolting. She rocks herself, arms tight around her stomach, tears stinging her eyes.

7

can't stop myself

Bryony's been going on about Luc's private view party to Blythe for days. She's been so excited it's driven him nuts. What shall she wear, what will he wear? He told her he would be wearing whatever he wore to work that day and she got in such a huff about it that he agreed to bring a clean T-shirt with him to change into. He's put it in the staff loos down the corridor, and mustn't forget to put it on, otherwise Bryony will go mad. She's convinced that, as they're Luc's friends, how they dress will reflect on him. Blythe knows Luc won't give a stuff about what they're wearing, particularly as by the time he gets there Luc's bound to be steaming drunk. By then he probably wouldn't bat an eyelid if Blythe turned up stark bollock naked.

Bryony and Cecillie are going to meet Blythe for a drink in the bar before they go up to the party and he'll join them once he's finished his shift.

He's on his own tonight; it's never very busy midweek and, in fact, today is quieter than usual. He's glad about that because right now, he's a bit distracted. He's waiting for the girls to arrive and every time the door opens, he looks up. Earlier, he knocked a stack of lemons off the back counter which pissed him off big time as he'd spent ages slicing them. Even though the girls have been to the bar before – Bryony a number of times – Blythe always feels unnerved when he's expecting someone he knows. It's OK once he's adjusted to them being there, but at first he feels clumsy and unnatural. Bryony thinks the bar's cool and she's thankfully seriously impressed by his juggling, which he always performs for her. She never notices cock-ups or mis-throws. In fact, juggling seems to turn her on a bit, and she's always encouraging him to go through his act, which of course he's more than happy to do, particularly back at his place where one thing leads to another.

The door begins to open again and this time he stops what he's doing because something tells him it's going to be the girls.

They both move confidently; as if they know they look good. Cecillie has her hair up in a tight shiny ice-blonde knot, her dress is scarlet and long like a sheath which dips and clings to every part of her body. She seems even taller, even thinner. Blythe's eyes are drawn to Cecillie straight away because she looks amazing, but after a second, he's searching for the woman he really wants to see and there she is, behind Cecillie, closing the door.

She's in black. Sweet Bryony. Her dress is short, very bloody short, he realizes as they start to walk towards him. Jesus, it must barely cover her arse at the back. The flesh on her thighs shivers with each step, the same soft flesh which locks around his body when they make love. She's wound a black scarf around her neck which contrasts with the almost translucent quality of her smooth, pale skin. Her hair, pulled back off her face, emphasizes her big eyes. His lovely, sweet Bryony.

He laughs when he sees their footwear. Cecillie's wearing a pair of pink, stacked flip-flops with a big, plastic, red flower on each toe-strap, and Bryony's got on a pair of chunky metallic silver and purple trainers.

He resists the desire to perform a superman leap over the bar, one hand on the counter, to hug them both. Instead he stands, grinning, waiting for them to reach him.

'You look fantastic. You'll do their heads in.' After kissing them hello, he sets to, making them their favourite cocktails, the taste of Bryony's strawberry-flavoured lip-gloss on his mouth, his nostrils momentarily holding a mixture of her perfume and the spliff they must have smoked earlier.

'We hope to,' Cecillie says. 'Luc said it was going to be full of posh gits.'

'If Jacques has anything to do with it, it will be,' Blythe mutters, then abandons what he's doing to attend to two women who have just come in. Regulars, who he recognizes. He makes an effort to chat as usual but he can't wait to get back to the girls with their funny stories and their teasing. After about forty minutes and three cocktails each later, they leave and the bar suddenly seems very dull. He feels impatient with the other punters, wishing away the two hours that he has to work before he can join the party. He doesn't normally drink behind the bar but, to cheer himself up, he pours out a large vodka and orange.

Arrows on the walls direct Cecillie and Bryony up the iron stairs from the back of the bar, along a narrow, well-lit corridor towards the hall. The entrance to this is through a pair of vast ballroom doors, ornately decorated in gold and blue, which are folded outwards. On both sides an English-style butler is serving kir and handing out a catalogue.

'Shit.' Cecillie lets out a low whistle as she glances through the prices.

'I didn't think they'd be worth that,' says Bryony.

'Neither did I.'

A large stone vaulting runs from each side of the doorway along the length of the ceiling. Suspended from each of these, on wires, are Luc's paintings, forming a short avenue into the main room which, from where they're standing, seems to be full of people.

Cecillie hurries Bryony along. 'We'll find Luc first then have a proper look round.'

It's like being at a medieval ball, Cecillie thinks, taking in the elaborately dressed women. There's an amazing mix of colours: blacks, purples, whites, reds, a lot of silver and gold. The men's outfits are much tamer but still very, very smart; almost without exception in evening wear. The conversation is low, a murmuring hum, which accompanies the fluid mass of bodies.

Cecillie and Bryony stand at the edge. Beside her Bryony whispers, 'Why's everyone staring?'

''Cause we look so good, of course,' Cecillie says confidently, even though she doesn't feel it.

'It's very glam, Cec.' Bryony sips her drink, scanning the room. The face she turns in Cecillie's direction is wide-eyed and Cecillie's sure she must look just as stunned. She's suddenly overcome with the giggles and it starts Bryony off.

'I need this,' says Bryony, swigging back her drink in one go. Cecillie follows suit.

'Poor Luc,' she says. 'There's going to be a lot of brown-nosing here tonight.'

On each perimeter wall are hung the large paintings. Behind them, as backdrops, are long strips of crêpe paper of varying shades of metal – silver, pewter to bronze and gold. They're draped from ceiling to the floor where they gather in folds like plush cloth. At the top end of the hall are wide French windows leading onto a balcony terrace. The windows are open and there are a few people out there, sitting at the tables. To the right is a set of doors identical to the entrance except on a smaller scale. These lead into a room where waitresses are busily serving food and drinks. One of the waiters, carrying trays of champagne, stops in front of them; they place their empty glasses onto the tray and take a full one off.

'We'll have to go and find him,' Cecillie says. 'We can't stand here all night.'

'You first,' Bryony says.

A shout goes up. Luc is pushing his way through the crowd towards them.

'Cecillie! Cecillie!'

He's wearing his new jeans bought specially for tonight and a loose, white shirt which shows off his tan, his strong neck, his soft, brown floppy hair. He looks wonderful. He looks so good that Cecillie's heart stops, then bump-starts. For a moment she can't believe that he's hers; that he's stumbling and tripping through all these people, all these rich gits, in his haste to get to her. Surely, she thinks, now that he's achieved this, his life will be so different and what they have together won't be so important. It won't be enough.

He hugs her, whispering that she's the one person in the

world that he wants to see. She closes her eyes and feels how well they fit together and that seems to explain everything. Over his shoulder, when she opens her eyes, Cecillie is confronted by tens of faces, all staring in her direction. Luc's hand follows the curve of her dress from her shoulder, down her back, to her waist and it finally comes to rest, cupping her buttock as he kisses her neck.

The faces turn away, the voices start up again, it seems with greater volume and the group resumes its weaving and wending, the threads of black amongst the colour. Standing still in the centre of the room is Frédérique.

'I'm drunk,' Luc says as he holds Cecillie away from him to look at her. 'But not too drunk to know that you look fantastic.'

Cecillie glances back at Frédérique. Luc leans over and kisses Bryony hello. 'You both look wonderful.'

'You charmer,' Cecillie says.

'How's it going?' Bryony asks.

'It's going great, I think. I'm letting Frédérique do all the talking.'

'Speaking of which,' Cecillie says quietly in English to Bryony. 'She seems to be heading this way.'

Cecillie watches Frédérique move through the room, chatting and smiling at the guests. She looks confident and at ease and Cecillie's heart sinks a little. She is so pleased that Luc's got this chance but she hasn't been happy with the amount of time that Luc's spent over here, in Frédérique's company, particularly this last week when it was pretty frantic.

Luc's been very honest about everything Frédérique's said and Cecillie's tried very hard not to be jealous. Luc had invited Cecillie to go over to the bar anytime while he was here, but she knew that he'd prefer her to wait until this night to see it. It was an act of trust which she owed to Luc to stay away and she's glad she did, she thinks; he's holding her waist so tightly that his fingers are digging into her side. Luc couldn't hide anything from her; she'd spot it a mile off. Hidden in their group of three, she slowly brings her hand up, upwards along his thigh and then strokes the crotch of his jeans. She feels his cock harden instantly and laughs as Luc places his hand over hers to stop her, gently squeezing her fingers.

'Naughty girl.'

'Cecillie!' Bryony squeaks.

'Don't cause any trouble, you two,' Luc warns them as Frédérique approaches. 'Be nice to her, please.'

Cecillie moves her hand away from Luc's, but slowly, so that she knows Frédérique's seen.

Luc introduces Frédérique to Bryony who giggles. Oh god, Cecillie thinks, that means she's drunk already; the champagne must have gone straight to Bryony's head. Cecillie's feeling a bit pissed too. She grins at Bryony, then at Frédérique.

'Nice to meet you,' Frédérique says to Bryony.

'Beautiful dress,' Bryony remarks.

Frédérique looks surprised. 'Thank you.'

It's a dark-grey jersey dress which hangs flatteringly over her curves and flips out mid-calf. Metallic colours are obviously in, Cecillie decides, and Frédérique carries it off better than most of the other women here. She looks very elegant.

Behind Frédérique, Jacques appears. Cecillie's sure it's him. She hasn't met him before, but this man looks just how Luc and Blythe have described the infamous Jacques. He's dressed in a white suit; striking with his dark colouring. His hair is very sleek. He looks very smooth, Cecillie thinks, very cool. Exactly how she'd imagined him.

'I agree,' Jacques interposes. 'The dress is beautiful and so is the woman wearing it.'

There's a casual familiarity in the way Jacques touches Frédérique to allow him room to join their group, but Frédérique looks uncomfortable. Cecillie smirks and Bryony, catching her eye, looks like she'll burst out laughing.

'Don't be silly,' Frédérique tells Jacques.

'But I'm not, darling. Wouldn't you agree?' he appeals to Luc. And Frédérique, startled, also looks at Luc.

There's a long pause. Luc seems stupefied until Cecillie nudges him and he comes to life. 'Absolutely, yes,' he gushes, seeking Cecillie's hand and holding onto it. 'You look great. Beautiful.'

Frédérique flushes. Luc sways slightly, bumping against Cecillie's shoulder.

'And our two English ladies,' Jacques says, shaking their hands as Frédérique makes the introduction, 'are quite enchanting.'

The girls are lovely from their heads down to their ankles, but what absurd footwear! An aberration of monstrous proportions! What could they have been thinking of?

The young people start to chat among themselves. He doesn't bother to follow their conversation; he's pleased to get a private moment with Frédérique. He turns to her and quietly says, 'Is there something wrong with your necklace?'

'No.' She raises her fingers quickly to her throat, then lowers her hand and looks away.

'It's only, you're not wearing it, I thought . . .' He pauses, concerned. 'Don't you like it?'

'It's lovely.'

'Then . . .'

'I didn't think it would go. That's all.'

'But it would be perfect,' he says, surprised. His fingers are drawn irresistibly to touch her neck, so smooth, but Frédérique flinches, twisting her head away. He draws back his hand quickly. 'Frédérique?' he questions.

'I hoped you wouldn't notice. I forgot it, Jacques, that's all. I forgot to put it on.'

'It doesn't matter, darling. I thought that there was something wrong.'

'You'll excuse us,' Luc's saying. 'I'm going to show Cecillie around.'

'I can't wait until this is over.'

'Aren't you enjoying being the star of the show?'

Luc groans. 'You should hear what these people say to me. See that woman with that stupid gold turban thing on her head? She wants me to paint murals in her house. And some man wants me to paint his portrait, in his bedroom! As if I don't know what that means.'

'They're all after your body,' says Cecillie. 'How am I ever going to compete?'

'I have something to show you.'

Luc dives into the refreshment room and emerges with a full bottle of champagne and two glasses. 'Come with me.'

He leads her to a small alcove tucked in the corner on the

right; almost hidden by the paintings suspended in the middle of the room.

'Come in here,' he says.

Here, the crêpe hangings are copper-coloured and there's a single painting. Cecillie stares. 'It's me!'

'From our day at the beach. Do you remember?'

They've spent a lot of time on the beach together and Cecillie's afraid that she'll get the wrong day. She stares at the painting as if it will reveal the answer, willing herself not to fail Luc.

There's a blue border but most of the background is a very, very pale yellow. She is completely naked, elongated and painted a golden colour which has a glossy sheen, giving the picture an almost three-dimensional effect. Her hair flames white heat around her head, and the ends seem to melt away into the sand. There's something crazy about the painting. It seems powerful, as if it's much more than a painting of her.

'Do I always look like that to you?'

'No, it's a kind of distortion of how you are sometimes when you're out in the sun. You seem to attract the sun, pull it in to you, store it up and then shine it out again.'

'Do I look like that now?'

Luc shakes his head. 'Different.'

'What's different?'

'Darker. More real, more solid.'

And then she remembers. 'It's the one you stayed up all night painting and then Frédérique came the next morning.'

'That's it.'

He kisses her and pours them champagne. He pulls her to sit on the floor and they toast each other.

'I felt quite sorry for Jacques just now,' Cecillie says.

'He'll live.'

'Do you think they'll get back together?'

'The man doesn't even know they've split up yet!'

They drink down the first glass of champagne and Luc pours some more.

'They'll be all right,' Luc says. 'Despite what Frédérique says, they're made for each other.'

'Like us.'

'No one's like us.'

'Did you see her face? Tonight, I mean.'

'Frédérique's?'

'When you said she looked beautiful.'

'Christ! I felt such an idiot.' They both laugh.

'Do you think she's beautiful?'

'She is, I suppose.' He shrugs dismissively. 'I don't want to think about it; I'm not interested in her, I'm interested in hearing what you think about that.' He points up to the painting. Cecillie's painted image floats above her.

'It makes me feel really, really sexy, but scared too. It's a scary thing, Luc, seeing yourself up on a wall. Oh no,' she exclaims, hitting Luc playfully on the arm. 'No wonder everyone was staring – they've all seen me naked!'

'Not in the flesh. That's for me.'

He slides his hand along her leg. The muscle shivers under his fingers. 'I could fuck you right now.'

Cecillie giggles.

'I'm serious,' he says. 'Let's leave right now.'

'What about your show? What about selling your paintings?'

'That's Frédérique's job. I don't have a say in that part. Except with this one, of course – no one's having this.'

'You're keeping it?'

He nods and pulls her to him. 'I wouldn't give you away for anything.'

Cecillie puts her empty glass down. She runs her hands across the front of his jeans. 'We could do it right here. No one would know if you were quick, Luc. Just unzip,' she says, tugging gently at his flies. 'Just unzip and shove in.'

Frédérique watches Luc lead Cecillie over to the alcove. He'd told her earlier that he'd been looking forward to showing Cecillie her portrait, for weeks. The secret was burning him up inside. She'd smiled and nodded and tried to look understanding, all the time wishing that he'd stop talking about it. She could make an effort to empathize with Luc; she does it often enough with her artists, after all. But she can't. She can't get any further from the hatred she has for the painting. She hates what it stands for, she hates the stir it's caused this evening and she hates, above everything else, the fact that it's not for sale. How she would love to take a cheque, and hand it over to the greedy eyes of a fat, slobbering businessman. Not for sale.

When he'd first shown her the painting she'd immediately told Luc that there was no place for it in the exhibition; she felt that it wasn't good enough. Luc disagreed and took her comments badly. She could tell from his eyes that he didn't believe that the quality of the painting was the real issue. He thought that Frédérique was jealous. He didn't voice his opinion, however. He argued for the painting – told her it was the best he'd ever done, that it meant more to him than all the others put together. It was a personal celebration he said, and he wanted it at the exhibition as a surprise for Cecillie.

She had responded firmly explaining that if the painting was a private matter, it should be treated as such. It shouldn't take up the space of another, better painting. Particularly, as he'd indicated he'd no intention of selling it.

She changed her mind in the end. Not because she'd misjudged the work – she had Fernand's opinion to back her up on that – but because of what Jacques said. He hadn't a clue whether it was good or not, but once he heard that Cecillie would be at the party, he'd urged Frédérique to include it.

'They'll love it,' he said. 'The artist's muse on canvas and in the flesh. It'll make a good atmosphere.'

'I get the impression that she's rather unpredictable.'

Jacques was adamant. 'All the better. Bohemian anarchy, that's what half the people expect from artists, you know that better than anyone. Drink and drama. It'll up your sales.'

Jacques was right. From the moment Cecillie and her friend arrived, the mood of the party had changed, shifting up a gear. It could be, of course, thinks Frédérique looking around, simply the champagne taking effect, but people are beginning to enjoy themselves and, more importantly, she's getting the first serious indications from potential customers.

Frédérique turns back to Jacques and Bryony. 'I have to circulate,' she says and heads off across the room.

'It's a big night for Frédérique too, I suppose,' Bryony says as they both watch Frédérique immediately start socializing; she stops every now and then, smiling, laughing, shaking hands, kissing cheeks. 'I didn't realize it was going to be like this.'

'Like what?'

'I thought it would be a small party for friends, I suppose.'

'Do you think it's too much?'

Bryony looks at him, not understanding.

'Excessive, I mean.'

'I wouldn't know. I don't know how these things are usually done.'

Jacques had meant this evening to be lavish. He had meant the party to make as big a splash as he could manage. He doesn't like Luc's paintings. He finds them dour, drab and sulky. He hasn't told Frédérique that because what matters is that Frédérique loves them. For that reason alone, he decided, if he had anything to do with it, the exhibition was going to be a success. He's pulled strings and made use of even the lightest of contacts to get the sort of guests he thought it would be advantageous to attend tonight. Fernand was a big help, once he knew Jacques's plan. He'll certainly owe some favours after tonight. But, thank god, his efforts seem to be paying off. Even the mayor's here and that's a real coup.

But now he wonders whether he's gone too far, whether the stress will be too much for Frédérique. He knows that she's found the preparation a real strain. It's ironic how, since she's been working over here, Frédérique's been so busy that they've hardly spent any time together. He corrects himself – personal time. They've had plenty of business discussions but their relationship has received nothing more than a snatched moment of conversation and the occasional meal before Frédérique's hurried off, distracted and, he has to admit, rather edgy. He's enjoyed having her nearby though. When he's had a spare moment, he's sat in this room and watched her – not just directing the others in their work but really getting involved. Frédérique's enjoyment of the physical element of the arrangements – the picture hanging, the background arrangements, even the redecorating – was evident. He was surprised by that, surprised at, and attracted by, that physical side to her, her strength, her flexibility.

Frédérique, as if sensing Jacques's scrutiny, looks in his direction and her smile fades. He's left staring into her dark eyes until she looks away.

He turns back to the English girl that he's been left with. 'Let's have a drink on the balcony.'

'OK.'

Jacques guides her towards the far end of the hall, stopping briefly to take two glasses of champagne from a waiter and handing one to Bryony.

It's been a very hot day and the evening has a sultry feel, as if it may storm later.

All the tables are occupied so they stand near the door. Bryony leans against the frame. Close up, Jacques is surprised to see that she's very pretty, with large dark eyes, and a resemblance to Frédérique. A less sophisticated, less guarded version.

'You're quite adorable,' he tells her.

'That's the second time you've complimented me and I only met you fifteen minutes ago.'

He laughs. 'Well, I stand by my first impression.'

'Thank you.'

'I mean it.'

'Thank you again.'

'Do you like the paintings?' he asks.

'I haven't seen them all yet. But yes, the ones I have, I do like.'

'And what about the artist? What do you think about him?'

'He's great. He and Cecillie make a nice couple.'

'Ah yes, Cecillie. She's a very striking young woman.'

'She's certainly struck Luc. He adores her.'

'I've noticed.'

Bryony laughs. 'They certainly don't hide it.'

Behind Bryony, Jacques sees Frédérique hurrying across the hall towards the refreshment room. He pats the pocket of his jacket which holds brief, hastily made notes for a speech should he be required to give one. He knows, sadly, that this will not be the case. Any thoughts of sharing this evening have gone; any fantasies about he and Frédérique side by side, announcing their engagement must be wiped out of his mind. How stupid he was not to realize that, for Frédérique, this party is work. She is, quite simply, too busy to think about him. Their future will be dealt with separately, later. They'll have their own party, he decides, their own celebration.

'I like the colours,' Bryony's saying. Jacques forces himself to pay attention.

'It's the subject matter that I don't like,' he says. 'This heavy-handed attempt at social realism.' He stops abruptly. He hadn't meant to offer his own opinion. He hopes the girl doesn't pass his comments on.

'The people?'

'Yes.'

'Don't you like people?'

'Not ones that don't smile.'

'Maybe they haven't got much to smile about.'

Surely the girl isn't going to give him a lecture on ethics. That would be too much. 'Everyone has something to smile about,' he says irritably.

She folds her arms and studies him. 'Do *you*? I haven't seen you smiling yet.'

He tries to force a smile. It comes out, he's sure, like a grimace. 'What sort of person do I look like then?'

'You look fed up.'

He's taken aback. 'I'm sorry, I hadn't realized it showed.' He stares at Bryony. Her eyes are friendly and for a minute he's tempted to tell her about his concerns but quickly decides against it.

'I shouldn't have said anything. It's none of my business.' She turns and looks inside, stopping the conversation.

He'll remember to steer clear of girls in trainers next time. He takes the opportunity to see if her friends have reappeared, intending to pass her on to them. There's no sign. 'Do you know anyone else here?' he asks, hopefully.

'Not a soul.'

He resigns himself to her company for a little longer. 'Another drink, perhaps?'

'Yes, please.'

Jacques bumps into Frédérique coming out of the refreshment room with a glass of champagne. He takes her arm and leads her to a quieter spot at the side of the hall.

'How are you doing?' he asks a little hesitantly. He examines her face. She looks tired.

'Fine.'

'It's going well, isn't it?'

'Very well.' She smiles and sips her drink.

He takes hold of her hand. She quickly glances around the room and continues sipping.

'We've worked well together,' he says.

'Yes, it's going fine.'

'Yet more to celebrate.'

'What?'

'You and me. We're going to have so much to celebrate. It's going to be one hell of a party.'

'What is?'

'Our engagement party, I was thinking . . .'

'I didn't know . . . we hadn't . . . I thought we'd agreed to discuss everything afterwards.'

'But it'll soon be afterwards, won't it?' he says gently. 'After tonight.'

'Tonight is what I need to concentrate on right now.'

'OK, OK,' he relents, laughing. 'But you're not going to hold me off for ever. This week you and I are going to do some serious talking. I'll cook you a meal and we'll have all the time in the world.'

'That will be nice,' she says quickly.

'When? Tomorrow?'

'Oh, I don't know.'

'Name your day.'

She moves away. 'Let's sort it out later, Jacques.' She smiles briefly at him. 'I can't think further than now.'

'Frédérique . . .'

'I've got to find Luc. There are some people I need to introduce him to.'

'The last time I saw him he was dragging Cecillie off for a little privacy.' They both look towards the alcove. 'And they haven't come out yet.'

'Well, I'd better interrupt their private party and get Luc to do some of the work tonight.'

'They won't thank you for it,' he calls after her but she doesn't look back.

Jacques fetches a bottle of champagne and starts back to the balcony. On the way, he spots Fernand arriving. They shake hands warmly.

'Very impressive,' Fernand says, amiably. 'You don't want to work for the gallery, Jacques, do you?'

Jacques laughs. 'I think I've got enough to do with this place.'

'I thought I'd try your restaurant soon. I've heard good reports, and not just from Frédérique.'

'I'd be delighted. Ring me when you've got a date. Frédérique will give you the number.'

'Where is she?' Fernand asks, looking round the room. 'And how is she?'

'She's doing fine.'

'I've been quite worried about her, you know? Perhaps I shouldn't say so.'

Jacques shakes his head. 'Yes, I've been concerned too.'

'You know, you two . . .' Fernand stops mid-sentence. Jacques looks at him but he shakes his head. 'No, nothing.'

'Go on.'

'I was just going to say you make a good team.'

Frédérique hears their laughter before she reaches the alcove. She hesitates a moment before going in.

They stop laughing when they see her. An empty champagne bottle rolls across the floor as Luc stands up and, staggering, he catches it with his foot, knocking over two discarded glasses.

Cecillie's dress is hitched up so Frédérique is treated to a view of her thighs. Luc's shirt's pulled out of his jeans, and it's wet down the front where he's spilt some drink. The pair of them look as if they've just ravaged each other. And as they're both evidently very drunk, Frédérique realizes, with a sickening feeling, they probably have. God knows who's seen them in here – not the press, please, she thinks. She could do without that as a headline in the local.

Luc hauls Cecillie up and her dress slithers back into place. They stand grinning, holding each other's hands.

Frédérique's voice shakes. 'I'm sorry to take you away from your fun, Luc, but there are some people you ought to meet.'

'I'm sorry to take you away from your fun, Luc,' Cecillie mimics once they've gone. Like fuck she is. Left alone, Cecillie moves up close to the painting. She places the palms of her hands flat on it. It's cool, which is a surprise as the painting looks so hot it might burn. She begins to move her hands up it, from her feet, along her legs, up and up, feeling the bumps and smoothness of the paint. Someone appears behind her.

'Hey,' a man's voice shouts. 'You can't do that.'

She turns round. A man, with a glistening forehead, looks from her to the painting and back. 'Oh, I see, I'm sorry. Sorry to interrupt.' He exits quickly. Cecillie smiles but the spell's been broken. She takes one last look at herself and then heads back into the main hall.

The party has moved on a few paces. There are some signs of disarray – a number of flushed, shining faces, some loosened ties, slippage for a few expensive hairdos. It's very hot and very loud. Everyone seems to be shouting.

Standing on tiptoe, peering at one of the paintings is a little fat man in a bright yellow waistcoat and crisp white shirt.

'Monsieur Bayard!' Cecillie shouts as she heads towards him. She hugs him enthusiastically.

He steadies her and kisses her on both cheeks. 'I wondered where you were hiding.'

'I didn't know you were coming.'

'Your young man invited me. I had no idea it would be such an occasion – I feel quite underdressed and there are cameras everywhere.'

'That's the press,' Cecillie tells him. 'Luc says I've got to have my photo taken with him later.'

'And so you should my dear. You look quite wonderful.'

'I'm pretty drunk.'

'It's allowed. It's a very special evening.' He puts his arm through Cecillie's and she leans against him.

'It is special, Monsieur Bayard,' she says. 'I've never been so happy in all my life.'

The more champagne they drink, the better Jacques and Bryony get on. Jacques really should be circulating but Bryony seems to have been abandoned to his hospitality and he's rather enjoying her company. He'd forgotten how funny the irreverent youth can be.

He glances inside again. Frédérique's been walking Luc around the hall. They've just joined a group standing the other side of the French windows and he can see her clearly as she introduces Luc. She looks lovely, her face is earnest, her eyes are alive and sparkling. He watches how the group look at her, then at Luc, then at her, back at Luc who shakes their hands then stands motionless – no, not motionless, gently swaying. He's very drunk, the young idiot, but Frédérique's keeping it all together. He allows himself a moment of pride.

'Frédérique and Luc are getting on well,' he says to Bryony.

'Not too well, I hope.' Bryony spins round and looks inside. 'Cecillie said she'd kill her if Frédérique tried anything on tonight.'

'Tried anything on?'

'Oh!' Bryony spins back, blushing. 'I don't mean anything, she didn't think . . .'

Jacques is frozen to the spot. He's staring at Frédérique who's gazing at Luc as he's talking. Her face is soft and proud. My god, he thinks, she's making a fool of herself. He spots Cecillie coming up behind the group.

'I see your friend's heading this way with a little fat man. Would you like to join them?' Jacques asks Bryony.

'Yes. But, Jacques . . .'

'Go on.' He practically pushes Bryony inside.

'Come and talk to me,' Jacques says to Frédérique, hissing in her ear.

'Not now, Jacques,' she whispers. 'I'm with these people.' She smiles brightly at him, then back towards the group. Jacques stares hard at Luc who looks at him, then Frédérique, and finally at his feet before walking away.

'Talk to me. Look at me.' He emphasizes each word slowly. 'Who made all this possible?' he whispers fiercely.

'I know.' She shakes her arm free. 'And I'm really grateful.'

'Really grateful! That's not what I want to hear.' He struggles to keep his voice low.

'Jacques, we'll talk later.'

People, he notices, are looking pointedly away.

'We'll talk now.' He takes her by the wrist, hard and tugs her away. She stumbles a little then straightens up.

'Please excuse us for a moment, ladies and gentlemen,' he says, putting an arm over her shoulder and starting to steer her away. Frédérique's body is stiff against his. He guides her across the hall, into the refreshment room and then through a side door into the kitchens. As soon as the door is closed, Frédérique turns on him.

'What's this about, Jacques? I hope you realize you've just made a complete spectacle of us.'

'I thought you were doing that quite well all by yourself.'

She's never seen him look so angry. His face is pinched, his eyes are so dark that they look hollow.

'Are you drunk?' he asks her. 'I hope to god you're drunk.' He looks her up and down. She finds herself straightening her dress, her hands fluttering to tidy her hair.

'I don't know what you're talking about.'

'You are drunk, aren't you? Tell me you're drunk.'

'I am not drunk,' she shouts. 'What is this all about?'

He can't know, she's thinking, he can't know. It's about something else, some misunderstanding. But she can feel sweat seeping out of her skin, and her stomach begins to churn.

'They're all laughing at you out there,' he says softly, coming towards her.

She backs away and stumbles against the wall . . . 'I don't . . .'

'You and your artist.'

'That's why I'm here. That's why we're all here.' She smiles in desperation, willing him not to go on. She doesn't know what she will say; she isn't ready for this.

He leans on the wall beside her, twists her face towards him. His fingers press into her cheeks. 'Don't pretend, Frédérique, I've seen it for myself.'

'I don't . . .'

'He's not even interested in you. He's in love with Cecillie, anybody can see that. You said it yourself. Passionately in love.'

'Cecillie . . . she told you?'

'No . . .'

'I didn't know that Luc had told her.'

'I can't believe this.' He releases her and pushes off from the wall. 'Told her what?'

Frédérique's confused. 'I thought . . .'

'Have you slept with him?'

'No!'

'What then, what is there to tell?'

'I . . .' She hesitates. 'I said . . . I told him . . . I love him.'

He looks away. He's silent. A silence which tells Frédérique that this was not what Jacques was expecting. She wishes she could take the words back, wishes she'd found out what he really knew before she'd said anything. Jacques turns back to her. His face is blank, he looks into her eyes. 'You poor, stupid idiot.'

She hates him. At that moment she hates Jacques so much she wants to slap his face. She breathes deeply and tries to speak calmly. 'You can't call me anything worse than I've already called myself. But the trouble is, I can't help it, I can't stop myself.' She thinks she's going to start crying but something in Jacques's hostile face revives her anger and the desire to hurt. 'I love him.

It's there, it's real, and it's made me feel more alive than I've done for months, years maybe, since I can remember.'

She knows as she says the words, that she's gone too far. But it's too late. Jacques stares hard at her.

'What happens now?' she asks, deflated.

'Now?' he says woodenly. 'Well, we can hardly ask everyone to go home, can we?' He lets out a sharp bark of laughter and considers her for a moment, as her face reddens. 'But you know that of course, you were counting on that.'

Frédérique doesn't say anything.

He's the idiot, Jacques thinks, he's the fool to have misread the signs. He's tired suddenly, and wants Frédérique out of his sight.

'Go back to your party. It's what you wanted, isn't it? Go on then, enjoy yourself.'

'I'm sorry . . .'

'Go away.'

'I think it . . .'

'Frédérique, we have to get through this evening, so please, get on with it.'

She leaves through the far door into the corridor. She takes a few steps but then collapses against the wall, her legs trembling.

'Are you OK?' The redheaded barman is peering round the corner at her. 'Hey, it's you. Are you OK?'

'I'm fine. Please leave me alone.'

But Blythe comes round and leans up against the wall beside her: hot and solid.

'Want a cigarette?'

He rummages around for the packet.

'I gave up years ago,' she tells him.

In the quietness she can hear the low hum of the party inside, then the flick-flick as the man lights a cigarette.

'I always find it helps,' he says, exhaling loudly. 'Especially when I'm pissed.'

'I'm not drunk.'

'I am,' he tells her.

'Well, it would take more than a cigarette to help me sort out the mess I've made.'

'Is the party crap?'

She shakes her head. 'No, my life is.' It sounds so melodramatic that Frédérique laughs at herself.

'Oh, life,' Blythe says. 'I always find a fag helps with *that*.'

'Just a puff, then.' She takes the cigarette. The smoke rushes in, burning her throat, making her cough, her eyes sting, but she holds the smoke inside and can feel it fizzing around her body, dizzying her head. She lets the smoke out.

'Better?'

'You're always seeing me upset,' she says, looking sideways at him. He is very drunk, Frédérique realizes. His eyes are bloodshot and he sways slightly each time he takes a drag. Jacques would be furious if he knew his barman had been drinking on the job.

'Hundred per cent record,' he says. 'So far.' He slurs his final words.

'I'm not always like this but I've made a mess of everything.'

'This is to do with your friend and mine, I take it?'

She nods. 'But it's my fault . . .'

He offers her another drag of the cigarette but she shakes her head.

'I've got to go back in there and pretend for the rest of the night that it hasn't happened.'

'I could escort you in,' he suggests. 'For moral support.'

'Perhaps you could.'

'Is everyone still there?' he asks.

'Oh yes, they're all there.'

He crushes the cigarette butt on the floor. 'Ready?'

'Jacques! Jacques!'

He doesn't register that someone is calling him until his arm is touched and held onto. It's Bryony.

'Are you OK?' she asks him. Big, earnest eyes.

'Of course.'

'It um . . .' Bryony hesitates. 'It looked like there was something wrong.'

'There's nothing wrong.'

'I put my foot in it, didn't I? I'm always saying stupid things when I'm pissed.'

'You opened my eyes, let's just say.'

'I'm really sorry. I don't even know if it's true, it's something we've been joking about and everything.'

'That,' he says, managing a bitter smile, 'doesn't really make me feel better.'

Bryony looks so upset, he feels sorry for her. Over her shoulder he sees Frédérique come in with Blythe.

'Your boyfriend's here,' he tells Bryony.

'Where?'

'With Frédérique.'

'Shall we join them?'

'I'd rather not. But please, you go ahead.'

'Will you be OK?'

'Of course.'

'Are you sure? I feel responsible.'

'You're very sweet,' he says bending down and kissing her briefly on the lips. 'Thank you.'

'What the fuck?' Blythe stands behind Bryony. He can't believe that Jacques has just kissed her. They don't even know each other, for fuck's sake.

Jacques nods at Blythe and turns to go.

'Hang on a minute. I think you owe me an explanation.'

Jacques faces him. He looks him up and down and Blythe's anger rises.

'I don't owe you anything,' Jacques tells him.

Blythe pushes him sharply in his chest. He lands heavily against one of the hangings, ripping it as he trips over. He bangs his face against the wall before going down. There's a smattering of laughter in the room and then Bryony is copiously and noisily sick on the floor.

Cecillie runs over to Bryony.

'I feel ill,' Bryony says. 'Take me home, please.'

Cecillie puts an arm round her. As they walk, Cecillie takes a look behind. Jacques is being helped up by several men, Luc and Monsieur Bayard are trying to manoeuvre Blythe out of the way but he's standing wild-eyed, looking crazy. At the opening of the avenue, Cecillie stops. Blythe is being led, meekly, head down, by Luc. Monsieur Bayard has, rather proudly, taken rearguard position. They look such a funny mix that Cecillie has to resist the urge to giggle. Bryony's shivering.

Jacques strides up behind Blythe. Cecillie gasps. Everyone's watching. Jacques is furious, but it suits him. He actually looks quite sexy, with his hair a little freer, his clothes less precise.

'You're sacked,' Jacques says.

Blythe whirls round. 'Fucking sacked,' Blythe shouts. 'Fucking sacked. I fucking resign, you arsehole.'

Blythe pushes ahead of Cecillie and Bryony and runs out.

Cecillie has a sudden desire to take a bow and say, 'That's all folks.'

When they reach the doors, Luc says, 'I'll come with you.'

'No, stay,' Cecillie tells him. 'You've got to. Come and see me afterwards. Come back to my place, after it's finished.' Bryony's crying quietly, Cecillie can feel her body jerk each time she sniffs.

'I'll escort the young ladies home,' Monsieur Bayard says, placing a hand on Luc's arm. 'Don't worry. I'll take care of them for you.'

Once Luc's friends have left, the party seems to really get going. Jacques was right, Frédérique thinks, looking around at the gossiping groups. They do love – what had he called it? – bohemian anarchy. And poor Jacques ended up the brunt of it. She had wanted to comfort him but when she went over, he walked away. He's disappeared. She assumes he's up in his apartment. He's left her to it and she can't blame him.

If she's honest, she's better off without him here – she can concentrate on Luc without worrying about Jacques.

She guides Luc from group to group. They sell more than she imagined they ever would. Cecillie is a mini sensation. Frédérique's lost count of the times she's been asked about buying her portrait, and some of the other paintings are very popular too; she could have sold them several times over. She talks more than she ever thought she could. By talking, she thinks, she can get through the rest of the evening.

Luc doesn't know what all the trouble was about; Blythe was virtually incoherent. He kept repeating, 'That fucking arsehole,' and, although Luc's got an idea Frédérique knows more, when he hints at it she looks strangely at him.

'Let's deal with the business in hand, shall we? The sooner we do, the sooner we can all go home.'

Passed from person to person, with drinks and conversation constantly pressed upon him, Luc barely knows what he's doing. But he doesn't have to, he finds. Frédérique does it all for him. He only has to stand there.

'So, young man,' a pompous man asks him, 'would you call yourself an artist of the people or would you be more comfortable with street artist?'

Luc is repulsed by the man's thick red lips which he constantly licks as he stares at him. 'Neither,' Luc says, tempted to add that he should go suck himself, before Frédérique interrupts.

'With Luc,' she says, 'first and foremost is his art. The inspiration he gathers from the city is, in a sense, offered back to the city in the form of his paintings.'

He follows Frédérique like an obedient dog. He listens to her replying for him about his past which he'd forgotten, which he thought didn't matter, which he has never known; about feelings, ideas, beliefs which he could never have guessed at owning and which are now, apparently evident in his pictures. Most of it's crap. Real crap. He wonders vaguely whether

Frédérique believes any of what she's saying or if it's just sales pitch stuff. She's very good at it, he has to admit: people pay attention, are captivated when she's speaking. Could she seem so enthusiastic, so convincing if she didn't?

'Yes, his paintings do reflect both the city he lives in physically and that of his mind. So there are darker corners of each. We all have a secret side to ourselves, don't we?'

'Yes, the girl in the painting is a source of inspiration for him.'

'No, it's not for sale . . . I'm afraid.'

In the end he stops listening. He's bored. He strains to see how many red spots have appeared on paintings, attempting to convert these into actual money. It seems to be an awful lot. He halves the amount and it's still more than he's ever had. He and Cecillie will be able to live in luxury for ages. They'll have that time off together they've been talking about and really spoil themselves.

When the last few guests are hanging over the remains of the champagne, Jacques reappears, his cheek swollen and bruised.

'I suggest you leave me to organize the clearing up.'

Frédérique begins to protest but Jacques glares at her. 'I'd prefer you both to go. Now.'

Luc stands with Frédérique while she waits for a taxi. He doesn't want a lift, he tells her, he wants to get some air. He starts to run before the taxi sets off and, when it goes past him, he turns down a side street, without looking round.

He arrives breathless at Cecillie's apartment. He opens the door quietly into a dimly lit room. Cecillie has wrapped a T-shirt around the lampshade and she's sitting cross-legged by the open windows, smoking. Her dress is pulled up and bunched around her waist; her knees shine in the lamplight.

She puts her finger to her lips and points to the bed. Bryony's asleep in it. He can see her pale face, surrounded by the mass of her black hair. He can't remember seeing it loose before. She looks like a child.

Cecillie stands up, her dress stays hoisted around her waist; she hasn't got any knickers on. She goes into the kitchen and he follows, her firm, brown buttocks tempting him forward.

'Were you a success?'

'I think so. You look gorgeous.'

He sits down and pulls her onto his lap. She slips her hand inside his jeans, kissing him as she does so. He sinks his mouth onto the base of her neck and down onto her breasts. He can smell the musky scent of her skin under the stronger smell of fresh cigarette smoke. The bones of her bottom press into his thigh. He slides his hand down and feels the moistness between her legs.

He half-carries her into the other room, but stops suddenly when he sees Bryony in the bed. They hold onto each other as they stagger around the room, trying to stifle their laughter. Cecillie still has her hand inside his jeans and his balls ache.

He pulls a towel and a jumper off the back of the door and throws them on the floor by the window. Outside, the sky has begun to lighten to a silky grey colour.

Cecillie's skin is cool, but as they move together, stroking, pulling, pushing, she begins to sweat.

'Jesus, you two were at it last night. I don't know where you get the energy,' Bryony says, sitting up in bed. She pulls at the neck of the T-shirt that Cecillie helped put on her last night and looks at it for a second as if trying to remember how it got there.

Luc's making coffee. There are clatterings, clinkings, and a low humming coming from behind the screen in the kitchen.

'We thought you were asleep,' Cecillie says, lighting a cigarette.

'I was until you woke me up. With your pash.'

'How're you feeling?' Cecillie asks, joining her on the bed and sliding her legs under the sheet. She plumps the pillow up behind her and puts an ashtray on her lap.

'I've got a terrible headache.'

'Me too.'

'It was the champagne. I drank buckets.'

'You were quite spectacular with your timing and everything.'

'I guess.' Bryony shrugs, then adds. 'Did we spoil it?'

Cecillie shakes her head. 'Uh-uh. Apparently the posh lot like to see a bit of brawling.'

'Oh, Cec.'

Cecillie takes Bryony's hand. 'It's OK, Bry. It was a success. Luc sold lots of paintings. And Jacques only had a bit of a bruise . . .'

Bryony smiles but then her face pales. 'Oh, no! I've just remembered. Last night I kind of let on to Jacques about Frédérique and Luc.'

'Shit! When?'

'Just before Blythe went for Jacques. I was apologizing to Jacques about me putting my foot in it and he was really sweet about it; said it wasn't my fault.'

'Well, he only needed to watch Frédérique for a few minutes

and he'd have spotted it,' Cecillie says sharply. 'Did you see her? She was all over Luc the whole time.'

'I did notice.'

'Silly bitch.'

'God,' Bryony says, rubbing her eyes. 'I don't know why Blythe got so worked up about Jacques giving me a kiss.'

Cecillie pouts her lips and says in a French accent, 'Joos a leetle kees.'

Bryony hits her arm. 'Cec!'

Cecillie blows a wobbly smoke ring, looks at Bryony and says carefully, 'I didn't hear Blythe come back last night, did you?'

Bryony nods. 'Later, though. You were asleep.'

Cecillie stubs out her cigarette and puts the saucer on the floor. She lies on her side, facing Bryony. 'He'll get another job OK, won't he?'

Bryony sinks down in the bed and tucks the sheet around her waist. 'I don't know. He might take this as his cue to go travelling.'

'What will you do if he does?'

Bryony doesn't reply.

'Will you go with him?' Cecillie persists.

'I can't – I've got the boys.'

'You don't have to stay, though. And you'll be leaving them next month, anyway.'

Bryony plays with her hair, winding it into a coil which she twists onto the top of her head where it immediately begins to unravel once she lets go.

'Have you decided what you're going to do, Bryony?' Cecillie asks.

Bryony nods. 'I'm going home. I'm going to take my place at university. I want to be a teacher. I always have.'

'Does Blythe know, is that why . . . ?' Cecillie stops when Bryony shakes her head.

'I keep putting off telling him.'

'You'll have to say something soon.'

Bryony pushes her hair behind her ears. 'He'll take it badly, I know he will.'

8

explain love

'Blythe! You're early. We're not meeting Cecillie down there until eight.'

'I couldn't keep away.' He kisses her hello. There's a smell of onion about her.

'You'll have to wait,' she says, closing the door behind him. 'I'm not expecting Sophie home for another hour.'

'That's OK.' He follows her down the hall. 'I thought I'd enjoy your company for a bit longer and get refreshments thrown in for free.'

The boys come squealing out of one room and pile up at his feet. He says, 'Hello, boys.' They untangle themselves and hurtle away, brake noises squeal them around the corner and into the room they've just come from. It suddenly goes very quiet.

Bryony stops and listens. 'I hate it when they do that,' she says, before leading the way into the kitchen where the onion smell is overpowering.

Bryony fills the kettle and puts it on the stove, flicking the gas on quickly, then returns to a pile of brightly coloured vegetables that she's in the process of chopping. 'It won't take me a minute to finish these,' she says as she waves him to sit down.

Blythe watches the neat, quick way she works, her lips pursed a little as she concentrates. Periodically she slides the vegetables into a big bowl, until the unchopped pile has gone.

She makes tea.

'OK,' she says, sitting opposite him. 'What is it?'

He tries to look innocent but then grins. He's been bursting with the news all morning. 'You know Luc's mate who's here from Spain for the festival?'

Bryony nods.

'Luc's spoken to him and he'll give us a lift back to his place Sunday night – and we can stay there for a week or so, he doesn't mind. He's got this fantastic place in the middle of nowhere. Like a bloody mansion, Luc says.'

'Next week?' Bryony says slowly and he knows by the way she frowns that she's not chuffed about the offer like he is. She twists her mug round and round on the table. While he waits for her verdict, all his plans – his thoughts of walking in the mountains, drinking in Spanish bars, the precious time spent with Bryony giving her a taste of what they could do together – dissolve.

'I'm on my own with the boys all next week. Sophie and Henri are going away – I told you. It's been arranged for a long time.'

He'd forgotten and this annoys him as much as the fact that Bryony can't go. He tries to keep his voice reasonable. 'They can find someone else for a week, surely? It's a one-off, Bry.'

'You can't just dump kids like that, you know,' she says, angrily.

He responds in the same manner. 'Christ, Bryony. Can't you do something spontaneous for once? It's like going out with an old person. You're so fucking responsible.'

He's made her cry. He sees tears plop onto the table, onto her hand.

'I've agreed to be here until I go back.'

'*If* you go back,' he corrects her as usual.

A pink flush rises up from her neck. He has to look away as she begins to tell him what he knows he doesn't want to hear. '*When* I go back,' she says quietly and then louder. 'I'm definitely going home, Blythe. I've decided. It's what I want to do.' The last words she says a little flatly, then she sniffs and looks fiercely at him, tears in her eyelashes before she blinks them away.

'OK,' he says. 'OK.'

They both sit and drink their tea in silence. Blythe's mind is working over what Bryony's just said. Well, the words are going round his head but he can't take in their meaning. He's been waiting so long for Bryony's decision that now it's here, it's as if her words are a test run. He glances at her to see if she was testing his reaction to that particular string of words, before she gave him the good news.

She holds his look and smiles. It's the smile that hits him in the guts. It's sad, a little apologetic, but also determined. It's an *I'm sorry but I've made my mind up and nothing's going to change it* smile. Christ. He knew this would happen, he fucking *knew* she'd decide this way. He fucking knew it.

'Six weeks, that's all we've got then, Bryony. Six fucking weeks.'

'I know . . .'

'So with such little time left, don't you think it's important we should spend as much of it together as possible?'

'It would be nice, but . . .'

'Nice, but!' He explodes. 'Fucking nice, but!'

She puts her hand out to him, to calm him down, but at the same time she's swivelling round towards the door to check whether the boys are in earshot. She wants Blythe calmer, but because of the boys, that's all.

'Fuck them, Bryony,' he says, childishly. 'What about me?'

'That's not fair.'

'I don't feel very fair.'

He stands up.

'Where are you going?'

'To get some fags. I'll come back in half an hour when you'll be ready for the festival, I take it?'

Bryony catches him up in the hall.

'Don't be like this, Blythe. What about the following week, I can talk to Henri and Sophie and sort it out. What about that week?'

'We won't have a lift that week. The guy won't even care who we are by then.'

'We could go somewhere though. Or you could go on your own. I wouldn't mind.'

He doesn't look at her until he opens the door and steps outside. 'That wasn't really the point of it.'

The bar is one of five buildings set on the beach on a short concrete promenade. The others are two hotels, a water sports hire shop, and a hairdresser's with a private apartment on top.

It's a popular beach for young people. There have been raves here most weekends since June. It's *the* place to be on the festival weekend. So Cecillie said. It seems she was right. When Blythe and Bryony are dropped off by their hitch, there are already loads of people wandering around, sitting on the beach, on the promenade, walking to and from the town.

'Where've you guys been? We've been waiting ages.' Cecillie's standing at the front entrance of the bar as arranged. She's holding a bottle of beer. 'Luc's gone for a pee. I haven't been in to dance yet. I've been waiting for you two.' She gives them each a hug as she speaks.

Blythe shrugs her off and heads for the toilets. Cecillie and Bryony watch him part stagger, part swagger through the crowds of people.

'He's touchy. And pissed?'

'He's been drinking vodka all the way here.' Cecillie looks sharply at Bryony who sighs. 'I told him I couldn't go to Spain.'

'With Luc's mate?'

Bryony nods. 'And I told him I was going home.'

Cecillie offers Bryony the beer bottle. 'What did he say?'

'He said we should spend the time we've got left together and I said I had the boys to think of – which I do – and . . .' Bryony drinks some beer, it's warm but comforting.

She hands it back to Cecillie who shakes her head. 'Have some more.'

Bryony gulps it down. 'I think I'll get pissed too.'

'He must have been expecting it, Bry. He's not stupid.'

Bryony shakes her head. 'He seems really shocked. I knew he would be, that's why I didn't want to tell him. I knew he'd be like this.'

'He'll come round. Once you start promising marathon sex

sessions during your holidays from university, he'll think it's a great idea.'

Bryony snorts into her beer. 'I need another one of those,' she says, placing the bottle on the floor behind her.

'Do you want Luc to have a word with him?' Cecillie offers.

Bryony shakes her head. 'Does Luc know all about marathon sex sessions, then?'

'Too right, he does. My thighs are killing me. Not to mention my other bits.' Cecillie grabs hold of Bryony's hand. 'You wait,' she tells Bryony as they head to the bar. 'You won't be able to walk for days at a time.'

Blythe has been gone ages. Bryony can't find him anywhere. They were supposed to be going into the town with Cecillie and Luc to get something to eat, but in the end the other two went ahead with Bryony telling them that she'd wait for Blythe and catch them up. But there's been no sign of him for over an hour. She's looked everywhere, pushing her way into each room, through the dance floor and out at the back where they're smoking spliffs in little huddles. He's disappeared.

She's fed up and angry and feels like crying. She's run out of money and she doesn't know anyone. Although she seems to be Miss Popular – people won't leave her alone. Wherever she goes, someone starts talking to her, or touching or trying to get her to join their group. Sometimes she has to wrench herself free.

Bryony decides to escape to the toilets for a while, but she's only been in there a few minutes when someone bangs on the door. She comes out, ignoring the rude comments from two pissed girls, and wanders the whole way round the bar again.

A man stops her as she walks past the bar, and holds onto

her waist with both hands. 'Would you like a drink?' He loudly orders two beers before she can reply. Bryony glances behind the man to check whether the bar staff have taken any notice of him. He's a lot older than most people here, and he looks a bit weird.

'On your own?' he asks, smiling. He's still got hold of her waist.

'With my friends.' She smiles nervously at a barmaid who rolls her eyes in sympathy.

The man laughs. 'We're all friends here tonight.' He puts his arm around her shoulders and asks her if she wants to dance. She agrees, thinking that she'll be able to get away from him in the crowd and they begin to push their way through to the dance floor. Then she catches sight of Cecillie.

'Excuse me. I've just seen someone.'

Cecillie's blonde hair is moving through the crowd towards an exit door. Bryony starts to follow her, the man grabs at her arm but she pulls away, other hands grab at her waist, her hair; faces peer into hers, stop here, join us, pretty girl, have a drink, kiss me. She carries on going, keeping Cecillie in her sights, like a temptress in front of her. Cecillie must have met up with Blythe on the way to the town, Bryony explains to herself, her heart lightening with relief, and they've all come back to fetch her.

There's a pile-up around the door, where Bryony hopes she'll catch Cecillie up. As she gets closer though, and sees wavy hair and a broad back she knows that it isn't her. Still, when she reaches the girl, she has to make sure. She puts her hand on the girl's bare arm. It's warm and dry. The face of a stranger looks round blankly.

'Sorry,' says Bryony. 'My mistake.'

She follows the girl outside anyway because she doesn't know what else to do. She can't believe that Blythe has shit out on her like this, she feels abandoned and angry and very sorry for herself.

The bright moon gives a hazy visibility, almost like daylight. There are a lot of people around, walking up the track towards the main town, some heading to the beach, some just sitting outside, others dancing on the beach where the music is being tannoyed out.

She sees the weird man by the door and quickly tags along behind a large group of girls on the main track, hoping he hasn't spotted her. She'll make her way into town, she decides, and go to the restaurant as planned without Blythe. She glances nervously behind her but the man isn't there.

Then she sees someone she does know. Jacques. He's outside the posh hotel. She doesn't think before she calls out his name and rushes towards him.

'I hope you remember me. I'm Bryony. We met at the party. Luc's preview party.'

'Of course I remember. We had a nice chat,' he says, surprised that Bryony isn't showing any discomfort or embarrassment and instead seems pleased to see him. In fact she smiles up at him and says, 'It's really great to bump into you.'

Jacques wouldn't have remembered her name. For a second, he thought she was Frédérique, and the smile that began to form was frozen, unfinished. He hopes that she didn't notice his disappointment.

'I've lost everyone,' Bryony's saying, glancing around. 'I'm out looking. It's a bit strange here tonight.'

'It usually is on festival night. Where is your excitable boyfriend these days?' he asks. It doesn't escape his notice that Bryony's been crying. Her eyes are rimmed red and her face looks very pale.

'I've lost him, too.'

'I'm sure he'll turn up soon,' Jacques attempts to reassure her quickly as he sees dangerous signs of fresh tears starting.

'I'm sure he will,' Bryony replies overbrightly.

'Look,' Jacques begins, with a wry mental note that he appears destined to play host to Bryony whenever they meet, 'I was just going to a restaurant up in the hills near here. Would you care to accompany me?'

'Thanks, but I'm supposed to be eating in town.'

Jacques pulls a face. 'The food there is all indescribably bad,' he tells her. 'And you'd be doing me a great favour, to be honest. I don't like to dine alone and especially not tonight. We could keep each company. The two lost souls.'

Now that Bryony's hesitating, it suddenly seems important that he doesn't end up sitting in the restaurant on his own. And he remembers too, that before the party went disastrously wrong, the two of them had got on rather well. He notices that she's wavering and he throws his last attempt, with a smile. 'Please?'

She looks very solemn. 'OK, thanks. But I can't be too long, or the others will worry about me.'

'We wouldn't want that, would we?'

The restaurant is on top of a small hill which is reached by a narrow and winding road, leading off a sandy track in between the bar and hotel on the beach. Jacques's car slowly zigzags its way up. Bryony looks out at the rocks shining white in the moonlight, looks down at the lights from the bars on the beach, and at the ghostly shapes and black shadows moving across the beach and wandering down the sandy tracks.

The car's comfortable. The quiet of the smooth engine, the seats which feel large, deep and soft, make it like a tiny sanctuary after all the noise and crowds. When the journey is over, she doesn't want to get out.

There are not many customers and Jacques, who is obviously known by the waiters, is led immediately to a table on the balcony outside. The promenade is clearly visible, and the heavy bass of the bar music plays underneath the softer, insipid tunes from inside.

'We always seem to end up on balconies,' Bryony says, then blushes as it only now dawns on her that in her relief at seeing Jacques's familiar face earlier, she has been horribly insensitive. 'I'm really sorry about what happened at the party,' she adds quickly.

Jacques looks surprised. 'I wouldn't expect you to apologize,' he replies. 'After all, it was better . . .'

The waiter arrives with the wine Jacques has ordered, providing a distraction from having to voice, and relive, the scenes of that night that have been constantly in his mind ever since.

'So what did you mean – two lost souls?' Bryony asks, sipping her drink. She looks much more relaxed. 'Why are you on your own tonight then? I would have thought you'd be with friends.'

'I was, but I needed a break from someone.'

The someone was Frédérique, or rather, the spirit of

Frédérique – since the real thing hadn't put in an appearance. He'd come down to the hotel convinced that she would be there because it's their usual haunt, it's where all their friends have gathered on the festival weekend every year since he can't remember when.

Frédérique hadn't rung to say she'd be there, but neither had she been in touch to say she wouldn't. He hasn't heard a word from her since the party. She's left him in suspense for over a week, unsure of what to do next, positive at the start of each day that she would contact him, disbelieving each night when she didn't.

The more he thought about it, the more he'd convinced himself that it would be typical of Frédérique to alleviate a difficult situation by having the cushion of their good friends around them, good food, good wine. But she wasn't there when he arrived and he drank on and on at the bar, joking and chatting but all the time keeping an eye out for her.

A couple of hours later, he overheard one of the women whispering to another, with an assessing look directed towards him, that Frédérique had phoned her to say that she wasn't coming this weekend. She was visiting her parents instead.

That was when he decided to go out for a meal, rather than eat in the hotel restaurant. He'd prefer to leave everyone free to get the gossip out of the way without his presence.

He thought he needed to be on his own, but having the company of Bryony, he realizes, is better, it'll stop him from agonizing over the situation. Unlike his friends, Bryony's detached from his problems with Frédérique and she's sweet, he thinks, watching her fingers playing with her hair, her thick eyelashes visible as she concentrates on the menu. She's a perfect excuse, he thinks, for him leaving the hotel. If anyone asks when he gets back, it will be easier to say he had dinner with a girlfriend than to say he dined on his own, and it might even put them off the scent for a while.

Their first courses arrive. Jacques has chosen oysters, Bryony artichoke hearts.

'Tell me, why do you stick with your crazy boyfriend?' asks Jacques as he prepares to eat.

'Blythe's not crazy!' She continues to defend Blythe. 'He isn't. He was angry, that's all.'

'You don't need to tell *me* that.' Jacques makes an elaborate gesture towards his cheek. Bryony peers at Jacques's face; there's a faint yellow bruise underneath one eye.

She waves her fork at him. 'He wouldn't like me being here with you.'

'Why? Can't he trust you?' Jacques gives her a lecherous smile.

'He doesn't like you,' she says, ignoring him, trying to explain. 'I mean, how you behave.'

'How do I behave?'

'Self-importantly! *Like the big I am,* I think he said.'

'I worked hard to get that bar going. I still work hard.' In spite of himself, Jacques feels offended. He sits back in his chair.

'Blythe thinks that you rub everyone's noses in it.'

'That's his problem. I'd say he was jealous.'

'I didn't mean to be rude,' Bryony says, realizing too late that the wine is making her garrulous. She may have overstepped the mark.

'I don't think it was unreasonable firing him, given the circumstances.'

'No,' Bryony agrees. 'He was definitely out of order.'

'He's a good barman, mind you,' Jacques admits, resuming his meal. 'One of the best I've ever had. He certainly knows his job.'

'Perhaps you just brought out the worst in him.'

'I repeat my earlier question, Bryony. Why, when your young man is unpredictable and dangerous, do you stick with him?'

Bryony knows that he's playing around and doesn't expect a serious reply, but she tells him the truth, anyway. 'I love him.'

Jacques places his fork carefully on his plate and wipes his mouth with a serviette. 'Ah – love,' he says. 'I'm interested to hear what you, as a woman, think about love.'

'It's no different for a woman than it is for a man.' Bryony gives Jacques a sharp look to express her dissatisfaction with his question. Jacques only laughs.

'It is in my experience,' Jacques says as he pours them some more wine. 'Very much so.'

'And I don't think you can explain love anyway: you see someone and you think, great! Or wow! Or oh my god! And that's it.'

'You don't think that love can come from less, um – explosive – beginnings?' he asks.

Bryony considers this for a moment. 'Yes, of course it can. But I think you still know deep down. It's just the wow factor's been suppressed until later, the right time or whatever, and then . . .'

Bryony stops talking. Jacques seems oblivious to her, absorbed in his thoughts. He drinks down his glass of wine and pours himself some more. Bryony, with alcoholic courage, gets the urge to push him further, sensing that his reserve is crumbling. 'How's Frédérique?'

She's hit the target. He looks shrunken and subdued. Cecillie would be proud of her, thinks Bryony, imagining them picking this over later.

'I haven't seen Fred for a while,' he says, quietly. 'She's spending the weekend with her family.'

Bryony's pleasure in her manipulation of the conversation is short-lived. Jacques's obvious distress quickly arouses sympathy in her. She tells herself off for being cruel and tries to make amends. 'She seems a very nice woman.'

He answered without any hesitation. 'She is.' He adds, 'You look rather like her in fact.'

'I thought that, too. Except she's very glamorous!'

Jacques brightens up a bit. He leans across the table, confidentially. 'I suppose you're wearing outrageous footwear again?'

Bryony laughs and sticks one foot out from under the table. She's wearing yellow plastic platform sandals.

Jacques affects to shudder. 'I think only the English could wear such things and be proud.'

Bryony excuses herself to go to the bathroom. Jacques watches her walk back to the table. She clumps along in her sandals, her arms held out from her sides as if she's trying to keep her balance. When she's seated, Jacques tells her, 'With a beautiful Italian shoe, you would be quite lovely.'

'Thank you, Jacques. But you don't have to bother with all that.'

'All what?'

'I'm not going to sleep with you. I'm not interested, you see.

I'm only interested in Blythe and I can only ever go for one bloke at a time. I'm like that. And anyway, I know you don't really fancy me. You're just going through the motions because I'm here.'

Jacques should be affronted by Bryony's assumption that he has any sexual interest in her, but he's fascinated by her candour. He has never met a girl who is so direct and it's refreshing.

'On the contrary, you are an extremely attractive woman,' he flatters her. 'And besides, I think that there's nothing wrong in enjoying yourself sometimes.'

He isn't serious. He has no intention of seducing her, of sleeping with her, as she put it.

'Well, I think you only like me because I look like Frédérique and she isn't here.'

He's amused by her comment, but wonders whether there's a grain of truth in it. He's always gone for a certain type of woman – a Frédérique type. But although Bryony may resemble her, Bryony's very different to Frédérique and to the women he usually mixes with, not only in how she dresses, but in her attitude too. He toys with the idea that there would be fewer complications with a softer, sweeter kind of girl.

Bryony continues. 'It's just easier, don't you think, less messy, if there's not sex tied up with it.' She sits back in the chair and looks straight at him. 'We can just enjoy a meal and keep each other company. And that's that.'

'It certainly could get messy, as you say, if your brutal boyfriend found out.'

The waiter brings them the next course and Jacques pours more wine.

'That's settled then,' he says.

'To no sex!' Bryony raises her glass.

Jacques toasts her back. 'No sex.'

'So.' Jacques pauses in eating for a moment. 'How did you manage to lose Blythe this evening?'

'He was angry with me.'

'Why?'

'It's a long story.'

'We've got the rest of our meal ahead, and at least another bottle of wine to get through.'

'OK.' Bryony puts down her knife and fork and shifts her chair forward. 'The thing is I'm due to go back home to England soon. I've got a place at university, starting in October. I met Blythe here three months ago and I guess it's kind of the real thing, like we were talking about. I want to be with him, but it's important that I go back.'

'And he doesn't want you to?'

'He wants me to travel with him instead. He's been getting worked up about it for days, ever since he lost his job, and he's running out of money and getting bored having all this free time. He hates the thought of England. I mean, *really* hates it. I think he was depressed and everything there. He's been pressurizing me to make my choice.'

Bryony sighs and Jacques feels a sudden rush of sympathy, of warmth. 'Decisions are difficult.'

'Except I've known all along really what I was going to do, but I couldn't bring myself to tell him before. I got annoyed with him today and came out with it – I'm definitely going home.'

'I see.'

'He says it'll be difficult only seeing each other in the holidays.'

'It will be. But not impossible.'

'And then he started giving me a hard time about how we should spend our final days together, which is easy for him to say but I au pair for two little boys so I told him that I can't just give them up like that.'

Jacques murmurs agreement.

Bryony continues, hardly pausing for breath. 'He said, on the way over tonight, that if I'm going to carry on working then there's no good reason for him to stick around here, so he's going to move on somewhere and find work. I thought we could carry on seeing each like we have been, on my days off and some evenings, but he's really fed up so he won't listen. He does need to earn money and I won't leave my job. So we're in a stalemate.'

Over coffee, Jacques has an idea. 'Perhaps we could help each other,' he says slowly.

Bryony looks surprised. 'How?'

'If I said Blythe could have his job back, for the next few weeks, then that would take the pressure off, wouldn't it? It would be like it was before.'

She looks doubtful. 'I don't know if he'd agree.'

'I'd leave that to your powers of persuasion. If he takes the job, you could take some time off, perhaps?'

'You're right. This family I work for, they're very nice people, and they wouldn't mind me having a few days' holiday if I let them know in advance.'

'That's more like it!'

Bryony plays with her spoon, tapping it against the saucer. 'But how will that help you?'

'One, I get a good barman back for the rest of the tourist season. And two, you do me a favour.'

'Which is?' she asks. She looks unconvinced.

'I believe it's common knowledge in your little group that Frédérique and I were supposed to be getting married.'

'Yes, I know.'

'Well, apparently she's changed her mind. She's not told me that exactly yet,' he says rather bitterly. 'I think I was rather supposed to assume that to be the situation. She's in love with someone else, as you also know.'

'Luc.'

Jacques nods. 'She won't see me but she'd see Luc. You could get Luc to talk to her. Explain how absolutely pointless it is about him and put in a few good words for me.' He laughs half-heartedly.

'Do you really think that would do any good?'

Jacques shrugs. 'I've no idea. But I'll try anything at the moment.'

Bryony touches his hand. 'I'm sorry. I don't think I could ask Luc,' she tells him gently. 'Cecillie wouldn't like it. She doesn't want him seeing Frédérique unless he really has to.'

Jacques parks the car at the front of his hotel. He points along the promenade. 'Isn't that Blythe over there?'

Bryony peers across him. 'Yes!' She hurries to open the door. 'I'd better go quick. Before he disappears again.'

As she gets out of the car, Jacques calls her back. 'My offer still stands,' he says. 'Even if you don't talk to Luc.'

She leans inside and they shake hands. 'That's very kind, Jacques. And thanks for dinner. I enjoyed it.'

'So did I.'

She turns and waves to him before running towards Blythe.

She slows down as she approaches and calls out. He spins round and staggers towards her. 'Where've you been?'

'Where've you been, more like? I looked everywhere for you.'

'I've been around,' he tells her and she decides to let it go.

'Have you seen Cecillie and Luc?' she asks.

'They're dancing.'

'Shall we go in, then?'

'I want to talk to you.' Blythe puts his arm around her and leans heavily on her. 'Let's go and sit on the beach,' he suggests, already turning that way. She lets herself be guided by him, pleased that he's in a better mood.

There are a lot of people on the beach so they walk for a while until they reach an unoccupied spot against the promenade wall. They sit down.

'I wanted to say that I love you,' Blythe says. His speech is slurred and he's getting sloppy – a sure sign that he's very pissed. She reaches for his hand. 'I love you too.'

'And I'm sorry for being a prick.'

She laughs. 'That's OK.' She shifts up to sit close to him. 'I've got some good news.'

Bryony suddenly panics that Blythe will think she's going to tell him she's changed her mind about going back so she rushes on before he has a chance to formulate such ideas. 'I saw Jacques. I went for a meal with him.'

'That's good news?'

'He's offered you your job back.'

'He what?' Blythe removes his arm and leans forward to peer suspiciously at Bryony. 'Why would he want to do that?'

'So you'd have some money and be able to stay here until I go.'

'How does Jacques knows what's going on between me and you?'

'I told him. I talked about us and he talked about him and Frédérique.'

'I don't believe I'm hearing this. Jacques has gone soft in the head and is offering a job to a guy who hates him, who would like to punch his fucking lights out. Am I missing something?'

'For a favour.'

'There's no such thing as a free lunch, is there, Bryony?' Blythe's face looks accusingly at her, his voice spits disapproval. 'So, what favour are you going to do for Jacques, Bryony? Let me see – another kiss? A fondle perhaps? Or something more? Jesus fucking Christ Bryony, what the fuck have you already done?'

Bryony's earlier anger returns. 'Jacques treated me to dinner. We were just talking. I had no one else to talk to, remember? You'd just fucked off and left me. At least he knows how to be nice to me.'

She should have known better than to attempt talking to Blythe when he's so drunk. She tries to explain enough, very simply, to bring the conversation to a close.

'He wants me to ask Luc to talk to Frédérique, that's all and for that you get your job back. He said you're a good barman . . .'

'How generous of him.'

Bryony persists. 'And I thought I'd get some days off work so that we could have some time together.'

Blythe moans, his head collapses onto her shoulder. She realizes that he's crying. She takes hold of his hand; he's trembling. He suddenly pushes Bryony away and is sick. He lies down in the sand, shivering violently. She kicks sand over the vomit and sits listening to his heavy, noisy breathing. He's fallen asleep. Bryony crawls to the other side of Blythe and curls up against him.

When Bryony wakes up, it's early morning and she's freezing. Blythe's gone.

She spots him down by the water's edge, picking up shells and then throwing them back into the sea. His hair looks orange in the weak light and his T-shirt is being blown around him.

She stands up slowly; she's stiff and her head's thumping. There's wine and grease on her T-shirt and she's covered in sand. She brushes herself down and goes to the water. She kicks off her sandals and washes her feet, splashing around, then she washes her hands and face, wets her hair and dabs at the stains on her top. The water's icy. It makes her scalp ache. But she feels cleaner and sharper immediately.

She walks at the edge of the sea, carrying her sandals, towards Blythe. He hasn't stopped throwing shells. What Bryony had mistaken as a calm scene, she sees now is the opposite. Blythe hasn't acknowledged her, even though he must have seen her, or heard her splashing in the waves. She's almost beside him before he turns. His eyes are wide, spacey.

'I can't believe you could imagine I'd go and work for that bastard again. Under any circumstances.'

'It would only be for a short time.'

'I'm not doing it.'

'OK. I just thought it would give us . . .'

'A few days together. I know, you said.'

'Well it would.'

'A few days isn't enough though, Bryony, is it?'

'What do you mean?'

'I mean it's over, Bryony, done, finished, gone. You go to university and I go somewhere else. Nice knowing you and all.'

Bryony pushes her bare feet into the sand to try and steady herself; her legs are trembling. 'You're joking.'

'You chose.'

'We can keep in touch, meet up, there are all sorts of things we can do. Other couples do it.'

His mouth pinches up, his eyes shift away from hers. 'I can't.' He speaks softly. 'I'm sorry Bryony, but I know I can't. I'd let you down and we'd both be miserable. It would be the worst thing.'

'Don't you think we'll be more miserable if we split up? Or do you count on not feeling anything?'

'Bryony . . .'

'You said you loved me.' Her words are wobbling, tears are running down her face; she doesn't wipe them away. She stares at him, willing him to look at her.

'I do love you.' He tries to take her hand but she snatches it away from him. 'I'm doing this because I love you,' he tells her.

'That's just shit and you know it.'

'I really am sorry.' He stares out to sea.

'You fucking, heartless bastard.'

'This isn't easy for me.'

Blythe reaches down and picks up some more shells, he fires them one two three into the sea. Plop, plop, plop into the water.

'So that's it?'

Bryony waits. Blythe shoves his hands into his shorts pockets.

The only sign that he's feeling something is the light flush that creeps up his neck to his face.

'Do you know what I want to do right now?' she says. 'Smash your stupid head in. How can you be so bloody stupid?'

Blythe starts to run towards the bar.

'You bastard,' she shouts, launching her sandals after him. Sand sprays up as they land.

Further up the beach Blythe heads towards the town.

'You bastard,' she says softly.

9

i'm sorry too

'This is Jacques,' Frédérique thinks as the phone rings, startling her out of her nap.

She picks the phone up, hugs it to her chest, while she considers whether to press the TALK button. She knew that once she was back from the weekend with her parents, he'd call sooner or later. Her intention had been to make the first move; imagining in that way she'd have control of the conversation. But she kept putting it off. The same way she's avoided seeing him.

Frédérique was relieved when the ten days of Luc's show came to an end. It had hung over her, making every day one where she had to find an excuse for not going to the bar. Luckily, Fernand's impending departure on holiday was a good enough reason for spending a lot of her time at the gallery; she's been learning the ropes to be able to cover for him while he's away. Katrin and, often Fernand, had tactfully covered most of the work at Jacques's place between them, leaving Frédérique to keep her visits there to a minimum which she risked only when she was pretty sure Jacques wouldn't be around: a couple of mornings when he was meeting with his suppliers and a late afternoon when he was visiting his grandfather.

Following Fernand's increased involvement with Luc's exhibition, it seems that Jacques and her boss have struck up a friendship. A few days ago, Fernand told Frédérique that Jacques had said he wasn't angry, just concerned about her and he'd tried to encourage her to go and see him.

Frédérique would have liked to believe Fernand. She's been on the verge of turning up at the bar a number of times but it's hard to forget the ugliness of Jacques's face, the iciness of his anger that night, and it's hard to imagine what they have to say to each other. After that humiliation, how can he not hate her?

The phone has stopped. Frédérique settles back on the settee and places the receiver beside her. She's relieved but also deflated.

She yawns and wonders whether she should make some coffee but she can't face any more. She's been drinking it so strong and in such vast quantities every evening to keep awake that it's become more of a medicine than an enjoyment. It's the only way she can get through the nights – caffeine hits and short bursts of sleep on the settee.

She can't go to bed because of the nightmares she's been having. The content of the nightmares disappears as soon as she wakes, but she's left with the sensation of real fear, her body is covered in sweat and her heart is racing. She aches for a good night's sleep in her bed.

How long? she catches herself wondering. How long will she be able to get by? During the day she feels feverish, has dry lips and hot, scratchy eyes.

The ringing starts again. Without thinking, she picks up the receiver, accepts the call and says 'hello'.

There's a pause before Jacques speaks. 'Frédérique? I didn't expect you to answer.'

'Jacques.'

'How are you?'

'OK. I meant to ring, but I . . .' She stops mid-sentence. There's a long silence and Frédérique is about to hang up when Jacques speaks again.

'We're talking now,' he says gently. 'Which is a good thing.'

'Yes.'

Another silence. Frédérique's voice seems frozen but her heart has gathered pace. It's pumping away, demanding all her concentration. Until recently she hadn't been aware of it as such a physical part of her body, a thumping, moving, working organ that is increasingly making its presence known.

'How was your family?'

'The same as usual, you know. Only a little bit worse.' Frédérique sighs.

It had been a dreadful weekend. Her parents were obviously expecting to hear some important news to explain her sudden visit. The kind of good news she knows that only a few weeks ago she'd been about to announce to them. She didn't want to upset them by telling them how near she'd been to making their dreams come true. They've always thought a lot of Jacques. She could imagine them coming out with statements like: *you've thrown your last chance away, you're running out of time, you should settle for what you can get, Jacques is a good man, a decent man, more than you deserve.*

It had been hard to maintain normality in their company.

She'd spent two days wound up so tight that she was constantly on the verge of tears.

She falls back on an old cliché and recognizes it as a truth: Jacques is not the right man for her. They are not right for each other. It's good to have established that at least, before any plans went too far.

'That's a shame,' Jacques says and she immediately feels guilty about his sympathy.

'It was quiet at the beach, this year,' the decent man, her last chance, continues.

Frédérique sits up straight on the settee, places her feet firmly on the ground, neatly together, and makes a big effort. 'Was it? Was everyone there?'

'Yes. Except you, of course.' Frédérique hears in his voice a sort of quiet appeal, almost – she realizes, a queasy panic rising – a flirtation. She waits, speechless, her effort curtailed abruptly.

'I wish you'd told me that you weren't going,' he continues. The hurt is evident in his tone, but the softness remains. 'I heard it from Sylvie or Aurore, or someone. In fact, I seemed to be the last person to know.'

'I didn't know how to tell you,' she admits.

'I understand. It doesn't matter, Frédérique.'

'I needed to think, Jacques. That was all. Everything was getting on top of me.' Her voice sounds shrill even to herself. 'I thought you'd still be angry,' she tells him.

'Not any more,' he says and adds, 'Frédérique, I know it's going to be hard, but we need to talk.'

'Yes.'

'Shall we do that?' he asks.

She understands suddenly that it's hard for Jacques, too. It's taken humility to keep ringing her when she's been refusing to answer, it's taken courage to talk to her now. She smiles with relief at this awareness and feels closer to him – a remnant of their old friendship – so that when he offers to cook her a meal, although she's still nervous about meeting, she says yes because it seems that the time is right.

'Which evening suits you?' she asks.

They arrange for Friday.

'I look forward to it.' She can hear her voice, bright and breezy, the higher pitch of lies. She's glad that he can't see how she's trembling. Friday, two days away. It will give her some time to prepare herself.

But, when Friday comes, she's far from ready. She's spent a hectic day, trying to finalize some gallery business with Fernand before he goes away, and she doesn't leave work until half past seven. She quickly showers and makes a brief effort in front of the mirror, dabbing on some mascara and a couple of coats of lipstick. She searches through her wardrobe but there's nothing suitable which is clean. Everything is waiting to go to the dry-cleaners. She pulls out her green wool dress which, after a brief examination – it's a little creased across the back – she decides will do. As she smoothes the material with her hand, she begins to make a mental list of the other chores that are becoming urgent: she ought to do some proper shopping instead of grabbing a packet of coffee and some cheese and bread every now and then. When she was showering she discovered she'd run out of conditioner, which she's always considered an absolute necessity. Now her hair, drying, feels too fluffy, out at all angles. She must pull herself together. She will be able to, when she's seen Jacques. After they've got that cleared up, she'll start to piece the other parts of her life together, too.

She manages to flatten her fringe with hair gel before she leaves.

Jacques is waiting for her at the bottom of the stairs leading to his apartment. He must have been watching out for her. He smiles enthusiastically as she approaches. His open, generous smile that she liked to think he granted only to a few, special, people. Despite the pep talk she's been giving herself all the way here, she feels her spirits sink. She forces herself to greet him as normal with a quick kiss on the lips and a cheek pressed to his. The scent of his aftershave is overpowering.

There's an awkward moment when they both turn to go up – Frédérique's hip squashes against his and they have to twist to accommodate each other. Jacques steers Frédérique in front of him, his hand on her back.

She had forgotten how tactile Jacques is. He likes to draw people's attention to something with a touch on the arm; emphasize a point during a conversation with a gentle tap on their hand. She's never minded it before, has in fact enjoyed the frisson that those momentary contacts have given her. Now she wants to shrug him off, to distance herself which she does, by quickening her step, almost involuntarily. She doesn't think he notices.

Jacques fusses around, settling Frédérique in the kitchen, at the table, with a glass of wine as he prepares a Chinese meal. One of his specialities. She's only eaten a ham baguette during the day and the wine both soothes her nervous stomach and makes her feel light-headed.

She watches Jacques's hands as he chops and crushes ingredients, measures and tests the sauce. He burns the first lot of ginger. It sticks fast to the bottom in little charred pieces but he won't let her clean the wok, instead he hustles her back to the table where he tops up her glass. While he frowns in concentration over the meal, Frédérique looks at him. The acrid smell of smoke, the loud whir of the extractor fan on the highest setting, gives her a sensation of cover so that she is able to take her time studying him; his familiar, angular face, his smart shirt sleeves, rolled back perfectly to just below his elbows. His appearance is exactly as she's always known it. She glances round the kitchen and through to the sitting room. It's all clean and tidy and white. Everything is in its proper place. Nothing has changed.

Jacques glances at her and gives her a quick salute as he raises his glass. The meal seems to be under control now. He looks relieved.

They chat over the sound of sizzling food. About how busy they both are; how there seem to be even more tourists this summer. Frédérique tells him that she'll be in charge of the gallery for two weeks while Fernand takes a holiday. Jacques already knows that which puzzles her for a moment until she remembers that her boss has seen much more of Jacques recently than she has.

They discuss safe topics: the continued dry weather, the local government scandal, the increase in taxes, until the meal is ready. They eat quietly, rather quickly at the kitchen table. Afterwards they go into the lounge.

Frédérique sits in an armchair and Jacques takes the settee.

'Let's talk,' he says.

'Do we have to?' Frédérique asks. 'It's been a nice evening. Can't we leave it at that? Go forward from there?'

'No,' says Jacques, pressing his temples with his fingertips. 'I need something more definite than that. We both do.'

He looks at her, expectantly. Frédérique says nothing. She feels hostility towards Jacques rising. Surely what happened at the party was definite enough? It was Jacques, after all, who had told her to leave and, she thinks, pointedly, to leave with Luc. But what he means of course, is now. What do they do now? She doesn't know how to say it, can't bring herself to say that old cliché – I want us to stay friends.

But isn't that exactly what she wants? She finds it almost impossible to imagine her life without Jacques. The practicalities of it are tricky enough: one of them would have to find different places to go, perhaps even a different circle of friends. She'd have to build up a completely separate life from Jacques. The thought is terrifying but, at the same time, she acknowledges that it also feels quite liberating. She is, for the first time, able to recognize the limits their relationship has imposed on each other, even before they stepped over the line from friends to lovers.

The CD which has been playing comes to an end. They sit in silence. The sound of music from the bar comes from beneath them; a low humming.

Jacques speaks again. 'I'm sorry about the way I behaved at the party.'

'I'm sorry too,' Frédérique says and adds hurriedly, 'I mean with how I behaved. It wasn't the right moment to talk.'

Jacques smiles. Maybe, she thinks, maybe this is going to be easier than she'd expected, all she has to do is keep saying sorry and Jacques will apologize too and they'll have understood each other.

'Remember,' he starts, then stops. 'Remember when I asked you, your . . .' He pauses and looks embarrassed. Frédérique's heart starts to race. 'Remember when I asked you to marry me, you said yes?'

'Of course, but . . .'

He interrupts her. 'You said yes because it felt right.'

Frédérique struggles to push her mind back to that evening. She can't remember exactly how their conversation went, but it revives some of the emotion she'd felt then, the sensation she'd had of the battle being over and how she had reached some peace. She remembers and blushes for it. Now she feels embarrassed that she should have treated herself and Jacques so cheaply. It was sad and wrong to have rushed into agreeing to marriage, even to have contemplated a relationship where there was no passion purely because they were lonely. They deserve better than that.

Jacques is still talking. 'Don't take this the wrong way, Fred, but I think you'd reached crisis point and it was all too much for you.'

She looks at him, confused. 'What was?'

She watches him visibly breathe in, preparing himself. Although she has no idea what he will say next, she feels her shoulders tighten.

'I think that you became overinvolved with Luc at a vulnerable time. I think you've confused what his art means to you, what he – as an artist – means to you with how you feel about him personally.'

Frédérique stands up, wanting to break the cycle of the

conversation so that they don't work themselves into another scene, another horrid, damaging scene like before. What a cheek, she thinks. The patronizing, egotistical cheek of the man. She goes to the window and looks out at the lights in the buildings across the road. If only you knew, she warns him mentally, if only you knew. She almost misses what Jacques says next.

'I'm not underestimating what you feel for Luc,' he's saying, and her heart stands still. 'He obviously means a lot to you – right now. But I know you, Fred, I think you can concede that? I know you so well and I want you to try and hold on to what we've been talking about, what we'd been moving towards. A future, a real future. Marriage, children. Frédérique?' Jacques comes towards her. 'Look at me,' he says, turning her round.

She won't look at him, she tells herself. She concentrates on his shoes until they become blurred. She closes her eyes, feels her unsteadiness, and tries to keep her balance. Jacques holds her and for a few moments she allows herself the comfort of the body of another person. Not talking, just resting. But Jacques starts to speak again and she steps away, feeling like a traitor for her lapse.

'I'm offering you a future.'

'Oh, Jacques.' She doesn't want to hurt him, but she can't let it go on. 'I'd love to be able to go back in time, but it's impossible.' She takes his hand. 'What you're asking is impossible.'

He squeezes her fingers gently. 'It isn't,' he tells her. 'We need some time, that's all. Time to let everything calm down.'

She looks at his face, tries to read the emotion there but fails. She notices that his eyes are a little bloodshot.

'What do you think, Fred? Would you be prepared to wait?

Not to end it yet? But to have some distance from each other temporarily, give us time to find out what we really want.'

She considers this. Surprised and touched by his generosity, she realizes that neither of them can contemplate a life without each other. Is it selfish, she wonders, to agree to this because she wants to keep Jacques as her friend? After all, she wouldn't be committing herself to anything.

When she says 'yes' her immediate thought afterwards is that now she'll be able to sleep again.

Frédérique hasn't had much to drink, but she isn't comfortable about driving home. Jacques offers her a lift and, although she would have preferred to take a taxi, she doesn't feel she can refuse. Downstairs, the bar's in full swing. The music is loud, there's laughter and a warmth coming from the room that makes her realize how cold it was in Jacques's apartment. She's frozen to the bone.

It soon warms up in the car and Frédérique falls asleep before Jacques has even left his street.

She wakes with a start. She's been dreaming, reliving once more the evening that she found the hanged man, except the swinging body was at the other end of a long, white room, facing the window, away from her. It seemed to take hours to walk across the floor. When she reached the body, she spun it round and saw that the man was not a stranger, but Luc.

'Better?' Jacques asks.

She nods but she feels woozy and unnerved. She peers out of the window to try and ascertain where they are.

'There's one more thing. A condition I suppose you could call it,' Jacques says. 'If we're going to give ourselves a proper chance, I'd like you to pass the handling of Luc's work over to Fernand.'

So that's the trap. She catches her breath. She should have known it couldn't be this easy.

'That's fair, isn't it?'

'I can't,' she says.

'What do you mean you can't?'

'I can't give that up.'

'He doesn't want you, you know.' Jacques's voice is louder, harsh now, his knuckles white as his hands grip the steering wheel. 'Are you going to throw away everything for something that's never going to happen?'

'It's not about that,' Frédérique tries to explain. 'You don't understand.'

'So you won't do it?' Jacques asks, his jaw clenched.

'No.'

The car lurches to a stop. 'Get out,' he tells her.

'Jacques . . .'

'Get out, get out,' he shouts, thumping the steering wheel.

Just like a movie, she thinks as she watches his car roar off down the road, skidding slightly as he hurls it round the corner. Well, that's pretty conclusive, she tells herself and laughs out loud. But her laughter dies into the silence of the dark boarded-up buildings, the deserted street.

She doesn't recognize where she is. From the pungent odour of fishy sea, she'd guess she was close to the docks. Jacques must have been driving around while she was asleep because this area isn't on the way to her apartment. Her watch says ten to two. She puts a hand out for her handbag but her fingers fish around in the air. It's in Jacques's car. No handbag means no phone, no money, nothing.

She starts to walk towards some lights, heading she hopes into the centre of the city where she'll be able to catch a taxi; she's got money at home. Her high heels clop loudly in the emptiness. She remembers reading somewhere that rapists can tell if it's a woman on her own by listening to the tapping of heels. Her alarm growing, she stares around her, her mind stretching, her eyes widening in an effort to recognize some place, the name of a street or shop that will indicate where she is. But she doesn't know this quarter at all. It's a mass of compact buildings and rat-run alleys. And it's very, very quiet. She continues on. Ahead, the street forms a small square before it branches out into three more streets. She recognizes it and the hairs on her neck prickle. There used to be a club there that Jacques and his crowd frequented at the time when she fell in with them. The club was right in the heart of the ethnic district, and their group wasn't particularly welcome but they liked the risk, the danger – until one of them had his arm slashed.

Frédérique considers taking off her shoes. Then she could run quickly, noiselessly, she reasons. But she wouldn't know where to run to, she thinks, her heart sinking. She's better off keeping her shoes on. That way she looks more confident, not as desperate as she's beginning to feel.

She takes a side street to the right. After a few minutes she knows it's a mistake: she's in the middle of a maze of narrow, shadowy streets, indistinguishable from each other. She can hardly bear to keep going, only hope stops her from sitting down in a doorway, curling up and hiding. Hope that she will somehow pass through into light and safety.

Every crevice and gap and jutting brick wall hides a potential assailant. Each hazard she passes leaves the horror behind her, but with a greater one ahead. Her heart is banging away at the base of her throat. She struggles to breathe, fights to stay calm, to walk indifferently, confidently past, through and towards. She gasps at a rustling close by and crosses the street, away from the noise, glancing to her side. She's never been so pleased to see rats.

There are lights a few metres away. She walks towards them, her mind singing already with relief, believing the ordeal to be over. There's a strong scent of spices and the muffled sound of voices, a shout, some laughter.

The street widens into another square and Frédérique can make out three, maybe four food stalls manned by black women who are cooking in the open, waiting for the dockers to finish their shift, and to catch those leaving the clubs. There's the sizzle of hot fat, the murmur of the womens' voices and their rolling laughter.

As she emerges into the open she feels like she's walking onto a stage. The women stop talking. Her smile hello, her request for help, is frozen. She knows that they would help if she just asked, but their cold stares, the palpable distrust wipes out her remaining courage. It's easier to walk past than to stop. Her dress is wet under her arms and across her back, and her breath is coming out in tiny, painful pants. She's halfway across the square when she hears the first soft call.

'Ooh, La France.'

'Ooh, Missy Money,' comes the next which is picked up by the others. 'Ooh, Missy France. Ooh, Missy Money.'

'Ooh, Missy France. Buy a little something from my stall.'

There's a burst of laughter, but she keeps walking, aiming for the street opposite, trying not to run.

Her lips are moving to the words that she's repeating in her mind. 'Please god, save me, help me someone, Luc help me, help me, Luc, Luc, Luc.' It forms a chant. And, as if by chanting and wishing, by the power of her mind, she recognizes the name of a street, which leads onto another street which leads, finally – thank god – to Luc's apartment. She's only a few minutes from safety.

Out of a doorway steps a black man. He walks straight in front of her so that she has to stop.

'Miss France,' he says in heavily accented French. 'What you doing here alone? It's too dangerous.'

Frédérique whispers, 'I've not got far to go.' She forces herself to look at his face. He's smiling. Her whole body is trembling. Surely he can see, smell her terror. She can smell it herself; her dry, stinking breath, her sweat. Inside her head she keeps up the chant. Luc, Luc, Luc.

'It's dangerous for a girl like you. I can walk with you.'

'No.' Panic streams through her. 'Really, I'm nearly there.' She names the street where Luc lives and the man nods gravely. He starts to dig around in his pockets. She thinks that she might faint.

'I have a sister. The same age as you. Perhaps a little younger, I won't let her walk round here at night. Here, take this.' He holds out something to her. She takes it. It's a short stick, sharpened at one end, like a crude knife, very light.

'Keep it in your hand,' he instructs her as he bends down to scrape up some muddy sand from the edge of the pavement. He presses it into her other hand. 'For the eyes,' he says, demonstrating how to flick it into someone's face.

'Thanks. Thank you,' she stutters as the man steps back into the doorway.

He calls after her. 'Goodnight, little sister.'

'Goodnight. And thanks,' she calls back. One hand is clenched around the dry rough stick, in the other she can feel the grit as she squeezes her fist tight. She has only to get to the bottom of this street, only a few more doorways to pass, only a few more dark slits of alleys to walk in front of.

But her nerve has finally run out and she runs, her shoes clattering. She stumbles against the door. She can't find the buzzer in the dark so she knocks, loudly, spilling the sand.

'Oh my god,' she thinks. 'What if he isn't in? What if Luc isn't in?' She knocks again. Louder. She's convinced that there's someone behind her; they've been summoned by her noise. She clutches the stick but doesn't dare look round. Luc, she calls, Luc, let me in. But they're only words in her mind, which is splitting with fear. She's unable to speak; her tongue is solid in her mouth, choking her, stopping the air in her throat.

When the door opens and Luc appears, she can't move until he puts his arms around her and takes her in. The shadows behind her fall away and she's safe. Thank god she's safe.

'Thank you, Luc,' she says. 'Thank you.'

He leads her to the bed, helps her to lie down, takes her shoes off and goes to fetch her a drink of water. She listens to the sound of the tap running.

Shivering, she pulls her dress up over her head, takes off her bra and slips under the sheet, fitting herself into the warm shape he's left behind. All she has to do is to lie there for a few minutes and he'll be back. Luc will be back.

* * *

But she doesn't remember him returning with the water; the next thing she knows is that it's daylight, she feels incredibly thirsty and, when she turns over, Luc's bare back is centimetres away.

She hardly dares move in case she wakes him. She wants to prolong this time for as long as she can. She lies still and looks around. His bedroom is small, cluttered but not dirty. The walls are full of photographs and postcards, there are three crates stacked on top of each other for his clothes and a sparse, but touchingly neat pile of towels and linen; there are books and sketch pads on the floor, and one big, faded armchair.

Luc's still asleep. She wants, desperately, to touch him. She reaches out a tentative hand. She's surprised by the coolness of his skin. She passes her fingers lightly up his back, feeling the bones of his spine, and across the dips and ridges of the muscles on his shoulders. His skin begins to quiver under her touch. Before she thinks about what she's doing she's moved up against him, pressing her warm breasts and her stomach against his back, breathing in the salty, resinous smell of his skin. She hears him sigh, long and low and then he turns over.

She feels the shock of surprise as his leg winds around hers, one arm holds her tight across her waist, a hand slides down her back, and then up to her neck. She mirrors his movements, down his back, down to his buttocks and back up.

His fingers sidetrack to her breast where they skim over her nipple before gliding away. They stroke the curve of her stomach, her bottom, where they find a way inside her knickers. She moves her head up and kisses his chest, his neck, and then his mouth. His lips gently touch hers. Her whole body is throbbing.

'Frédérique,' he murmurs, as he places another soft, quick kiss on her mouth, then on her forehead. 'Frédérique,' he repeats, more clearly. 'I'm going to stop.'

Her body stiffens. 'Oh, don't. Please.'

She tries to kiss him again, but he takes first one hand and then the other and presses them together on the bed as he slides away.

'Shit, Frédérique, I'm sorry. It should never have happened.'

'But I wanted it to happen,' Frédérique says, her voice rising. She looks at him to see if he's laughing at her, but it's pity she reads on his face. 'I wanted you to make love to me.'

'I'm sorry,' he says.

He strokes her hair as she buries her face into the pillow to cry. Then she feels him get out of bed, hears him getting dressed and clattering around in the kitchen. Soon she smells coffee and she knows that she can't stay there for ever.

There are blisters on her feet which hurt when she puts her shoes on. She feels sordid in her stale clothes but she enters the kitchen with as much dignity as she can muster.

'Hi,' says Luc, as he pours her a bowl of coffee and places it on the table in front of her.

'Hi,' she replies as she sits down.

'When you've drunk that,' he says, lowering his eyes. 'I'll walk you home.'

10

one thing led to another

At seven o'clock on Saturday morning, when Jacques wakes up fully dressed on his bed, he immediately reaches for the phone lying beside him and tries to ring Frédérique. There's only her answer phone in reply, as there has been since last night when he first started calling. As soon as he realized that he'd thrown Frédérique out into one of the worst areas of the city, he'd driven back to fetch her and found that she'd disappeared. He drove up and down the road and into some of the streets leading off it, but even though it was less than five minutes since he'd been there, Frédérique had gone. He got out of the car and shouted her name at the top of some of the alleys which were too small to drive through. Nothing. Then he started phoning. He used his mobile constantly to see if she had returned to her apartment. Always the answer phone. With his heart pounding, he drove to Frédérique's place in case she was so angry with him that she was refusing to pick up the phone. There were no lights on and no reply when he buzzed long and hard on the entrance bell. He waited outside in his car for a while but then decided to go back to the area where he'd left her. No sign. And still the answer phone. In the end, as it was getting light, he returned to his apartment and sat on the bed with the phone next to him. He can't remember how many messages he left before he finally fell asleep.

This morning he leaves another urgent one for her to call him and then, as his mind sorts through the various possible scenarios, he phones again: 'If you don't want to talk, that's fine, just let me know you're OK and put the phone down. I won't ring back, if you don't want me to, once I know.'

He has horrific visions of her lying dead somewhere in the sludge of the stale dock water, or in hospital having been attacked.

He tries ringing the gallery as soon as it opens at ten: she hasn't arrived yet, he's told. He paces the flat then wanders downstairs to check whether the staff have tidied up the bar properly before leaving last night. He shouts at one of the cleaners who has left a bucket in his way, before returning to his flat to phone the gallery again.

It's half past ten: Frédérique has not been in and hasn't phoned in, either. Saturday is their busiest day and Frédérique rarely misses one. The chatty receptionist, whose name he can't remember, confirms this odd behaviour. 'It's not like her is it?' she remarks. 'Perhaps she's got car problems. I'll tell her you called as soon as she gets in.'

'Oh my god,' he says as he puts the phone down. He knows that Frédérique's car is still parked outside the bar. 'Oh my god.' He feels nausea slosh in his stomach so he stands in the bathroom, waiting to throw up. It subsides to a dull ache. He has a drink of water from the cold tap and, because he hates feeling so powerless, so useless, he decides to drive over to her flat once more. Outside, he glances briefly to the left to check that Frédérique hasn't been to collect her car. It's still there.

When he's fastening his seat belt, something lying on the floor of the passenger side catches his eye. It's the strap of Frédérique's handbag, which she must have tucked in the foot well beside her feet. He pulls the bag out and places it on the seat.

An icy sweat freezes him in place. He licks his lips and tries to swallow. All the time he's been picturing Frédérique alone where he left her, he's been reassured by a certainty that Frédérique's sense, her practicality would get her out of the situation he'd put her in: probably by catching a taxi, perhaps even staying in a nearby hotel until morning. Now, seeing her handbag, it hits home. He not only abandoned her in a dead-end part of the city, but left her without any cards, keys, money or, as he opens the bag and takes a quick look inside, mobile phone. Nothing. If she isn't home when he gets there he'll have to inform the police, so that they can start searching for her. *He's* done this, he tells himself, *he's* done this to her.

Please god, he thinks as he starts the car, please god, I'll do anything as long as she's OK. He drives badly, because he keeps looking at the handbag, and finds himself addressing it as if it were a dog about to be restored to its mistress. 'Nearly there,' he says. 'Nearly there.'

As he reaches the top of the park and turns left towards her apartment block, he sees her. She's walking along the pavement with someone whom he quickly recognizes as Luc. 'Thank you, thank you, thank you,' he shouts, drumming the steering wheel with the palms of his hand. 'Thank you, thank you.'

He watches Frédérique's gently swaying walk, sees her face

as she turns to speak to Luc. He's too far away to be able to see how she's feeling, but close enough to remind him how much he loves her. He will prostrate himself before Frédérique, ignoring the presence of the great and wonderful Luc; he will beg forgiveness, he will offer himself up to her. Any wish, any action she asks of him, he will perform. He owes her so much.

He feels dazed with relief. He slows right down as he approaches them, and is about to beep the car horn when he notices Frédérique's dress. It's the same one she was wearing last night. There's no mistake because it's the same one she'd had on the night that he proposed to her and he'd been surprised – but pleased – to see her in it again. He'd taken it as a conciliatory gesture, a subtle reference to their engagement. A positive start to the evening which had then ended so badly. So badly in fact that she's dressed in yesterday clothes which can only mean one thing. Frédérique hasn't been home. She must have stayed the night with Luc.

While Jacques had been out of his mind with worry, Frédérique was happily screwing without a thought for him. He's shaking so much that he can't continue driving.

When Frédérique and Luc enter the apartment block, Jacques waits, praying that the concierge, who holds spare keys, is absent and that Frédérique will have to call him to arrange to get her handbag back. Jacques imagines casually mentioning that he has it with him, that he is – in fact – right outside her place, this very moment. 'What luck, isn't it Fred. Isn't it?' he hears himself saying.

But nothing happens and, after a few more minutes, he forces himself to start the car and go home.

Bernadette is cleaning his apartment when he gets in. He

tells her to leave, almost pushing her out of the door in his haste to be rid of her. He stands in the middle of the sitting room with Frédérique's handbag under one arm and listens to Bernadette's laborious footsteps clanging down each step. He's waiting for Bernadette to be out of hearing, so that he can shout and scream but by the time he's sure she is, the desire's left him. He hurls the bag across the room where it lands on the settee with a thud.

What hurts him most is the realization that Frédérique must have gone to Luc. It's extremely unlikely – almost impossible – that she happened to bump into him last night. Unless, of course, when he saw them, they'd only just met. The spark of relief this thought brings fades instantly. It's even less likely that Luc would be hanging around Frédérique's part of the city and, besides, the way they were walking together, the way they were chatting certainly gave the impression they'd been in each other's company for a while. And of course, there's the dress.

So, he calculates, Frédérique went to Luc rather than return home, perhaps because she needed someone to talk to, or maybe – and Jacques finds this thought agonizing – maybe just for help. Jacques doesn't know Luc's address; he could have delivered Frédérique to Luc's front bloody door for all he knows. But obviously one thing led to another.

The irony of Jacques being the cause of them actually getting it together makes him charge across the room, looking for something to hit. He punches the settee cushion before sinking down on the seat.

He rubs his eyes. They're heavy with tiredness. He resolves to lie on the bed and sleep. It would at least prevent him from thinking. But as soon as he lies down, he's tortured by images of Frédérique making love with Luc. The thought of Luc touching her has him fighting for breath. His rage is choking him, but picturing them together gives him an erection at the same time. He feels dirty; a dirty fool.

He gets up and collects two bottles of wine from the kitchen. He switches on the television in the lounge and sits down in front of it.

By Sunday evening, Frédérique still hasn't called. Jacques hasn't left his apartment since Saturday morning, so he knows that Frédérique's made no attempt to ring him, although he still hopes that she might. He carries his mobile with him everywhere and he's even turned the sound off the television in case he doesn't hear the apartment phone when he's in the kitchen or having a pee. He hasn't dared risk taking a shower. But the only call he gets is from a friend who he cuts off quickly, pretending that he's on his way out. As he puts the receiver down, he glances at the meal Bernadette brought him yesterday evening from the restaurant at his request, which now lies congealing on the coffee table. He didn't touch it: the smell of the food makes him feel ill and the real reason he wanted to see Bernadette was to ask her if Frédérique's car was still outside. He'd had to go into full details – the make and colour, the registration number, the position it was parked in – before Bernadette was happy about going outside to check. She phoned him from the kitchens, shouting over the noise, to say that it had gone.

Jacques is working steadily through his supply of wine. At moments he feels almost pleasantly numb; he can almost laugh at the absurdity of his situation. Frédérique doesn't know I know, he repeats to himself, she doesn't know I saw her with him. Sometimes when the music from downstairs permeates through, and he hears the chatter and laughter of people arriving at the bar, he feels a kind of fragile peace, a remnant of his sense of achievement that the success of this place, which he's created, can bring.

But for most of the time, his mind boils with anger, feeding its rage by reliving the events of Friday night and Saturday morning. When he's like that, he hates any noise, however tiny, interrupting his concentration.

At half past nine on Monday morning he rings the gallery. Someone tells him that Frédérique's in a meeting. He leaves a message to ask her to call. By midday she still hasn't rung back. He has no right to be angry, but he is. For all she knows he could have spent the last two days ringing round hospitals, and alerting the police. She's thoughtless and selfish, he decides. He rings again.

This time, she's at lunch. She's happily enjoying food while the very idea of putting anything solid in his mouth sickens him. He drinks a bottle of wine before phoning again.

She's in a meeting. She's happily getting on with her daily routines, her life, while his has stopped dead. Dead, like he thought *she* might be. He keeps phoning, and gets the same story: she's with a client, with a customer. The message is that she's not available, he isn't stupid – he understands that she's telling him to keep away.

Jacques continues to drink. By late afternoon, he's very drunk.

'I know she's there.'

'I'm sorry?'

'Don't play games with me. Tell Frédérique she has to phone me or I'll keep phoning every minute and her precious artists won't be able to get through. Tell her I *know*, tell her I saw her. Tell her that.'

'Frédérique *isn't* available.' The phone goes down.

'I'll show you,' Jacques mutters as he fumbles to redial, 'I meant what I said.' But when the call goes through, the answer phone is on. The gallery is closed.

He throws down the handset. It lands on top of Frédérique's handbag. He reaches for the strap, pulls it towards him and sits the bag on his knees. It's big and quite heavy. When he opens it, he's impressed, but not surprised, by the neatness of the contents. He takes out her mobile phone. He switches it on and it rings immediately, startling him so that he drops the phone and unbalances the bag. Frédérique's belongings cascade onto the floor. He rights the bag, picks the phone up and switches it off.

He sits contemplating the pile of woman's things at his feet before scooping them up and shoving them into the bag. When he's finished, he looks inside and decides that it won't do. He slides down to sit on the floor and shakes the contents out again. He's amazed at how much there is. A packet of stockings, a make-up bag which he opens and pokes around in, touching the smooth plastic cases of lipstick and mascara; there's a pair of sunglasses, tampons, umbrella, a fountain pen, a mirror, a cardholder with her business cards, a pair of knickers which he squashes quickly down to the bottom, a purse, contraceptive pills, two condoms, a fat personal organizer. It all looks very familiar and yet completely alien to him. It's like a home from home, a bag of everything you could possibly need. Except that the one night that Frédérique did need it . . .

He concentrates on what he's doing to stop his thoughts going down that route. His clumsy fingers look excessively large in this world of tiny items: a packet of tissues, a copy of Luc's exhibition catalogue, which he resists tearing up; a postcard signed Isabelle – her sister; three shampoo sachets; a travel toothbrush and paste such as they hand out on aeroplanes; nail file, and finally a small card which seems to have come loose from something and, when he turns it over, has 'Cecillie' written on it, not in Frédérique's handwriting, not French-style writing, so he assumes it's Cecillie's handwriting. He can't imagine what Frédérique is doing with it.

He leaves the personal organizer out until last. He hesitates before opening it, then begins flicking through the pages of the diary. They are full of notes, lists of various appointments, and calls to make marked in different colour pens according to Frédérique's method for dealing with business. He flicks forward to the most recent pages to find that these are all virtually blank, except for the odd, illegible scribble. On one she's written in red capitals 'MUST' and nothing further, on another, a small 'J'. He checks the date: it was last Friday. The 'J' would surely mean him.

He wonders why, in this strange block of empty pages, the only entry should be him. What is the significance of that? What the hell does it mean?

There's a noise outside and he turns guiltily to face the door. But when he listens harder, it's all quiet. He finds the addresses at the back of the organizer, goes straight to the entry for Luc and stares at it for a while before getting up, fetching his diary and noting the details down using Frédérique's pen. There's no telephone number, only an address. He returns the organizer and pen to the bag, closes it and goes to fetch another bottle of wine from the kitchen. He doesn't want to risk sobering up – he's got an important visit to make.

On his way over to the gallery, Jacques is convinced that Frédérique will be there. Fernand's away on holiday, so she'll be working late to prove herself capable of being left in charge. When he arrives there, however, the building is in darkness. He tries the door, but it's locked. He feels absurdly let down, but his mood quickly changes to excitement, a kind of triumph: he has a key! Fernand had given him a spare last week when he brought back Luc's unsold paintings from the show. He contemplates the key on his key ring. Now he's here, Jacques tells himself, he might as well go in.

The alarm bleeps frantically as soon as he unlocks the door. He panics as he punches the code in, not sure if he's remembered it correctly. But the noise stops and he's struck by the tremendous silence inside. It's very light downstairs – the moonlight is flooding through the large windows at the rear of the room.

He wanders around the ground floor but Luc's paintings aren't there. The gallery feels eerie which he attributes to the disturbing, watchful figures of some of the sculptures. He can't help feeling that they disapprove of his presence.

His footsteps echo on the bare wood of the stairs, his breath sounds in his ears. It's dark and he trips up when he misjudges the final step. His heart races and his hands are clammy. He wipes them on his trousers.

He finds Luc's paintings in the main room; seven, he counts.

Before he takes a proper look at each one, he tries to wipe any preconceptions he holds from his mind. He takes his time, standing for a few minutes in front of each. But he sees the same blocks of dismal colour, the same crude characters with their miserable faces as he's always seen. He knows that he'll never like these paintings.

There's a picture at the end which hangs slightly apart from the others. It's much smaller and because of the poor light, he has to stand very close to be able to study it properly. When he does, he's surprised to see Frédérique's face, ghostly white, looking out from an olive-green background.

He doesn't remember this picture being in the exhibition and he's sure that Frédérique has never told him about it. No wonder. For a start, she looks ridiculously childlike with her big, trusting eyes and secondly Jacques knows what it entails. Hours of posing for sketches, sitting in Luc's apartment, or maybe he went to her place. Hours of intimacy. God! What an idiot he was to have imagined that Friday was the first time. If he'd seen this image before of Frédérique gazing at Luc with those starry eyes, he'd have had all the evidence he needed. They must have been laughing behind his back for a long time.

He goes downstairs to the kitchen and bangs the cupboard doors open and closed, searching for alcohol. He can't find any. What he does find, in one of the drawers, is a sharp knife. He tests the blade on his fingers.

Upstairs, he doesn't hesitate. He's surprised at how tough the first painting is. He has to stab it several times with real force to penetrate the canvas. There's a popping noise as the knife bites through. Once there's a hole, he cuts and rips the painting, knocking it off the wall. He moves along the line. Stab, pop, rip, slashing and stamping on them when they're on the floor. At last it's the turn of Frédérique's picture.

A cold rationality hits him. It isn't Frédérique's face, it's Bryony's.

He wonders how he could have ever made that mistake. He leans against the wall.

When he staggers back down the stairs, he's met by a tranquil, moonlit scene of perfectly placed paintings and sculptures. His drunkenness has deserted him and common sense tells him that to damage only Luc's paintings will raise suspicions. The idea of randomly destroying more exhibits is hard to contemplate, but in the end he knocks over a couple of the judging, vigilant sculptures, takes a few paintings off the wall and places them on the ground, stamping on the frames and – to make maximum effect with minimum damage – he pushes everything off the reception desk. Next he picks up a heavy bronze sculpture, retrieves the key for the French windows from the kitchen and goes into the garden. He desperately needs to piss so he relieves himself at length against the wall.

He launches the sculpture at one of the windows. The noise is horrific. He rushes back into the gallery, replaces the sculpture on its stand, locks the windows from the inside, puts the key and knife back in their places, resets the alarm and leaves the building.

Frédérique knows that something's wrong as soon as she opens the door of the gallery. It just doesn't feel right. The place sounds different; there's a different echo, a different silence. The door is wrenched out of her hands and opens wide, banging against the interior wall. It must have been the draught from the smashed window, she realizes later, which tugged it away from her.

She stands in the doorway, surveying the broken glass, the smashed ceramics, the pictures and papers on the floor, before she thinks of Luc's paintings and runs upstairs. It's worse there. Much worse.

They lie in mangled heaps of coloured canvas and paper and splintered wood. She squats among them, moaning to herself, keening and rocking from side to side as she mourns the ruined paintings. She picks up pieces of floppy canvas and presses them to her face. On the wall there's one intact which Frédérique takes down and cradles in her arms. One, only one left.

She wanders disorientated through the gallery, her mind blank until she comes to, standing with her hand poised on the telephone.

After the police have gone, Frédérique and Katrin start the long job of clearing up. Frédérique calls their insurance company who rattle out a list of instructions as if it's an everyday occurrence. Not for me, she wants to tell them, this has never happened to me before.

And yet, once she gets going, she's soon working efficiently, much more effectively than she's worked for weeks. The soggy mass of her brain suddenly begins to function.

She calls in the two women who cover reception for one day a week and the team sets to, sweeping up the glass, photographing and cataloguing the broken items – thankfully not as many as first appeared – and answering the phones. News has gone around quickly. It'll be in the local papers this week, Frédérique's sure about that.

She's relieved that at least Jacques has stopped phoning, and grateful that she's too occupied for her mind to wander in that direction. She does, though, take an opportunity to apologize to Katrin who has been the recipient of Jacques's constant and awkward phone calls to the gallery. Katrin shrugs and pulls a face, interrupting Frédérique's confused and garbled explanation.

'Men,' she says. 'They're like children.'

And Frédérique, although she feels guilty about how she's treated Jacques, is glad to have the opportunity to nod, smile, shrug and move on to the next unpleasant task, which is contacting Fernand, on the first holiday he's had in three years.

'But what about the alarms?' he asks, the shock evident in his voice. 'Didn't they work?'

'They came in through the back, through the garden windows,' Frédérique explains. 'Over the wall! The police said they get in anywhere, these days. They see it as more of a challenge.'

They'd never bothered to alarm the back of the building, believing it inaccessible.

'My god! That's all we need, vandals with aspirations.'

Frédérique tells him that there's nothing he can do, no point in him coming home early. She promises she will let him know if the situation changes. She assures him that she'll have everything sorted before he gets back. She knows that he'll come anyway, but she has to say it.

'Don't give anybody any money,' he tells her after he's stopped swearing. 'There might be all sorts of hidden costs and people will demand the moon if they get wind there's money up for grabs. Leave that part to me.'

Frédérique draws up a claims form for the artists concerned, their agents and a couple of buyers who had left items in the care of the gallery, and spends most of the afternoon on the phone notifying them. She leaves messages for those that can't be contacted.

'Vultures,' she says, once she's seen the manager of another gallery to the door. 'Bloody vultures.'

Katrin brings her a baguette and she eats it at her desk while she makes a list of everything else she needs to do.

She sends Katrin to drive over to Luc's place to give him a message, and if it's convenient, to bring him back with her. Frédérique would have preferred to have gone in person but she can't leave the gallery; she's waiting for Fernand to ring in for an update.

Katrin shows Luc into Frédérique's office. He's wearing a clean T-shirt and a pair of shorts. He looks nervous, jangling his keys in his hand.

'It doesn't look so bad out there.'

'We've tidied up a lot.'

'Were you here first?'

'Yes, I found it all.' Frédérique stands up. 'Luc, I'm sorry. Your paintings were destroyed.'

'Katrin told me.'

'Oh, I asked her not to.' She touches some forms lying on the desk, looks at him. 'I wanted . . . I thought I'd better tell you.'

'We had nothing else to talk about in the car.'

'I suppose not.'

'Can I see them? I'd like to see them.'

'Of course.'

Frédérique leads him to a side room where she's laid the paintings out on the floor as best she can, together with any identifiable pieces that have become detached. There are huge gaps in all of them and a pile of canvas which nobody has had time to go through and match up.

The untouched picture still hangs on the wall in the main room.

Luc squats down in front of his ruined work, like Frédérique had done earlier. She can't help staring at the muscles of his thighs, thinking that only a few days ago those legs had wrapped themselves around hers. He sifts through the heap of scraps, holding some of them into the light; a couple he places next to the painting they belong to. All Frédérique can think about is how his fingers moved across her body. She hates herself for these thoughts but she can't stop them. Every movement he makes reminds her of the kisses, the caresses, the way he held her. She wants to leave him alone because it's breaking her heart to watch him, and yet she doesn't want to miss a moment of time with him.

'How could they do it?'

'I'm sorry, Luc. It must be an awful shock.'

'A shock?' He looks puzzled, waves his arms around and shoves his hands through his hair. 'It's a bloody nightmare!'

She wants to comfort him, but she doesn't dare touch him. She has forfeited all rights to behave instinctively, naturally towards him.

'I know how you must be feeling . . .' she says lamely.

He looks at her, shakes his head. 'I don't think you could possibly begin to imagine.'

'I am really very sorry.'

'You had my favourite . . . Sainte Catherine . . .'

'I know.'

'All that fucking work, all that fucking heartache.'

'You'll get money of course.'

'I don't give a shit about that.'

'I know, but I have to say it.' Her voice is trembling. She feels that somehow she is to blame. She should have taken better care of them; it was her job to keep them from being exposed to this assault. She always felt before that she was on Luc's side, today she feels like the enemy.

'Do you think the police will catch them?' Luc asks.

'They didn't seem very hopeful,' Frédérique tells him. 'They don't usually catch vandals, do they?'

'Thank god the one of Cecillie wasn't here.'

When Frédérique gets home, she turns on the answer phone and stands over it to listen to her messages. She didn't clear it yesterday and there are several: all from Jacques. She fast-forwards and resolves once again to phone him. She should have called before and left a simple 'I'm fine' message, like he suggested. She knew, though, that as soon as she made contact, those few words wouldn't be enough for him. A day's worth of talk wouldn't be enough for Jacques.

She presses play. '. . . listen. Frédérique, I saw you with Luc and I want to know. I have the right to know what's going on. I know I shouldn't have . . .' She presses pause, her finger hovering over the play button. She doesn't understand. When did he see her? She presses play. '. . . left you by the docks, but I was angry and I know you're angry with me but I want to talk, please talk to me, please . . .'

She stops the machine, then she rewinds and listens to the whole message. He saw her with Luc. The painful memory of that night returns and she cringes again with the humiliation it brings with it. The following message from Jacques is so quiet that she has to turn the volume up. He's crying. 'I'm sorry. I was crazy, I didn't know what I was doing. Frédérique, I'm really sorry. I'm really sorry, I'm sorry.' She rewinds and replays it. She isn't sure what it's about and yet at the same time she knows she's hearing one of the most terrible things she has ever heard.

The machine bleeps at her. Her fingers rest on the buttons. Then she wipes all the messages.

11

good news

The tapping on the door brings Cecillie to her senses. She doesn't know how long she's been sitting on the toilet. Just sitting, thinking of nothing. She's numb, even her bottom feels numb where it's been pressed into the toilet seat. There'll be a ridge on her flesh, she thinks, as she stares at the door handle which is being turned and rattled and turned again.

'In there still?' calls Madame Pasquet in her high, wheezy voice. 'Are you ill, my dear?'

'Yes,' shouts Cecillie above the flushing cistern. 'I'm sorry, just coming.'

'Stomach,' Cecillie says apologetically as she's confronted by Madame Pasquet in her pink dressing gown, a towel folded neatly over one arm; tucked under the other is a bulging, flowery bag of toiletries. She has to squeeze past as her neighbour pushes her way into the bathroom, as if Cecillie might change her mind and go back in before she's made it. She hadn't realized the time. There's an unwritten rule that Madame Pasquet always takes her bath at eight in the morning.

Back in her apartment, Cecillie opens the French doors and

stands out on the balcony. She shades her eyes against the intense August sun. Although it's early, the air is already hot and heavy. It's impossible to stay outside all day at the moment.

She looks across at Max's balcony and wonders about going to talk to Bryony about what's happened, but the shutters are closed. Bryony's not up yet. It beats Cecillie how Bryony manages to get any sleep in a dead man's apartment but she claims it's peaceful. Cecillie isn't convinced.

No, it wouldn't be a good idea to trouble Bryony right now; Bryony's got enough of her own problems to deal with. It's amazing how well Bryony's coped with the split from Blythe in the end; especially with him behaving like a complete prat. The way Blythe's disappeared is typical of how stupid he's been over the whole thing. Cecillie had never imagined he could act so mean. Bryony was so distraught at first that Cecillie didn't think she was ever going to get through it. None of them did; they were all worried to death about her. It was a relief when Bryony moved next door so they could keep an eye on her.

Cecillie looks longingly at her unmade bed. She can't imagine how she ever managed to spend all those late nights, dancing, making love, just staying up talking and drinking. She is so tired all the time, she aches for sleep. These last couple of weeks it's been so bad that she's planned her days around naps, and her evenings so that she gets as much time asleep as she can.

But it's still not enough.

A few mornings she's woken up so late that Luc's already gone back to his place to work, and the coffee he left for her on the floor beside the bed has been stone cold. She slept alone in her apartment for a couple of nights, to try and catch up on sleep, but she missed Luc and in the morning had the same tiredness, the same queasy, hungry feeling hanging over her.

'Shit,' she thinks. 'Shit, shit, shit.'

The first time she had an inkling that she might be pregnant, she pushed it aside, out of her mind, and hadn't thought about it again until recently. It was easy to dismiss; she's never on time and quite often misses a month. It's never mattered before. In fact, Cecillie has always welcomed those missed months as a bonus. Who wouldn't be pleased to get away without having to bother with all that? And they haven't been stupid, her and Luc; they've always, always used condoms.

But time's been moving on and she *feels* different.

Her suspicions began in earnest this week. Each time she went to the toilet, she checked whether she'd started. She'd been going to the toilet more frequently, she now realizes, and a couple of times had even fooled herself into thinking she could feel the mild stomach ache which announces the arrival of her period. But nothing. Last night, hunched over her pocket diary, she had finally worked it out. It took a while, her weeks were amazingly similar, blurred by the haze of summer living. She carefully pieced it together by significant events and memorable dates: parties, Bryony's birthday, Luc's exhibition, the city festival. She counted the weeks, she counted the days. She hasn't had a period in all the time she's known Luc.

Cecillie goes back inside and tidies up. She makes her bed, washes out some underwear, wipes the surfaces in the kitchen, sorts through a pile of magazines where she discovers a packet of photos she'd forgotten about.

She begins to make coffee but the smell of the grains brings on the nausea so quickly that she decides on a coke instead. It's a strange feeling this sickness, not powerful enough to make her feel she's going to throw up, thank god; she hates being sick. No, it's a prickly, roaming nausea which tightens her stomach and throat and makes her head spin gently.

She lies on the floor, hoping to catch some air from the open windows, and takes out the photos. They're Bryony's. Most of them are of the little boys Bryony used to au pair for; one shows Blythe in action at the bar. They'd all laughed about that one, Blythe included, because he looked such a poseur. There's a couple of Bryony and Blythe together. Cecillie looks hard at these, but can only see and remember how happy they'd seemed. She was shocked by how quickly it all changed but Luc said that he'd been expecting it; not because Blythe had dropped any hints to him but because he thought they were always too different, with different agendas.

It had unsettled Cecillie for a while; she'd needed Luc's reassurance that the same thing wasn't going to happen to them. It wasn't, he told her. He loved her. And she loved him.

But how could Blythe not love Bryony? Cecillie thinks. How could Blythe not want to be with someone as nice as Bryony just because she wants different things?

The rest of the photos are of their group, outside bars or cafés, some in Cecillie's apartment, some at the beach.

Cecillie selects the ones that she's in and lays them on the floor. She tries to put them in chronological order. Some are easy – her skin's paler, her hair darker. In most of them she's either drinking or smoking or both. She studies them, wondering as she looks at each, is she pregnant when that one was taken, or that one, or that one?

Luc only appears in a couple of them. In both, the two of them are sitting round a table, smiling at the camera, at Bryony she supposes. In the first, they're holding hands, in the second, Luc's arm is around her. In that one she's leaning on him, leaning in towards him to fit in the picture, their heads gently together. She holds the photo towards the window and peers at Luc. Is this a father, she wonders, is this man ready to be a dad?

She wakes up on the floor, with the photos sticking to her face. She's sweating. She sits up, checks her watch, it's gone midday. She remembers half-waking some time earlier, but went straight back to sleep again with the warmth of the sun on her arms and back.

Luc's supposed to be coming to meet her at three. She should tell him then that she's pregnant. But she isn't ready, she hasn't prepared herself properly. She skirts quickly over the fact that she has no idea what such preparation would entail.

She hurriedly washes her face at the kitchen sink, finds her keys and goes out.

As she rides along, the air is so warm it's as if someone's blowing a hairdryer on her, and it's dusty, too; she can feel it coating the inside of her mouth. The city is parched, being bleached to the bone by the sun, while her skin gets darker. She looks at her arms and finds it hard to believe they will fade back to the colour on some of the photos, from when she first arrived here.

She drives to the big oak tree in the centre of the city, leaves her moped propped up at the kerb and sits under the tree where she lights a cigarette. She doesn't really take the smoke down, but the sensation of the cigarette's presence in her fingers makes her feel better. She finishes half before stubbing it out on the arm of the bench and flicking the remains to the ground. A tiny wisp of smoke rises from the squashed pulp and Cecillie fights back the immediate desire to get another cigarette out of the packet. Her thoughts swing between the idea that the baby, the uninvited guest, will have to take its chances and the horror of what damage it could do, if . . . But she doesn't go on with the if. Her mind cuts out. She's stuck in a limbo of only her knowing that she's pregnant, and nobody else; it feels unreal as if she'll never progress further than being two months' pregnant, or however long it is, for the rest of her life. Forever pregnant!

She takes a deep breath and forces herself to guess Luc's reaction. In other situations she's sure she could predict his behaviour, his response; like now, she can see him vividly in her apartment, lying on her bed reading one of the old magazines, drinking a coke while he waits for her to turn up. He'll be wearing jeans and a white T-shirt and he'll have taken his trainers off. She can see his strong, bare feet in incredible detail, the wide big toes, the wiry black hair that sprouts on each one, his smooth, brown skin. She knows him that well. But telling him about the baby, she can't picture it at all. She's frightened that the news will be too much, especially after what happened last week.

He'd been devastated after seeing his ruined paintings at the gallery. He sat down on the edge of her bed and told her about the state they were in, the vandals, all that Frédérique had said. At first she had thought he was OK about it; he spoke very calmly, he even made some joke about how he'd probably receive a lot more money from compensation than he would have done by selling them. When he stopped speaking, she'd gone over to him and hugged him and that's when he had started to cry. All she could do was hold him, feeling his body twitch and rock and shake. She hated him crying, she felt so useless; and it seemed to go on for hours. She doesn't want to be the cause of pain like that to him.

The tramp, tramp, the clack, clack of shoes and the murmur of voices, catches Cecillie's attention. She looks up. It's the end of the lunch hour and all the office workers are returning to work. Men dressed in suits, women in neat skirts and fitted blouses, or formal dresses. She is slap bang in the middle of the real world. She stares at them trying to spot signs of responsibilities. Are the dark shadows under the eyes; the necks and faces flushing an uncomfortable pink from being belted and buttoned in on a hot afternoon only in her imagination? People stare back at her. Some of the men smile at her, none of the women do; they look straight through her or away. She's probably a mess, she certainly feels dirty; she didn't wash properly this morning, having been rushed out of the bathroom by Madame Pasquet.

She leans back against the tree. The lumps and bumps of the bark dig into her skull. She desperately wants another cigarette. Above her the branches are intricately patterned spiralling up towards the sky with the leaves so dense that only a peephole of blue is visible. It seems to move above her, at first gently, then to spin and spin. She feels light-headed, the rush of familiar queasiness. She hangs her head forward.

The streets are quiet; deserted again, now that everyone's safely inside their offices. Grey figures flit occasionally past the windows of one of the blocks which are otherwise blank and oddly bare. Unadorned with shutters, they are cold and unwelcoming.

Shivering, she decides she's had enough shade and is ready for a bit of sun again.

The café is quiet. There's only one couple sitting outside. Cecillie observes them as she settles herself at a table. The girl has brutally short hair and patterns shaved, or perhaps tattooed, on the sides of her head; Cecillie can't quite make out which. The man looks older, with the same short haircut. They sit unspeaking with hands linked on top of the table and their free hands holding cigarettes. There's a dog asleep, curled between their feet. They look as if they're recovering from the night before, as if they've nothing else to do. Any other time Cecillie might have gone up to them, shared a cigarette, chatted a little, been a part of their lives for a while, because she's always felt very much part of that kind of world. She's no longer sure if that's true so she stays where she is.

The sun is slowly warming her skin and it feels good. When the waiter appears beside her she's ready to order a lemonade and a toasted ham sandwich. She feels saliva in her mouth as she speaks, anticipating the flavours. After he's gone, she closes her eyes.

She can visualize the scene, as if in the fish-eye lens of a camera. The street curves in front of her, the oak tree is on the left, the couple on her right. In the centre, in the foreground, is the outline of the back of her head and the tops of her shoulders. She's indistinct, blurry. The focus is on the backdrop and the extras playing their parts. The couple at the table murmur, cars pass, a door slams. She doesn't need to open her eyes to know what's around her, to recognize the daily life of the city.

Then the view changes. She is now clearer. She sees herself

as a stranger would, as perhaps the waiter saw her a few minutes ago. A young blonde woman, with a pack of cigarettes on the table in front of her, a young woman waiting for the food and drink she's ordered to arrive, a woman without anything urgent to do, without any worries.

The lens pulls the young woman in as the focal point; she's caught in a close-up. Cecillie sees her smile, the incline of her body as her hands reach towards the cigarettes. She looks relaxed and then shit!

The waiter puts a plate on the table, breaking Cecillie out of her thoughts. She has to screw her eyes up for a second against the glare of the sun. She stares at her meal and tries to recall the time when she felt like that girl but she can't.

Across the street, shutters are being opened after the siesta. In one of the buildings, a woman leans right out and the bright red varnish on her fingernails flashes as she extends her arms out to push the shutters apart. It's like a curtain opening on a play and, as if that was the signal, the cast appears from nowhere.

There must be at least forty because each table is soon occupied. People push up against each other, shoulders against shoulders, arms rest against arms and on the backs of chairs. They shout across to each other, bodies constantly sitting down, getting up. Cecillie's table is taken over. She nods her agreement when a woman asks with gestures whether the other seats are free. Cecillie notices the waiter dragging out some more chairs from the side of the café which are quickly snapped up, and there's a sudden appearance of two young girls, encased in brilliant white aprons, who carry plates of toasted sandwiches, trays of drinks, and who are treated with smiles and jokes by their customers.

The woman who spoke to Cecillie is joined by another woman and two men. Two couples, Cecillie assumes. They order food from one of the passing girls and then turn to Cecillie.

'Sorry about our noise,' one of the men says in stilted French.

Cecillie replies in French that they shouldn't worry. The café is doing good business.

'American,' the woman says in English, gesturing generally. 'On holiday.'

Cecillie nods and is rewarded with broad smiles.

'We love your city,' the other woman says. 'It's a wonderful place.'

The others join in with praise. They mention the *mairie*, the maritime museum, the public art galleries, theatre, cathedral, parks. They go on listing places and buildings in the city until Cecillie wonders if they'll ever stop. But their enthusiasm is also infectious and she responds warmly.

'Thank you. I love it too.'

It's a good moment. She's happy and buzzing with pride, not only because the tourists mistook her for being French but also to hear the city talked about in such favourable terms. Why not? She does love it. It feels like it belongs to her.

When Cecillie gets back to the house, Monsieur Bayard is standing in the doorway of his apartment.

'Salut,' he says extremely cheerfully, as if he's been waiting for someone to turn up. It soon becomes obvious that that's *exactly* what he's been doing, as he immediately embarks on a conversation.

'Where are you kids these days?' he asks. 'Why do I never see you or Blythe or the little one? Even she doesn't come to see me any more. Have I done something wrong?' He chuckles and grins at her.

'No, of course not.' She smiles back.

'Good,' he says, looking at her. 'Do you think I could persuade you to share some wine before you go upstairs? Do you have time? My wife's still not back and it would be good to have some company.'

Cecillie hesitates for a moment. 'OK, thanks.'

Monsieur Bayard gestures Cecillie to sit down. 'Every year my wife stays with her niece for two months,' he tells her. 'And every year, I get lonely.' Monsieur Bayard sighs. 'My niece has some troubles so she'll be away for even longer.'

Cecillie sits on the leather sofa that she's sat on so many times before, and sips the glass of red wine that he gives to her. It tastes good, warming her inside.

'Now, tell me,' he says, sinking down in an armchair. 'Why are you looking so drawn? Too many parties, huh? You kids do too much partying!' He laughs.

But Cecillie doesn't laugh. She fidgets while she tries to think of something to say. 'I'm tired,' she says, eventually. 'I suppose all the fun has caught up with me.'

'Oh,' he says.

He's peering at her, over the glass poised in front of him. He catches her eye, winks and smiles. He has a silly smile; it puffs his cheeks out like a hamster and shows his gold tooth at the front.

'I'm pregnant,' Cecillie says and waits to see how she feels, now that she's finally said the words out loud. But the wave of emotion doesn't happen, instead she watches Monsieur Bayard as if she's watching a silent film. She sees how his face alters, his smile disappears, his eyes pop wider, a parody of surprise, his smile reappears; then she looks away.

He sits beside her, taking hold of her hand, which feels hot against his cool fingers.

'That's good news,' he says.

She can feel tears starting. She sniffs loudly.

'A baby is good news, Cecillie.'

'Is it? I really don't know.'

She searches her pockets for a tissue, finds one and blows her nose. Monsieur Bayard leans back on the settee so she has to turn in her seat to face him.

'But it makes it all so serious, huh? What about Luc? What does he say?'

'I haven't told him yet.'

'Oh,' says Monsieur Bayard. 'Am I the first to know?'

He beams again when Cecillie nods.

'I'm honoured. But Luc will be so pleased.'

'I'm not so sure.'

'Of course you are sure. He will be over the moon.'

'Well, I'm not.'

'I can see that. The tears.' He dabbles at his face with his fingers by way of explanation.

'It's so stupid. I feel so stupid.'

'Of course you are stupid,' he says. 'But that's what happens to a lot of people, to my wife and myself, to maybe even your parents, but it is also the most natural thing in the world to happen. So that it's not such a nightmare, Cecillie. It is not so bad.'

'But I'm not ready.'

'Not many people are. My wife, now, she was furious,' he

says. 'Really,' he confirms, urgently, seeing Cecillie's questioning look. 'Furious. Uh-huh. I'll tell you why. She had just spent two hundred francs on a new dress. Two hundred francs was a fortune in those days and she had been saving up for this dress for months and then pfuuh, she was pregnant. She only wore it once, then she got too big and she couldn't wear it again. She never got back down to that size.'

Cecillie laughs.

'It was a beautiful, silk dress,' Monsieur Bayard sighs and shakes his hand to show his appreciation. 'Really tight, showing every curve. So you can see there was no way she could wear it when she was having a baby. But she would have waited, you see, waited so that she could wear the dress out, get her money's worth, before she even thought about a child.'

'I don't want to be fat,' Cecillie says, her voice coming out in a whine. 'And I want to choose when I'm ready.'

'Of course, my dear,' Monsieur Bayard replies, picking up her glass and handing it to her. 'It changes everything. But that doesn't mean it will be for the worse. It could make things better. Something to share with your young man, someone to care for, to love. And they love you back, too, Cecillie, don't forget. It will be good, Cecillie. It will be good.'

Those words are the first she remembers when she wakes up early in the morning on Monsieur Bayard's leather settee, covered in a multitude of colourful blankets. Her neck is stiff and her back's cold. She doesn't remember falling asleep, doesn't remember Monsieur Bayard removing her trainers which she can see are placed neatly on the floor, beneath her feet.

She's folding the blankets into a neat pile intending to make off quietly when Monsieur Bayard taps on the door and comes in. She's never seen him in his pyjamas and dressing gown. He looks quite hilarious, like Hercule Poirot on the television. She hopes he mistakes her amusement for a smile of thanks for his hospitality.

'I hope you feel better,' he says peering at her.

'Oh, yes,' she replies. 'Much better, thank you. In fact, I must go now,' she says. 'And see Luc.'

'Good girl.'

As she's leaving, Monsieur Bayard gives her a hug. Because she's taller than him, his head presses into her neck and she can smell the sweetness of his hair oil; some strands stick to her skin as she draws back.

'Thank you,' she says, eager to get away before the nausea starts. 'Thank you. I must go now.'

In her apartment she finds a note on the kitchen table from Luc:

Weren't we supposed to meet today?! Did I get the time wrong? Come round tonight or see you tomorrow at the café. 3-ish? With love, Luc. I MISS YOU!

She sits down and, placing one finger on the middle of the note, she pushes it around the surface, sliding it into each corner, lining up the edge of the paper with the edge of the table.

If she sets off now, she could be at Luc's place in fifteen minutes, and five minutes after that she would have told him that she's pregnant and they would have talked about it and she would know what to do.

But when she's out on her moped she loses her nerve and

takes a long route round the city, ending up by the docks, on the other side of the river from Luc's quarter. If she crosses the bridge she'll only be a short distance from the café. It's not quite ten o'clock. Luc won't arrive for hours and although three o'clock seems impossibly far away, she decides to wait for him there. She can spend the time looking at the river, chatting to Maurice. It's better to wait, she convinces herself, rather than disturb him from his painting. She knows how fragile his concentration is these days, how little it takes to knock him off track. No, she tells herself, the best thing for both of them is to wait.

But as she cuts the engine and coasts down to the parking area she sees Luc is already at one of the tables outside, with his long legs stretched out in front of him, and his hands around a cup of hot chocolate; his persuasive, talented hands. She feels a lurch of desire, but she's a bag of nerves by the time she gets off her moped and kisses him hello.

'I don't know why,' he says, softly. 'But I had this urgent need to get here as soon as possible.'

'Luc,' she blurts out. 'I'm pregnant.'

She bites her bottom lip and waits for his reaction. Luc's face is uncomprehending at first, then he jumps up, grinning. 'Cecillie, that's great. No, that's brilliant.' He kisses her with a loud smacking kiss. 'You're beautiful, you're wonderful,' he says, dancing her around the tables.

She is stunned by how happy he seems. And he's not faking it either; Cecillie knows that look: from on the beach, or after making love, or the few times that she's got him silly with drink when he just sits around in a haze, grinning whenever Cecillie comes into focus. Lovesick, Bryony calls it and Cecillie used to get a kick out of seeing him like that. Now it makes her feel tearful. He pulls her down to the chair next to him.

'What's wrong?' he asks.

He's stroking her hand; she can feel his fingers moving up and down on her skin. It irritates her and she fights the desire to withdraw it. She asks him directly this time, 'How do you really feel?'

He doesn't answer at first. 'Pleased, definitely. But scared, too. Shit scared.'

'I'm worried,' she puts in quickly and takes a deep breath. This is what she's been so afraid of saying, this is what she's been reluctant to acknowledge. 'I'm worried that it will ruin everything.'

She can see him considering, assessing it all and waits, tensely, to hear his verdict.

'Yes,' he starts, slowly. 'Yes, it will change some things, but I don't think it'll spoil them. We'll be able to go to the beach, teach the baby to swim, you'll be able to take it out on the moped with you, when it's older; give me some peace while I paint.' He's teasing her, gently.

As he speaks, the hope inside her is building. She's seeing herself washing the baby in Luc's sink; the paint, the turps, will scent the baby's skin like they do Luc's. She's setting out on the moped with a toddler fastened in a seat behind her, down to the quays to watch the ships come in; to point out the oranges, like masses of garish bubbles on top of the crates. She's sitting with a drink and cigarette in this café while the baby is passed from adult to adult. A child who speaks French and English, who is beautiful, and clever and good.

But she isn't stupid; she knows reality isn't that easy. Hasn't she after all witnessed how badly it can go wrong in her own family?

'What if the baby doesn't sleep, what if it's ill, or something's wrong with it, what if I don't know what to do? What if I'm a crap mother?' Cecillie scrabbles for the cigarettes and lighter in her pocket. She puts them on the table but doesn't get one out.

She sees her own mother. They're in the kitchen making Cecillie breakfast. Her mum's eyes are red from crying and her hands tremble as she butters the toast. Suddenly she runs out of the room. Cecillie waits for a few minutes but when she doesn't come back, she gets the marmalade from the cupboard and finishes preparing her own meal.

'No way,' he says, shaking his head. 'You'll be great, I know you will. You'll be a great mother.'

His words startle her. They start a burning down in the depths of her stomach. She grips hold of the table with her free hand. 'I don't think I can do it. In fact I know I can't.'

'You always say you want to go with your body, to listen to your body.' He puts his hand on her stomach. 'Well, listen to it now. What it's telling you.'

She wriggles in her chair, so that Luc is forced to remove his hand. But as soon as it's gone, she wants it back.

'It'll be fun.' He puts his arm around her, draws her to him so that she can feel the warmth of him. 'Lucky baby to have us two for parents.'

'I suppose,' she says. 'I suppose it might be OK.'

She gets a cigarette, lights it, inhales deeply then offers the packet to Luc. He shakes his head, tuts, takes the cigarette out of her mouth and stubs it out.

'We'll get somewhere nice,' Luc is saying. 'Somewhere bigger with a bathroom and a room for the baby. I can afford more rent now.'

'You couldn't do that, Luc. You can't leave your place.' The idea shocks Cecillie. She hadn't expected this at all.

'We can't have a baby without a bathroom.'

'They have loads of kids in those places, you're always saying so. They manage. . . .'

'They *have* to manage, but if we can afford it, Cecillie, it's not only stupid but it's playing at that life; it's an insult if it isn't for real.'

'But you wouldn't be you if you didn't live in this quarter, in your flat with your painting room and everything. It's who you are.'

'I'm not talking about moving out of this quarter. And I don't think having a bathroom will make me a different person. God, Cec, I'm talking about a new place, together, that's all. A fresh start with my new family and –' he pauses '– with my painting.'

Cecillie shakes her head. 'I want you to carry on as before.'

'You know I haven't been painting properly. Every time I go in my room, I'm reminded about what I've lost. I can't continue like that, I need a new direction.'

It was days before Luc had been able to face going home after his paintings were destroyed. They'd spent the time quietly together, in Cecillie's apartment, reading, making love, cooking huge meals. And although he goes there every morning to work, she knows that really it's been a pretence that they've both kept up, because it's clear he isn't achieving much at all.

Cecillie knows this not only because his mind drifts off sometimes when he's with her and he seems sad and confused but also because the turpsy, oily scent is fading from his skin and his clothes are often clear of paint.

Luc continues, excitedly. 'This could be exactly what I need. This will be a completely new beginning. For both of us. It'll be great.'

'I want us to stay the same,' Cecillie says, fighting back the tears. 'I want you to stay the same.'

Luc gently strokes her face. 'Nothing stays the same, Cecillie,' he says in a lower tone. 'But I promise you it'll be better, much better.'

Cecillie is surprised by the surge of desire his touch brings. She didn't know that she could feel pregnant and sexy at the same time. She wants, with a terrible urgency, Luc to make love to her.

'OK,' she says, distracted by the ferocity of her feelings. She sits on his knee and Luc kisses her for a long time.

Luc bounces his legs underneath her. 'Come on,' he says. 'I want to take you somewhere.'

Inside the church Cecillie shivers from the cold. There are a lot of people here, the odd voice sounding loud against the murmur of hushed voices.

Luc leads her down the aisle towards a small crowd of tourists. Behind them are tens of candles high up on the altar. At first, Cecillie thinks that they're not alight because the flames are almost transparent in the glare of the sun through the side windows.

'Here, take this.'

Luc hands her a candle and lights it with a taper from one

at the altar; then he lights his own from hers, tipping them together like glasses in a silent toast. They are standing in the middle of a group of people but it feels as though they've created a space just for the two of them.

'After I first met you,' Luc says in a whisper, 'I came back here and asked the city to make you mine. Now we're going to thank the city for our baby.'

Cecillie fights more tears. They seem to come much too readily these days, even when she's happy.

'And afterwards –' he bends towards her, speaks close against her ear so that she can feel his lips tickle the skin '– I'm going take you home and make love to you.'

'OK,' she whispers back. 'OK.'

She feels like a little girl in front of a birthday cake waiting in trembling excitement to blow out the candles and make a wish, except that she's holding the candle in her hand, watching the flame flicker and dance; and she knows that the candle must stay alight for this wish to come true.

Luc closes his eyes, so she copies him. She concentrates and begins her wish; she hopes it will all be OK, that's what she says in her head, over and over again. I hope it will all be OK.

She peeks at Luc. The flame plays a ghostly pattern across his face. He must be making a long list of all the things for his new start, she thinks. Or maybe he's simply taking some time to consider the news. The good news. She takes hold of his hand and leans against him.

12

feel empty

After Frédérique has rung twice on Jacques's doorbell, Bernadette his cleaner appears on the stairs.

'He's in, Madame,' she calls up. 'But he told me no visitors. He hasn't let me clean all week.'

'Have you got your key?'

'Yes, Madame.'

'Can I have it? I'll go and check on him.' She waves aside Bernadette's hesitation. 'I'll take responsibility for anything that happens. He could be seriously ill.'

Bernadette climbs the stairs slowly, unwinding the key from the bunch she keeps under her overall. She looks relieved as she hands it over. 'I have been worried, Madame,' she says. 'But I didn't know who to speak to.'

Frédérique waits for Bernadette to start back downstairs before putting the key in the lock. She calls into the apartment. 'Jacques. It's me, Frédérique. I'm coming in.'

There's silence. She closes the door behind her.

The place is in a terrible state. There are glasses and bottles covering the coffee table and a large red stain on the pale carpet which sets her heart pounding before she realizes that it's wine. Her bag's on the settee with all her belongings scattered around it. She instinctively wants to collect them together, but first she must find Jacques.

He's lying on the bed, propped up on pillows. He looks awful. His face is unshaven and sunken like an old man's; his hair is sticking up at all angles. Frédérique stands over him. He doesn't show any surprise at her appearance in his flat.

A cigarette is burning in a wine glass beside him. It hisses as she stubs it out in the dregs.

'Oh, Jacques, what a mess.'

'Are you referring to me, or the apartment?' Jacques mumbles.

She resists remarking on the smell in the bedroom: underneath the stink of stale cigarettes is the fustiness of an unwashed body. His clothes are dirty and creased as if he hasn't changed for days.

'I'm sorry,' he says, quietly.

'Are you ill?' she asks.

Jacques shakes his head, then puts his hand up to his forehead. 'Well, I've got a headache.'

'I'm not surprised,' she says, taking in the cluster of empty wine bottles by his bed. 'Have you eaten anything?'

'I don't know. I don't think so. I don't want anything.'

'I'll cook something while you go and shower.'

Jacques doesn't respond. Frédérique goes into the bathroom and turns on the shower. She fetches a clean towel from a cupboard and leans against the bedroom door frame.

Jacques hasn't moved. She has a feeling that he's waiting for something.

'Come on,' she says, putting on a jovial voice. 'Get up. It'll make you feel better.'

'Are they coming?' he asks. 'Are you getting me ready for them coming?'

'Are who coming? Who are they?'

'The police. I've been waiting for the police.'

'I haven't told the police.'

He flushes red from an emotion she can only guess at: embarrassment, gratitude, relief? She throws the towel at him. Jacques's hands clutch it as it lands on his stomach. She turns away because she doesn't want him to catch sight of her face and see evidence of her own confused feelings. She needs to be strong.

There's a rustle of bedclothes as Jacques gets up. She watches him walk unsteadily down the hall, as if he's an invalid, or extremely drunk. Frédérique hesitates about offering to help him undress, unconvinced that he'll be able to manage on his own.

'Will you be OK?' she calls after him.

He nods, before closing the bathroom door.

In the lounge, Frédérique tries to collect her thoughts. She's shaking. She was prepared for Jacques's defiance, even for his anger, but she wasn't prepared for this: his defeat.

She picks up her belongings, fishing down the sides of the settee to retrieve a pen and some make-up, feeling under the settee for any stray items. She puts the bag by the door ready to take with her when she leaves.

She gathers all the dirty glasses and crockery she can see, scrapes congealed food off plates into the bin and loads up the dishwasher; she fills two carrier bags with empty wine bottles and starts on a third. Finally, she examines the contents of the fridge.

By the time Jacques emerges from the shower, the apartment has regained some order; the washer is humming away and Frédérique has prepared a cheese omelette, some orange juice and a large pot of coffee.

Jacques looks more like the Jacques she's accustomed to; clean-shaven with his hair combed neatly back, in glossy wet waves. He sits down at the table. A waft of aftershave reaches her across the room. Its familiar scent conjures up memories of happier, cosy chats in this kitchen. She concentrates on serving up the food.

'Frédérique . . .' Jacques begins.

'Eat first,' she interrupts him. 'Then we'll talk.'

She hasn't eaten properly herself all day and the omelette tastes surprisingly good. They finish their meal in silence. Then Jacques speaks. 'I need to know – are you going to tell the police?'

'No.'

'Have you told anyone?'

She shakes her head. 'What would be the point?'

'To punish the idiot who did what he did, I suppose.'

'I . . .' Frédérique hesitates. 'I wouldn't want anything to happen to you.'

For the first time since Frédérique arrived, she and Jacques look each other in the eye. It doesn't last long. Jacques offers a thin smile, before turning his attention back to his cup of coffee.

'Thank you,' he says.

Frédérique clears the table. As she reaches over to take Jacques's plate, he takes hold of her wrist and says, 'That's the best thing I've heard you say for a long time.'

She twists her arm away, the cutlery clattering violently on the plate.

'I've been angry, Jacques.'

'I can imagine.'

'You wouldn't believe how angry I've been.'

'And now?'

'Now?' She considers revealing that her reason for coming over was to exact some revenge; to somehow make him pay, to hurt him. But that desire now seems futile, it seems that he has suffered enough.

Frédérique glances at him. Jacques is staring into nothing; preoccupied with his thoughts. His body looks stiff, brittle and she surprises herself by wanting to comfort him.

'Now I feel empty and, I don't know – sad, I suppose,' she tells him.

He makes no response to her statement and she can't bring herself to say it again. She feels they were rather inadequate, insubstantial words that won't stand up to repetition.

She puts the plates on the work surface near the sink, then returns to sit down at the table. Jacques looks up.

'Have you seen him? Luc? Have you seen him since the paintings were . . . ?'

'Yes.'

This time Jacques doesn't look away and Frédérique forces herself to face him.

'What did he say?'

'Not much.'

'Was he angry?'

'Of course. Angry, upset, and . . . relieved,' she says, flatly.

'Relieved. What do you mean?'

Frédérique feels her anger flare up against Jacques's eager interest but it fizzles out as soon as she speaks. 'He was relieved that the one of Cecillie wasn't there.'

'I see.'

'I did too.' She bites her lip. 'It's all been an absolute disaster.'

'Fred?' Jacques puts his hand on top of hers. She grips it tightly.

'I have missed you, you know,' she says. 'To talk to, to talk things over with.'

'Me too.'

She sees with horror that Jacques is crying. She holds on tighter to his hand. 'We've both made complete fools of ourselves,' she says, 'haven't we? Complete fools.'

13

the right decision

Bryony can't remember much about the days immediately after Blythe ran off and left her on the beach. She knows that Cecillie and Luc took her back to Cecillie's apartment, she knows she went from there back to her house, but she doesn't remember how or when. She lay in bed for over a week while her body burned up with flu. Sophie and Henri didn't make a fuss about having to cancel their trip. Although Bryony made a weak and muddled attempt to argue against it, in the end she had to admit that she wasn't in a fit state to care for the boys. The family was very kind to her; Sophie brought her home-made vegetable soup and ice-cream that Bryony often couldn't eat. The boys came to see her too and Fabien read her his favourite story about the donkey and the chicken over and over again; it's imprinted on her brain now, and snippets of its rhyming prose keep returning to her at odd times of the day.

That this short period of her life happened, she knows, but the memories have a hallucinatory edge; the boundary between reality and dreams is very woolly. The one certainty during that time was her body. Each single part of her hurt, even her knuckles, her toes, her eyelids. She slept and cried and ached and lay in her bed while the family moved about the house.

Then the illness eased so that she was, at last, able to get out of bed and keep an eye on the boys for a few hours; enough for Sophie to get to her office and keep everything ticking over there. By the time Sophie returned, Bryony was exhausted and would sleep all evening. The fourth day she was up, Henri came home with bad news. His father was seriously ill, and he had to leave immediately to be with him, and then – as death was imminent – he phoned to say he would have to stay to sort out his father's affairs which were intricate and rather confused. Sophie decided to join him with the boys and the plan quickly developed into the family being away for six weeks. Sophie asked Bryony to accompany them, offering it as a holiday for Bryony – a time for recuperation before she returned to England, not as work.

Bryony was tempted by the description of the big, old house near the woods and the little wooden sailing boat on what she pictured as a lake but which they all called the pond. It sounded very beautiful and peaceful and Bryony knew that the family really wanted her there but, in the end, she elected not to go.

She doesn't regret the decision. Well, that's not quite true. She regrets letting the boys down. She remembers all too clearly Fabien's face crumpling when she broke the news to the two of them. Patrice burst into tears. She protects her weakened body from the waves of guilt and despair by closing her mind to any thoughts of missing them. Children don't always understand; children feel betrayed, she knows that and it hurts. Henri and Sophie were sympathetic and made it easy for her, never questioning her decision once it was made. She's grateful to them but she doubts whether she expressed it fully.

She's grateful, too, to Monsieur Bayard who has let her move into the apartment next to Cecillie for however long she needs a room, for however long it takes to sort herself out.

Bryony had intended her stay to be very short but it's been nearly two weeks since she arrived and she's no nearer to booking her ticket home.

She hasn't admitted it to anyone yet but she can't leave Blythe behind. All the time that she remains in the city, and is living in this house, she feels close to him. Once she leaves, the tie will be broken; her relationship with Blythe will be dead. She'll only have memories mingling in with the memories of the boys, of Cecillie and Luc and everyone else here. Blythe will be no more real than the others.

Anyway, Bryony finds Max's old apartment restful. The walls are white, the bed is thin and modern, the wardrobes and cupboards are all white-painted chipboard. There's no hint of spookiness, in fact the atmosphere is cool and bright. She enjoys waking up late and letting the sun burst in when she opens the heavy shutters; she likes lying in bed listening to the sounds of the street at night and she likes being part of the household, with her friend next door and Monsieur Bayard popping in often, even though he's not comfortable in the apartment. Cecillie laughed when Bryony described how he paces about the whole time, and can't keep his eyes off the area of the ceiling where Bryony assumes he must have found Max. Monsieur B is effusively pleased that Bryony is staying there as he won't now need to say that the last tenant in these rooms killed himself.

This morning Bryony is getting dressed when Cecillie taps on the door.

'Fancy going out?' Cecillie asks, hovering at the doorway, her hand sitting protectively over her stomach. She won't come in. The apartment has bad vibes she says, so Bryony always goes next door to chat. It's sweet how Cecillie's suddenly become superstitious, extra careful since she had her pregnancy confirmed. She's determined to do everything right and keeps pumping Bryony for advice. Fortunately Bryony has a vast store of pregnancy and children stories from her array of sisters, sisters-in-law, cousins, and aunts, so she's able to oblige Cecillie with plenty of examples and sympathetic tales to confirm what is likely to happen, what is normal. She enjoys these times with her friend, she hadn't realized how interesting pregnancy could be and they have a good laugh about the funnier – usually the yuckier – aspects of the whole process. Cecillie's so excited about the baby that it's hard for her happiness and enthusiasm not to rub off.

'I'll be with you in a minute,' she tells Cecillie.

She washes quickly and glances at herself in the mirror. She lost weight during her illness and it shows in her face which, to her mind, is paler than ever. When she gets back to England no one will believe she's recently spent a whole year, or particularly a hot summer, in southern France.

In the few moments it takes to pass Blythe's door, Bryony and Cecillie pause in their chatting. They don't mention his name, but Bryony knows that Cecillie, like herself, is wondering whether he's in there or not.

Neither they nor Luc have seen Blythe in the weeks since he and Bryony split up. At one time, Cecillie and Luc were convinced that Blythe had left without saying goodbye, although Bryony maintained that he wouldn't do that; then Cecillie formulated the idea that Blythe might have died in his room and went off in a panic to persuade Monsieur B to open his door. She returned with the news that Monsieur Bayard had seen Blythe the week before and heard him a few times late at night and that Blythe had also pushed his rent under their landlord's door, so although Cecillie is not yet a hundred per cent convinced, it confirmed Bryony's opinion that Blythe's still around. She's always believed this without requiring any proof – for a strange reason: whenever she's passing on her own, she leans against his door for a few minutes, and she would swear she can feel the heat of him inside.

The gentle breeze outside the blue café is a perfect antidote to the stifling heat. Earlier, Luc had been to view a couple of apartments.

'One was a hole,' he's saying. 'But the other one's a possibility.'

The murmur of Cecillie and Luc discussing a new home is comforting background noise as Bryony drifts away into her own thoughts. Then, as if it's welled up from inside and spilled out, Bryony utters Blythe's name. She sits, dazed, feeling foolish in front of her friends who have stopped talking and are staring at her.

Blythe's name is forever in her mind; it crackles through her brain and clings to her lips. Sometimes when she's alone she lets his name pulsate in the space around her, repeating it again and again, listening to it as if the name were alive. She experiments; speaking softly, sometimes loudly, or drawing each syllable out until it's become purely a word. Or letters in a word. Dissected. It's never happened in public before.

She attempts to cover up her slip. 'Blythe used to love watching the river,' she says quickly. But it's a scrappy bit of nothingness which she knows doesn't deceive either of them. The Blythe which escaped from her lips a minute ago, was so abrupt, it's obvious that nothing was meant to follow it. It was a cry intended for him. Where are you?

Cecillie squeezes her hand. Luc disappears into the café and when he's gone Cecillie asks, 'Do you want to talk?'

Bryony shakes her head. It's crazy that she should be feeling like this, she tells herself. How many times over the last few weeks has she kept vigil in her room? Alert to the sound of Blythe's apartment door, to any movement outside. How many times has she haunted the streets, the places where Blythe usually goes, hoping to catch a glimpse of him?

'Why are we both still here? Me and Blythe I mean,' she asks Cecillie, who shrugs. 'After all the hassle he gave me about getting out of the city, why's he hanging around?'

'Maybe he's got stuff to sort out,' Cecillie suggests.

If he left, Bryony tells herself, it would release her, too.

Bryony declines Cecillie's invitation to the beach and makes her way home.

As she approaches the house, Blythe suddenly appears at the top of the narrow alley which runs down the side of the building. She's startled by the sight of him and stops in her tracks. Blythe's gawping at her, separated from her by a few feet of pavement.

Bryony's drawn towards him. As she gets closer, Blythe averts his eyes. She has the impression that he's trying to block out her presence, or will her into walking straight past him into the house. But she's so relieved to see him – even though she never doubted he was still around – that when she's level with him, she takes a step forward.

Blythe's face is expressionless. She could almost believe he's frozen there, a wax model. She puts a hand out and he retreats a short way into the alley.

'Well, what do you want?'

She's confused and shocked to hear his voice. It seems so long ago since she's heard it. She scans his face. His mouth is pinched, his eyes are hard in the darker light of the alley. There's no softness there, she realizes in panic. She doesn't know this Blythe, has no idea how to talk to him. When she doesn't reply, he pushes past her. She doesn't attempt to call him back.

She closes the shutters in her apartment and crawls into bed. She waits for the horror of illness to descend on her again. Some time later Cecillie knocks at the door but she can't answer: her throat has seized up, her body's too heavy to move.

Bryony hears Cecillie talking to Luc on the landing before the fever takes over. It swirls through her body, bringing pain and the sweats. She curls into a ball and drifts in and out of sleep. Whenever she wakes up she starts to cry; a crying which hurts her stomach, her eyes, and her face which is so tender she can't bear to rest it on the pillow.

By the morning, the fever has run its course. The thought of home rushes in on her. It makes her cry again but this time because she knows that soon she'll be with people who love her, somewhere where she matters. At a lucid point during the night, she had come to the decision to leave. She thinks of sitting, talking with her mother in her warm kitchen with a cup of tea and a plate of custard creams, the desire to be there is so sharp that it takes her breath away.

She opens the door to see if the bathroom is free. The door opens immediately and Cecillie emerges.

'Bryony! Where've you been? I was worried about you.'

'I've been ill . . .'

'Oh no.' Cecillie rushes towards her. For the first time Bryony notices Cecillie's put on weight; her breasts bounce under her vest top as they never have before.

'I'm all right now. In fact . . .' She takes a deep breath and smiles. 'I've decided to go home.'

'Oh, Bryony.' Cecillie's fingers touch hers. 'I'll miss you.'

'I'll miss you too,' Bryony replies and the tears threaten again.

'Oh god, don't start me off,' Cecillie says, waving her hand in front of her face. 'Come out here so I can give you a hug.'

'I desperately need a bath,' Bryony says. 'Keep me company?'

Bryony runs the water while Cecillie makes herself comfortable on a towel on top of the toilet seat cover. Bryony pours in loads of bubbles and oils and the small room fills with perfumed steam. She undresses and gets in, wincing as the heat scorches her feet, but she perseveres, lowering herself slowly until there's only her head above water level. 'I've been thinking about my mum,' she tells Cecillie. 'I hadn't realized how much I miss her.'

'You'll see her soon.'

'I can't wait.' Bryony sinks down into the water to soak her hair. When she comes up, Cecillie is sitting on the edge of the bath, with the shampoo bottle in her hand.

'Might as well practise on you,' she says and begins to lather Bryony's hair, rubbing gently round and round on her scalp.

Cecillie swirls the water over her head, raking through the strands of hair with her fingers as she rinses off the shampoo before finally squeezing it into a coil and securing it in a bun with a hairband. Cool water trickles down Bryony's back; she sinks down, grateful for the heat of the bath. Cecillie resumes her seat on the toilet.

'I hope that's how I am with my baby. Really close like you and your mum.'

'You will be.'

'What if it doesn't want to see me, like I am with my parents? Won't that be awful?'

'Your family was damaged by the accident. That won't happen to you and Luc.'

'It's frightening how much I love it already,' Cecillie says. 'Sometimes I can't imagine how Luc and I will manage and other times it seems so wonderful.'

'It *is* wonderful.'

'Luc keeps me going,' Cecillie says. 'If I didn't have him I think I'd flip out.'

Bryony points to Cecillie's stomach. 'This baby will have the best mum and dad ever,' she assures her and Cecillie giggles.

Later, in the afternoon, when Bryony's packing she thinks back over the weeks she's spent living in the house and recognizes the ridiculous way she's wasted time waiting for Blythe. She cringes at the thought of how patient her friends have been; she blushes too, about her behaviour yesterday with Blythe.

After her bath she went out to buy her ticket to fly home. It's sitting in her handbag next to her passport in readiness for the end of the week. She phoned her parents and she's focusing on the memory of the warmth in her mother's voice, to keep up the momentum for making the final break. The image of her parents' kitchen, her mother, friends and family, all the people and odd things like beans on toast, English television, even some of her old clothes, her books and childhood toys left in her bedroom, send a tingle of anticipation, a soft longing to be back there, increasing her conviction that she's doing the right thing.

She has a final task before she departs. She wants to explain to Blythe her decision to go. She doesn't want him to hear it from someone else and she feels there should be a tidier way of finishing their relationship. She decides to write a letter. It isn't a long one, and she hopes it isn't embarrassing – for Blythe, that is. She has told him the truth – that she loved him, and loves him still. She's explained how much he's hurt her and how she feels he came to the wrong decision, that she will always consider he was wrong but that she accepts his right to feel differently. She writes that she enjoyed their time together and it will always remain a happy memory for her. She writes the whole letter quickly, without changing a word. Now that she's definitely leaving, she has a new confidence inside her.

She doesn't doubt that if she bumped into Blythe now, it would go much better, but she doesn't allow herself any dreamy images of him hugging her, holding her to him for one last time. That's too painful. And it's not going to happen.

After finishing the letter, she visits Monsieur Bayard. He's all smiles and welcome when he opens the door. 'Come on in. Come on in.'

'I only wanted to say . . .' She follows the waddling man into his lounge.

He offers her some wine. She didn't mean to stop, but he's

been so kind, so sweet to her that it's the least she can do.

'Now,' he says once they've sat down. 'What did you want to tell me?'

'I'm leaving. I decided yesterday and I booked it all today.'

He looks sadly at her. Remember, she tells herself, remember that he's always looked like that, sad puppy-dog eyes. It isn't anything personal, it isn't anything to set her off. So she doesn't cry; she looks over his shoulder, and studies the faded wall-paper, the bureau crammed with papers, and the photographs on the dresser.

'When do you go?'

'Friday evening.'

'Oh my god,' he says dramatically, his hand flapping suddenly towards his hair which he tries to smooth down. Her heart skips with tenderness for him. 'I'm sorry to hear that. I shall miss you.' He sighs elaborately. 'The summer goes, and all my little friends start to go, too. Oh well, it happens.' He shrugs. 'Every year they say the same thing, they'll never leave and then – pfuh, they're gone.'

'I'm sorry,' she tells him.

'You two girls have been my special girls.'

'You've been wonderful, Monsieur B.'

'It's been my pleasure, my dear,' he replies, tapping his glass. 'Forgive me, my interference, but are you going to say goodbye to Blythe?'

'I've written him a letter. I'll put it through his door later.'

Monsieur Bayard brightens up. 'Why don't you bring it down to me?' he asks. 'I'll give it *personally* to Blythe and I can tell him what a silly boy he is, at the same time. Perhaps tell him to come and see you?' He winks at her. 'Use my influence.'

Bryony can't imagine anyone less likely to persuade Blythe than Monsieur Bayard so she says hurriedly, 'That's very kind, but I think I'd rather do it myself.'

As she's leaving, he takes her hand and says, 'I think for you, it is the right decision to go home.'

She smiles gratefully. 'I do too.'

When Monsieur Bayard has closed his door she stands briefly in the hallway. Across from her is Blythe's room. Later, she promises herself, she will deliver her letter and then she will have finished here.

14

let me talk

Blythe is sitting on his bed when he hears the front door open and Cecillie start to make her way up the stairs. She no longer sprints up them. He hears the care in her tread, the firm squeak of trainer on the stone. He has the idea that she might hold on to the banister these days too, pulling herself along. That's not the only change he's noticed: Cecillie sleeps in the afternoons, for an hour or two before Luc gets there. He hears the gentle murmuring as Luc wakes her up, the soft paddings around the room before they turn the radio on. Neither of them gets drunk much either, or shouts, or dances around, or sounds like they used to. It's all quieter, it's all softer. They seem to have infected the atmosphere of the whole house; it's more subdued, more tranquil. Except for the buzz of the news. He hears the tenants nattering on the stairs, outside their doors; he hears the general concern and the excitement. Cecillie's pregnant, Cecillie's pregnant. She's always being accosted by the old women – Madam do-da upstairs, and Madame Dufosse across the way, not to mention the biggest old woman of them all, Monsieur B. The funny thing is that from Cecillie's voice you'd think she was as interested and serious as they are. She chats for ages. He's amazed. It's as if she's become the house mascot and Luc, the wonderful Luc can do no wrong. The old biddies twitter around him whenever they see him. He's like a god, thinks Blythe sourly, like some bloody god bestowing his magnificent seed.

Blythe feels a tickle in his nose, the tickle becomes intense. He's going to sneeze. He looks around for something to blow his nose on to stop it but there's nothing to hand. The sneeze burns; his eyes are watering. He grabs at the bottom of his T-shirt but too late, it's a bitch of a sneeze, the *aah-choo* fills the room, a gob of snot splats on the wall beside him. Jesus! He wipes it off with his T-shirt.

He's left with a high-pitched ringing in his ears which clears after a few seconds. The building seems unnaturally still. He must have missed Cecillie entering her apartment. There's no sound of her moving around above him; no creaking of the floorboards and there's no music. She's not in there. She can't have gone into the bathroom either as he would have heard the annoying squeal of the hinge. So where is she?

The knock on the door makes him jump. He lies motionless.

'Come on Blythe, I know you're in there. I heard you sneeze a minute ago.'

Shit. If he doesn't answer, he thinks, she'll go away. She raps loudly, an irritating tune.

'I'm not going away, until you open this door.'

What a line he thinks and sighs, swearing under his breath. What fucking timing. He gets off the bed and opens the door a crack. He peers at Cecillie.

'May I come in?'

'Sure.' He flings the door wide open and so hard that it bounces against the wall with a bang. He retreats back into the room, leaving Cecillie to close the door behind her. He assumes a cross-legged position on his bed, leaning back against the headboard.

'Blythe, why's it so dark in here?' Cecillie asks, looking at the window which is shuttered up.

'I like it like this.'

There's a silence that Cecillie breaks.

'So?' she says.

'So, what?'

'So I merely wondered what the fuck you've been up to,' she says and then with a hand on her stomach, she looks down. ''Scuse the language, baby.' Then back up at Blythe. 'Well?'

Blythe shrugs.

'I mean you kind of disappeared completely. Luc's been missing his manly chats with his ol' drinkin' partner.'

She's watching him, head to one side, arms folded, as if she's expecting a reply. Sweat begins to form in his armpits. It's nothing to do with you, he wants to say. Why don't you concentrate on breeding – as that's what you're so interested in these days – and *leave me alone.* He savours the viciousness of the words but doesn't speak.

He takes a cigarette out of the packet which he offers to Cecillie who declines. He lights up and pulls on it heavily. That's better. The curl of smoke heads towards Cecillie. She waves her hand around then asks, 'Do you mind if I open the window?'

She's doing it before he gets the chance to reply. 'Hey, I don't want everyone to know I'm here.'

'I'm going to tell them anyway, stupid, and I can't stand the smoke, it's making me feel ill.'

'Shit, I forgot.' He looks at the ash forming on the end. 'Do you want me to put it out?' he asks half-heartedly.

'It doesn't matter.'

He squints his eyes up against the light.

'Over here you know,' Cecillie says, 'the doctor was telling me, if you smoke less than five a day when you're pregnant, or it might be ten, anyway, they consider you a non-smoker. They even write that on your record – non-smoker.' She huffs and puffs as she pushes the window up. Wide open. He can smell the outside. Fresh. He's not sure that he likes it though, he's not sure that he likes Cecillie being here. Disturbing him, winding him up, asking questions. He blows the smoke strongly out of his nostrils away from her direction. The draught pulls it towards her. Cecillie continues. 'I've gone off it anyway and I don't want to take any chances, and Luc is being particularly un-French about it and has a fit if I so much as look at a cigarette.'

'I've cut down too,' Blythe tells her. Although it's only because he's stopped smoking when he's been in his room, thinking that the smell would give him away.

Cecillie sits down on the bed and Blythe feels a shock of intimacy as the mattress sinks beneath her weight. She shuffles back against the wall, her legs stretched out.

'It's weird but, since I got pregnant, it's like my sense of smell is incredibly sensitive. Things either smell really beautiful or really awful, nothing in between. And I get confused, too.' She pauses as she settles herself. 'It's like I can smell colours. Luc is really jealous. He says he'd kill to feel like that. He thinks that his painting would take on a new dimension.

But to be honest, I find it bloody exhausting all the time.'

'You don't look much different.'

'Don't I?' Cecillie narrows her eyes. 'Are you sure?'

'Well, you've got bigger tits and you look kind of knackered but that's about it.'

'That *is* about it.'

They laugh.

'I never thought you'd go through with it.'

'Why not?'

She looks away, and he realizes that he's upset her. He rushes on. 'At first, I mean, I didn't think you'd want to be bothered. It's great, though, for you two, I know you're really pleased and everything, which is cool.'

'It wasn't planned,' Cecillie says, rather sharply.

'No, but you've really gone for it, that's what I was meaning. Like it's the best thing that's ever happened to you.'

He looks away and studies the end of his cigarette. He can sense Cecillie watching him. 'Luc's been great. I could have easily have freaked out about it.'

Blythe nods. 'So you're staying here then, this is it – where you're stopping?'

'Yes,' she says. 'That's been the easiest part, I suppose. I never thought I'd feel like staying in one place again so soon. But it felt right here from the beginning. And with Luc, I guess it feels like home.' Cecillie stretches and yawns. 'So what have you been doing then for the last three weeks?'

'I've been out or I've been here.'

Cecillie looks surprised. 'We haven't seen you.'

Blythe shrugs. 'I've kept myself to myself. I didn't want to see anyone.'

'Bryony, you mean.'

'I needed some space.' He flicks ash onto the floor.

'Oh right, nice one. What a mature and responsible way to behave.'

'Don't start on me,' he tells her. 'I thought it would be the best thing for everyone, for Bryony, I mean.'

'Come off it,' Cecillie sneers. 'The best thing you could have done for her was piss off travelling like you said you would. That's the *least* you could have done.'

It was a bad move letting Cecillie in; it was always going to come to this – her accusing him of behaviour he's unable to defend. He pushes a fist down into the mattress and pulls hard on his cigarette. Cecillie isn't telling him anything new, for fuck's sake. It was what he'd meant to do after all. But it seems as if finishing with Bryony took all his energy, and since then he hasn't been able to dredge up the strength to leave. It sounds so fucking pathetic, he can barely believe it himself. He knows it's gutless to hide away and that he's treated Bryony like shit, and that dragging out the end makes it difficult for both of them. But knowing all that and being able to do something about it are two different things entirely.

'It's a bit of a weird way to behave, Blythe. Have you been sneaking out the back or something?' Cecillie speaks softly and he appreciates the effort she's making to be nice to him.

He nods his head. 'I've found a secret passage!' he jokes, then adds, 'There's a storage room in the basement which leads to the courtyard where the biddies hang their washing, and there's a tiny alley on the right of that.'

Cecillie shakes her head. 'I didn't even know there was a basement.'

'It's huge, with mouldy walls that are falling down and it's full of crap. Old carpets, old beds, a pram, tins of paint and piles of other stuff, god knows what, hidden under plastic sheeting, and crusty sheets and blankets. It smells pretty shitty too.'

'Is that where you'd come from when Bryony saw you?'

Blythe hesitates, stares at Cecillie.

'She said you didn't exactly look chuffed to see her.'

'It wasn't that,' he starts to say and then stops.

He hasn't been out since that encounter, not wanting to risk another scene with Bryony like the last one. The whole incident had seemed to proceed in slow motion – them spotting each other, Bryony walking towards him, her stepping close to him. He was eaten up with the need to give her a big hug but as each slow second passed, it became increasingly hard to carry out, and the tension of wondering what the fuck she was going to say to him strung him out. In the end he'd taken fright and walked off.

'So,' says Cecillie, slowly, 'you're sneaking about the place like a wanted man in a bad film, and then holing up in here, simply to avoid Bryony. What do you do in here?' she asks, then adds hurriedly, 'No, don't tell me! I don't think I want to know!'

He grins at her. 'Nothing. I'm as quiet as a mouse and as good as a monk.'

'Don't you get bored?'

He shrugs and stubs out his cigarette in a glass on the floor.

'Do you get stoned?'

'I haven't even been drinking.'

'What about going to the loo?'

Blythe nods in the direction of the sink and Cecillie pulls a face.

'For pissing only,' he explains. 'And as for shitting; well, I've become a secret shitter while you lot are all snuggled up in your beds.'

'You're gross.'

'Thank you.'

'And bloody mad.'

'Language,' Blythe says and points to Cecillie's stomach. She giggles.

'Do you know,' Blythe says, relaxing a little, 'it *isn't* boring. Because I'm lying here without any music, I can hear everything in this place. You just have to be bothered to listen. There's never five minutes without some comings and goings, somebody coughing or farting, the doors opening and closing, the stairs creaking and clattering with feet and, Jesus, the noise of the plumbing; I'm thinking of telling Monsieur B to get it looked at. It sounds like it's on the way out, the death rattle, you know.' He pauses to pick up his cigarette packet. 'I can make out your moped or Monsieur Bayard's car, clashing his fucking gears all the time. So . . .' He lights up and drags the smoke down. 'So, I have this target, right? I concentrate on following, in my mind I mean, each person as they enter the building, and try to work out who it is by the way they close the door, or walk, or cough or fart . . .'

'Or sneeze,' Cecillie says, interrupting. Blythe ignores her.

'Or pause on the stairs, or which door is opening. I mean, did you know that the Dufosses still have sex? It doesn't last long, I admit.'

He doesn't mention how Bryony's walk is the softest of everyone's. He doesn't tell her how one time when he'd heard Bryony come downstairs, he'd stood by his door to listen closer and then got a real shock when he realized that Bryony was leaning against the other side. There were only a few centimetres of wood and paint between them and the blood was pounding so loud in his ears, he was convinced it would give him away. After she'd gone out, he couldn't breathe properly. He lay on his bed and had to physically contract, expand his chest, to take in air, as if he was learning to breathe again. He erases the unpleasant memory and returns to what he was saying.

'And d'you know,' he continues. 'I reckon that if I listen like that, for a whole day and night for a month, I'd know all there is to know about all the people in this building. I'd be on intimate terms with their habits, their routines, their daily fucking monotony. I'd know who has a shit in the morning, or in the evening or who fucks who when. Everything. All the rest will be frills and decoration. You'd be amazed, Cecillie, how noisy life is.'

'You're giving me the creeps,' Cecillie says. 'Do you listen to me and Luc?'

He shakes his head. 'You're too fucking boring.'

He's lying. He couldn't stop even if he wanted to. He's tried. These last couple of days, the house noises have been more like a curse. His ears are tuned in, and he can't tune out even for a few minutes. He remembers watching a film once where a man, a scientist, struggled to achieve x-ray eyes but once he had them there was no turning back, he couldn't do anything without seeing into everything around him, he couldn't even sleep because he saw through his eyelids. In the end he was driven mad and stumbled into a church where there was this priest spouting on about if thine eyes offend thee, pluck them out. So that's what this chap did. Blood everywhere. And Blythe knows what that feels like; for there to be no escape, no relief. Cecillie might have pretty much saved him from pulling his fucking ears off!

'She still likes you, you know,' Cecillie says suddenly, catching him off-guard.

'Does she?' he asks too quickly, blushing.

Cecillie's straight on to him. 'Are you fishing for compliments?'

'I was interested to know, that's all,' he mutters. His heart starts racing along, his mouth twitches into a quick grin, which he forces into a kind of frown. He needn't have troubled because Cecillie's next words are enough to wipe the smile off anybody's stupid mug.

'But you've missed your chance now,' she tells him as she pushes herself off the bed. He stares at her, waiting. Cecillie's half-kneeling, half-standing.

'She's going. Didn't you know? Haven't you been listening hard enough?'

'Fuck off, Cecillie.' He stubs out his cigarette. 'Back to England?'

Cecillie nods. 'She didn't want anyone else to tell you but with you avoiding her and everything . . .'

'When?'

'When what?'

'When does she fucking go, of course?'

'Day after tomorrow.'

'Are you sure?'

'Of course I'm sure.'

'Shit.' Blythe shifts violently on the bed. Cecillie straightens up.

'Are you going to see her before she leaves?' she asks him.

'I don't know.'

'Maybe you really are a bastard, maybe that's all there is to it.'

'Of course I'm a bastard, I'm a fucking man, aren't I?'

'Ha, ha.'

She looks down at him. 'You know, it's a real shame you two couldn't have worked it out.'

'Yeah, I know.'

'Yeah, I know?' she mimics him, dragging each word out. 'What does *that* mean, Blythe?'

'It means goodbye, Cecillie, you're boring the fucking pants off me.'

Cecillie goes to the door.

Blythe calls after her, 'Are you going to tell Bryony?'

'Tell her what?'

He hesitates, then says, 'I'd like to see her before she goes.'

Cecillie smiles knowingly and raises an eyebrow. Blythe shows her the finger. She sticks her tongue out at him. Another stupid grin on his stupid mug.

'Expect a visit,' Cecillie says, giving him a little wave as she opens the door. 'If she's stupid enough to bother with you.'

He hears Bryony come down about an hour after Cecillie left. In that hour he's tried to think about what he would say to her, he's tried to think what he would do, but mostly he's hung out of the window in a state of sweaty panic and his brain full of Cecillie saying *she still likes you, you know. Likes*, he tells himself. Only likes.

But now Bryony's standing outside the door – this time it's

only a temporary barrier until she knocks, when he'll . . . He steels himself. His heart is leaping with excitement. He can feel it – a constant twitching in his chest.

She hasn't knocked. He puts his ear against the door. There's a rustling and under the door comes a white envelope. She's leaving him a letter. A pulse of anger runs through him. Cecillie was wrong. Bryony doesn't want to see him. He stands on the letter before it's come right through, removes his foot as she withdraws it. Perhaps she'll try knocking now.

The envelope reappears in a different place. Blythe stamps on it as if it's a cockroach to be killed. It's tugged back and he opens the door quickly.

'Cecillie said you would come.'

'Cecillie?' Bryony asks. Her eyes are wide with shock. 'I haven't seen Cecillie. I was leaving you that.' She points at the envelope on the floor which is criss-crossed with patterns from Blythe's dirty trainers. 'It kept getting stuck.'

'I stood on it.'

'Oh.'

'I thought we could talk,' Blythe says. 'Won't you come in?'

Bryony hovers in the doorway. 'I don't know,' she says. 'Perhaps you ought to just read this. It has all I want to say in it.' She bends down and picks up the envelope, dusting it off before holding it out to him. He doesn't take it. He feels his face flush.

'Don't you want to hear what *I've* got to say?' he asks, suddenly.

Bryony looks past Blythe into his room. He glances behind him but there's only a corner of his bed, a pile of his clothes in view. He looks back at her. She's still staring off into the distance, her bottom lip, held by her teeth, is quivering.

'I thought, I was only thinking, that you might not have anything to say, to me.' Bryony's voice trembles and she hangs her head.

'Oh, Bryony,' he says. 'What an absolute bastard I've been.'

Tears plop to the floor.

'Please,' he says, softly. 'Let me talk to you. I've got a lot to say and it's all grovelling. Please.'

Without looking up, she steps inside. He closes the door behind her.

He almost loses his nerve but reminds himself that he's only got this chance so he breathes deeply and says, 'You'd like that, wouldn't you? To see me grovel.' He tries to make a joke but even to him it sounds flat. His eyes seek out the shape of her lovely breasts underneath her T-shirt. Desire jabs him in the groin. Will he ever be able to hold those again?

'I'm a stupid bastard. I think you even called me that yourself.' His voice has risen unintentionally; Bryony shrinks away from him and lets out a kind of whimper which slices into his gut.

He walks over to the window, his hands jammed into his jeans pockets.

'I'm sorry, Bryony. Have I told you that I'm sorry?' He speaks to the window.

'I think you did,' she says quietly behind him. 'You said you were sorry but it wouldn't work. It would never work.'

He faces her. She's moved back to the door. 'I always was thick, wasn't I?' he says.

How fucking useless was that hour of preparation? Blythe thinks, sourly. All he did was practise saying sorry and he's already said that bit and it's not enough. It isn't worth anything; it doesn't provide an explanation, it doesn't express how badly he feels for her, and for himself. It's inadequate. He's fucking inadequate. She's squashed up against the door looking like someone's flung her against it. She flinches if he goes anywhere near her. My god, he thinks, can he go through with it? Can he risk putting her through this again? She doesn't deserve it. He doesn't deserve her. What can he say? Will she say something?

Bryony looks uncomfortable under his scrutiny; she fiddles with the letter she's still holding in her hands.

'OK,' he says. 'OK. Here goes.'

He takes hold of her hands. The envelope crackles.

'Can I come with you? Back to England? Will you let me, Bryony? Will you forgive me for being such an arsehole?'

'Come back? With me?'

'Cecillie said you're leaving. I want to come too. If you don't want anything more to do with me . . .' He peters out as he watches her start to shake her head.

'It's not that.'

'It's not? Well, I've got an uncle who lives where you're going,' he says, rushing on. 'I'm pretty sure he'd give me a bar job and then in your holidays we could travel.'

'But you hate it in England.'

'Well . . . yes, but . . .'

'I don't want . . .' she begins.

'No,' he interrupts her. He can guess that sentence. I don't want you to. He drops her hand. 'I guess I've left it too late.' Yes, he realizes that now. What a dickhead, it's too late. His mind knows it, but his heart is yet to catch up with the bad news, it's still twitching away, ever hopeful. What a dickhead. What a loser.

'No,' she cries out. 'I don't want you to do something that will make you unhappy, that's all.'

'Bryony, I was wrong,' he says softly. 'I was so fucking wrong, I don't know how to make it right.'

Bryony wipes the tears away from her face and Blythe catches a glimpse of her fingers. He takes hold of both hands and examines them. Her nails are bitten right down, mounds of pink tender skin bulge above the lines of nail. He runs his thumb across each mound: they feel very soft, very smooth. His whole body aches for these little sore fingertips.

'I love you,' he says. 'I love you.'

15

not quite true

'Do you mind if I come in?'

Because Jacques's face is in shadow and Luc's mind is elsewhere, Luc doesn't take in, at first, that it's Jacques standing at his door. It's the BMW gleaming in the sun behind his visitor which finally gives it away. Luc is both irritated at being disturbed and curious as to why Jacques is there. The curiosity quickly fizzles out when it dawns on him that the sole reason Jacques would tolerate seeing him is because of Frédérique. He sighs. He's tired of that story, he thought it was over. His heart sinks wondering what Jacques will drag up, and the temptation to simply say I'm busy and close the door is very strong. Instead he invites Jacques in and leads him into the kitchen. He watches, annoyed, as Jacques brushes off the chair before he sits down and scans the room with barely disguised disbelief.

'It's a dump isn't it?' Luc says, antagonistically.

Jacques hesitates. 'It has . . . character.'

Luc laughs. 'I've had enough of it too, I'm leaving next month.'

'You're going?'

'Round the corner. A bigger place, you know – with amenities.'

Jacques frowns. Luc explains, 'I meant a bathroom.'

'I thought that was what you meant.'

Luc picks up his bowl of coffee from the table. There's some more in the jug on the hot plate but he hesitates about offering it to Jacques. He'd rather not prolong the visit.

'I usually work in the afternoons,' he tells Jacques. It's not quite true. Afternoon working is a fairly recent attempt to regain some control over his painting. He's been unable to resume his old schedule of working first thing in the morning; it doesn't help that he's mostly at Cecillie's at that time of day. They never spend the night over here these days; it's too difficult for Cecillie if she needs the toilet in the night, and too stuffy for her to sleep well.

He comes back to his place after lunch while Cecillie has a nap, and makes an effort for a few hours.

He's found that if he sketches his room and all the things in his room, it keeps his eye in; and lately he's also been sketching the changes in Cecillie's body from memory. He's fascinated by the way her stomach has rounded – just a little – not flabbily but taut; and by the changing colour of her nipples, how they're darkening and growing – he wouldn't have believed that possible; and by her breasts which, as they've become fuller, cast crescents of purple shadow onto her ribcage. He's also excited by Cecillie's slowing down, her lazy sensuousness. He has flashes of new paintings of her, this time with pinks and reds, peaches and yellow. He'll be ready to start on them as soon as they move.

He looks forward to beginning the first one. It will be a

bright afternoon, Cecillie will be asleep in the bedroom and the apartment will be quiet. In his painting room, he'll mull over the idea as he looks out over the top of the warehouse and across the quay, then he'll open one of the windows, lean out to catch a glimpse of Sainte Catherine's spire before settling down to work.

'I'm sorry to have disturbed you,' Jacques says. Luc gets the feeling that he may have said it before but he's only been half listening.

'It wasn't going too well today as it happens,' Luc admits. 'This is my third coffee break.' He relents. 'Would you like some?'

Jacques shakes his head. 'No thanks.'

Luc sits down opposite him. 'I don't want to rush you, but I do want at least to attempt doing something productive today.'

'Of course.'

Close up, Luc is struck by how different Jacques looks to the smart-suit image he has of him. Behind all the trappings, certainly in the artificial light of the kitchen, he looks like one of the dockers. Lean, strong – like someone who boxes, bare fisted, in illegal rings. If Luc were to paint him in overalls and a vest it wouldn't look at all odd. Except, he notices, that his hands are soft and unused, his fingernails manicured.

'You said you were leaving here?' Jacques asks.

'Yes.'

'Have you ever thought about going further afield?'

Jacques says it casually, but too casually. Luc doesn't answer at first; he's unsure where Jacques is heading. Jacques goes on. 'I understand your young lady is travelling.'

'Was. Cecillie's decided to settle here.' Luc never stops feeling grateful for this: for this woman who has plunged herself into the city and keeps surfacing with treasures that make him stop dead and take a second look. And she wants to stay. He loves her for that alone.

'I see.'

Jacques's flat tone surprises Luc. He realizes that the two of them have never been on their own together. Any talking has been in the presence of others – usually, now he comes to think about it, Frédérique. He definitely prefers there to be a third person. He's finding it difficult to judge the momentum of the conversation, to catch Jacques's drift, and he's bloody sure that there's a lot of reading between the lines to be done. Jacques has come with an agenda and Luc is only slowly, very slowly, getting the picture.

He's unsure of what will follow and he's already feeling wound up by the man without there being any definite reason he can put his finger on. He sympathizes much more now with Blythe's attitude to Jacques and mentally congratulates Blythe for knocking him over, then immediately feels bad about it. The guy obviously cares for Frédérique and is going through a rough time. Perhaps, thinking generously, on a one-to-one basis he's one of those people who unintentionally comes across negatively.

'I came here to talk to you,' Jacques says.

'OK.' Get on with it, then! he wants to add.

'I need your help, or to be clearer, I need your help to help Frédérique.'

'What's wrong with Frédérique?'

Jacques hesitates. 'She's in a mess.'

Luc's surprised. It's not the impression he's had at their recent meetings. In his opinion, Frédérique's emotional, slightly odd behaviour appears to have vanished – completely. All in all, she's been pretty cool towards him and very businesslike the last couple of times that they've met – no embarrassing personal declarations, no meaningful looks, which has, in honesty, been a big relief. Meeting in the gallery, never anywhere more informal, seems to have helped the situation. Luc's been making an effort too: he keeps the conversation flowing to fill the occasional embarrassed silences: usually with chat about art in general and sometimes, when Frédérique asks him, about his own work. He steers clear of mentioning Cecillie and their plans, not because it's a sensitive subject, but because it no longer seems appropriate. He gets the feeling that Frédérique has elected to forget about that particular shared past and he's more than happy to oblige.

Luc's earlier annoyance at Jacques rises again – on Frédérique's behalf, as well as his own. There's no need to go stirring up old stuff.

'She was heading that way before you came on the scene, you have to understand. I'm not saying it's your fault but, unhappily, the timing made the situation worse. And you still being around, well, that makes life difficult. For Frédérique.' Jacques pauses. 'While you're still here the gallery won't let you go. Your work's in demand, I gather, and if they think they're onto a good thing . . .'

'She can pass me on to someone else to deal with, what's that bloke's name? Fernand. I'm not fussy . . .'

'I didn't mean . . .'

Luc interrupts again. 'I need the money. The gallery, like it or not, is what I really need right now.'

'But unless you move away, Frédérique's . . .' Jacques presses his hands on the table. 'I feel that she's at a turning point, which she can't reach because of your presence.'

Luc swallows. He wonders how much Frédérique has told Jacques about that night, but then dismisses the thought as irrelevant. Frédérique, he reminds himself, is fine. 'Don't you think you're exaggerating? She seems OK to me.'

'It costs her to keep up that appearance.'

Luc sighs. 'I don't want to be rude, but are you sure it's not you who has the problem?'

Jacques's eyes narrow, his mouth sets hard. 'Me?'

'It seems like you're the only one of us who can't forget.'

Jacques looks deflated. There's a silence before he says, 'I wish it was.'

Luc feels stifled by the conversation. This afternoon, he can predict, will now be a total washout.

'I don't want to leave,' Luc tells him.

Jacques responds quickly. 'A year or two, maybe. It needn't be for ever.'

Luc shakes his head. How can he explain to this virtual stranger that this would be a lifetime to him? An exile. He can't even begin to contemplate it.

Luc's had enough; he wants Jacques gone, immediately. He's amazed at the nerve of the man and his casual assumption that leaving the city would be easy for Luc. Does he view Luc's life, his work, everything, to be that insignificant? He's about to speak when Jacques says, 'We could come to some arrangement.'

Luc almost laughs at his coolness. And then it all comes clear. The way he reads it is that Jacques is trying to buy off a rival, get him out of the city to be sure, leaving the way clear for him. The idea of Jacques as a bare-knuckle fighter doesn't seem so far-fetched. Here's a man who bargains hard. Luc needn't waste his time feeling sorry for him.

'You're offering me money?'

'Compensation.'

Luc attempts to control the emotion in his voice. 'I have no intention of leaving, now or in the future. This is my place, where I belong. End of story. Now, if you wouldn't mind?' Jacques stands up as Luc heads to the door. I'm much taller than Jacques, Luc thinks crazily, as if sizing him up for a fight, and he nearly flinches when Jacques holds out his hand to shake.

'Will you think about it?'

'I've thought.'

'Think again?'

'OK,' Luc says, just to get rid of him. The urge to get back to his painting room is overwhelming; talking about the city has flooded his mind with images. He needs to be alone.

'You're seeing Frédérique later, aren't you?'

'Yes.'

'I'll drop by the gallery and you can give me your answer then.'

Luc laughs. 'That doesn't give me long.'

'I want this sorting out as soon as possible. If you agree to go, we can discuss arrangements later.' And with that he's out of the door and into his car before Luc can reply.

He speeds off down the street, dust clouds behind him. Luc shuts the door and slams his hand against the wood. Arrangements. The stuck-up arsehole, the prick, the . . .

He attempts to curb his anger by repeating to himself, 'Who

cares? Who cares? Who cares?' It calms him and he makes his way into his painting room where he inhales the welcoming smell.

Luc's pleased to see that there's no sign of the distressed and hopeless Frédérique that Jacques had conjured up earlier. It gives more weight to his growing belief that it's Jacques with the issues, not her. He puts it down to simple jealousy and decides not to pay any more attention to Jacques.

'There's still a lot of interest in your work,' Frédérique tells him.

'That's good but I haven't got anything new.'

'It'll come,' she says.

The softness of Frédérique's tone alerts him and he glances at her. But it's only doubt thrown up by Jacques's earlier comments. Frédérique meets his eye and smiles, briefly. She's OK, he thinks; she's looking rather good, in fact.

'I sold the two paintings of yours I owned,' she says, then blushes and adds, 'I hope you don't mind?'

He shakes his head. That couldn't be a clearer sign, he thinks, that whatever Frédérique felt for him is over. He can't recollect which ones she had, but then he gets a vivid picture of them in her hallway the morning after she . . .

That was only a month ago, but it seems much longer; a lot has happened since then. Most importantly, his baby has happened. This thought compels him to walk over to the window where he expects to see Cecillie waiting. She's there on her moped looking up at him. He waves to her and she waves back. She looks fresh and cool in a white T-shirt and denim shorts. Her face is shining up at him, her smile is big for him.

He longs to be down there with her, and for them to take off for the rest of the day.

On the other side of the road, Jacques's car comes up level with Cecillie. Jacques leans out of the car window. He can tell they're shouting across to each other but he can't hear their voices. He's startled when Frédérique speaks.

'There's just a couple of other things . . .' she's saying and he's drawn back into the room, irritated that he'll have to deal with Jacques before he can enjoy his time with Cecillie. He sits down and waits for Frédérique to continue.

She's in the middle of telling him about some changes in gallery practice when there's the sound of someone running up the stairs, there's a swift knock and then Cecillie comes in, with Jacques close behind.

Before he reaches her she asks him, out of breath, 'Luc, what's this about leaving?'

'Don't worry,' he says, shooting a look at Jacques. Trust the prick to tell her. 'I said we're not interested.'

'You said you'd think about it,' Jacques interrupts.

'Did you?' Cecillie asks.

She looks worried then relieved when Luc says, 'Only to get him to shut up and go away.'

'That's not quite true,' Jacques says.

'What's going on?' Frédérique asks.

'He paid me a visit this morning,' Luc says.

'I'll explain later,' Jacques says hurriedly, glaring at Luc. Got him back, Luc thinks, pleased, and grins. He squeezes Cecillie's hand.

'Why would we want to leave?' Cecillie says, puzzled. 'Especially with the baby and everything.'

'The baby? What baby?' Jacques asks loudly.

Frédérique interposes. 'Cecillie and Luc are expecting a baby, I'm sure I told you, Jacques.'

'I hope to god he didn't get you pregnant too.'

Frédérique's hand flies to her mouth, her eyes widen. Nobody speaks.

Cecillie turns to Jacques. 'What do you mean?' She turns to Luc when Jacques doesn't reply. 'What does he mean?'

'It's OK, Cecillie, he's got it wrong. It wasn't like that.'

'What wasn't like what?'

'Cecillie.' Frédérique steps up to her and starts to explain. 'It was a misunderstanding, that was all, it was my fault. It shouldn't have happened.'

Luc can tell by looking at Cecillie that she's appalled by Frédérique's words. She's pale and rigid; her eyes are flicking from one person to the next. Her hand has slipped away from his. He tries to take it back but she folds her arms.

'What?' she asks. 'What shouldn't have happened? I don't know what you're all talking about.'

'They spent the night together,' Jacques tells her. 'One night. So they say,' he adds.

'Jacques!'

'Arsehole,' Luc mutters.

'Luc?'

Cecillie's reaching out towards him for support but stops, her hand flaps in the air between them. He grabs it, tries to force eye contact with her. He starts talking as quickly as he can but it isn't easy, there seems to be too much detail, too little time to cram in a satisfactory explanation. 'We didn't do anything. Don't worry, I'll tell you all about it later. Frédérique turned up in the middle of the night, lost or something. His fault.' He nods viciously in Jacques's direction. 'I had to take her in.'

'One night, that's all. It was a mistake,' Frédérique says.

Cecillie starts to cry. Her distress is terrible. Luc feels himself panicking. He attempts to put his arm around her, to comfort her but she recoils, turning on him, her face red and screwed up. She spits words at him. 'Don't touch me, you fucker, don't touch me.'

'OK,' he tells her. 'OK, but let's get out of here, Cec. Come on.'

He doesn't think she's going to listen to him but she follows him out and allows him to support her as they walk down the stairs. In the street, he tries again to hold her but she shakes him off.

'Cec . . .'

'No, no, no.' She scrubs at her face. 'Leave me alone.'

'Please, Cec, let's go and get a drink.'

Cecillie licks the tears away that have dribbled on to her lips. He sees the effort it takes to control her crying. 'I don't want to have a drink with you,' she tells him, coldly. 'I don't want to be anywhere near you right now.'

She gets on her moped, fumbles around in her pocket for the keys. He stops her hand when she tries to start the engine.

'Nothing happened for Christ's sake!' he tells her. He can't understand how they've got to this point. Nothing did happen. Nothing.

'One night, that's all,' she says mimicking Frédérique.

'Yes, but . . .'

He's distracted when Cecillie waves at Frédérique's office

window. He looks up and sees Frédérique and Jacques staring down.

'Fuck you,' he shouts at them and turns back to Cecillie who has started the moped, and is already driving off. He attempts to climb on the back but it unbalances the moped which wobbles dangerously, so he gives up. Cecillie accelerates away. He watches her disappearing down the road, her hair and T-shirt blowing out behind her before he sets off running to her apartment.

Luc knows before he opens the door that Cecillie isn't at home. Her moped isn't parked outside the front and she won't have bothered to push it inside during the day. He scans the room for signs that she's been back. It doesn't seem likely. He gets a coke from the fridge and takes it out to the balcony. It's a hot, bright afternoon. It would have been nice at the beach. The street below is empty. The rest of the house is quiet. It's still siesta time. He feels tired himself but can't contemplate a nap.

He thinks of Cecillie out there somewhere, in a café probably, trying to work out everything that's gone on, trying to make sense of what she's just heard. His body cries out to reassure her, his mind is impatient to get the chance to properly explain. Once she's here with him, he knows it'll be OK. They'll laugh about it in the end.

Fucking Jacques, fuck Jacques, the biggest prick in the world, he thinks, slamming his hand down on the railings. And fuck Frédérique too. Although, he tells himself, she did at least try to set the record straight there and then. At least he'll give her that. But how wrong, how damaging, how clumsy were the words she used, and perhaps, thinking about it now, it wouldn't surprise him if it had been a calculated attempt to get her revenge.

He's kicking himself that he didn't tell Cecillie immediately. He thinks back to that day and tries to remember why. He'd only stayed for a minute at Frédérique's apartment before coming straight over here to Cecillie. They'd had a really nice afternoon – like they were planning today – at the beach and a meal in a fish restaurant. He remembers it clearly now. He hadn't wanted to spoil it. That was his excuse at the time, but he sees that he was being stupid and cowardly; he had felt awkward about bringing the subject up, he hadn't been able to pick the right moment. The truth is that he felt guilty about what happened with Frédérique, he still does feel bad about it. He feels that, somehow, he should have prevented the situation going even the little way it did.

At the sound of a moped, he looks down expectantly, but it isn't Cecillie. He puts the coke bottle on the floor and wanders back inside.

He tries to rationalize why the apartment doesn't feel like it usually does. For one, it isn't as tidy as usual. There's a sweatshirt thrown over the end of the bed, some socks in the middle of the floor and in the kitchen, he'd noticed, the sink was blocked with a soggy mass of what looked like rice. He clears this up and shoves the clothes into the canvas laundry bag. He puts some music on but turns it off again almost immediately. The track sounded grotesquely cheerful.

He decides to take a shower and unhooks a towel from the back of the door, pressing it to his face, breathing in the lemon scent of Cecillie's soap. He rummages in her toiletries bag and takes out the soap dish and bottle of shampoo.

After he's showered, he dresses and goes downstairs to see Blythe.

Bryony opens the door when he knocks.

'Luc,' she says, letting him in. 'I haven't seen you for ages.'

Luc knows from Cecillie that Bryony and Blythe have made up and that Bryony has delayed her flight home so that the couple can return to England together at the end of the month. There are plans for a big celebration before they go. Bryony's skin is pink and her hair's down and messy. Luc must have caught them at an awkward time but they seem genuinely pleased to see him and they don't make him feel uncomfortable. Bryony kisses him and Blythe gets off the bed and says loudly, 'Luc, my man, have a drink with us,' as he shakes his hand. Luc notices a couple of bottles of wine beside the bed.

'I'm not stopping,' Luc says, assessing the situation. 'I only came to ask if you've seen Cecillie?'

'This morning, not since,' Bryony tells him. 'Why?'

'We've had an argument, nothing serious,' he adds quickly. 'But she's gone off and I wondered if she'd been back here this afternoon.'

'We haven't heard her,' Bryony says. 'And we've been here all day.'

In one way that seems like good news, because it probably means she'll return soon, but on the other hand he would prefer to know whether she's calmed down since she left the gallery; he doesn't like the thought of her driving when she's so upset. It's going to be a long wait.

'Have a drink, Luc mate, you look wasted.'

Blythe and Bryony are evidently concerned and Luc's tempted to stay with them, for some company, and for their friendship. But he knows, despite their welcome, he would be in the way. They need to catch up on time together.

'Thanks, but I'll wait upstairs for her.'

'How about a drink tomorrow, OK?' Blythe suggests.

'That'll be good.'

Luc meets Monsieur Bayard coming down the stairs.

'Cecillie still not there?' he asks him, already knowing the answer.

Monsieur Bayard shakes his head. 'Can you tell her I was enquiring?'

'I will.'

Luc passes Monsieur Bayard and is unlocking the apartment door when he realizes he doesn't want to be on his own.

'Would you like a cup of coffee, Monsieur Bayard?' he calls down. 'I'm about to make one for myself.'

Monsieur Bayard is soon puffing up behind him. 'What a good idea,' he says happily. 'Another excuse for me not to get on with what I am supposed to be doing.'

'And what's that?'

'Paperwork. Taxes. I loathe this time. I always loathe this time,' he says despairingly, settling down at the kitchen table. The effort of conversation suddenly weighs heavily on Luc and he regrets inviting Monsieur B in. He can't think of any small talk.

He clatters the coffee pot and cups as he puts them on the table. He sits down. They face each other, avoiding each other's eyes, splashing sugar cubes into the cups. Monsieur Bayard clears his throat and Luc, startled, looks at him, expecting him to speak.

Monsieur Bayard hesitates, then asks, 'Is everything all right?'

Luc nods half-heartedly, then shakes his head.

'Will Cecillie be back soon?'

'I don't know.'

'Ah.'

'We've had an argument.'

'I see.'

'This guy, Jacques, you know the one who owns the bar?'

Monsieur Bayard murmurs acknowledgement and Luc continues, 'He's really fucked it up.' Luc rubs his hands across his face.

'What did he do?'

'It's a long story,' Luc says, trying to formulate it all in his head, unable to tell Monsieur Bayard that another woman spent the night in his bed and that nothing much happened except he didn't tell Cecillie, and she had to hear about it from Jacques and Frédérique, the woman who's been desperate to get together with him, the woman in fact who spent a night with him. It doesn't sound so innocent when it's put like that.

'I just want her to come home so I can put it right.'

'I'm sure she won't be long,' Monsieur Bayard says, nodding.

They sit in silence.

'Tell me, have you resumed your painting, hmmnnh? I was so sorry when Cecillie told me about the vandals.'

'I haven't done very much lately,' Luc says and feels compelled to continue. 'I'm finding it hard to concentrate. But it is coming back. Slowly.'

'It was the shock, I suppose,' Monsieur Bayard says.

Luc shrugs.

'I liked your paintings, but the one of Cecillie, I'm *so* glad it wasn't damaged. I thought it was very, how shall I put it . . .'

he taps his fingers on the table. 'Bold. Very bold. My god,' he adds, 'I thought she looked magnificent.'

Monsieur Bayard is beaming at Luc. He smiles back. 'Well, thanks, Monsieur Bayard. That means a lot.' He feels lightened, exhilarated. There's a sense of pieces locking into place and a thrill passes through him. He understands with the force of absolute truth that his path with Cecillie is key at this point. The city may return to him later, but for now he must focus on his sketches of Cecillie and their baby growing inside her. Soon, he hopes, she'll be back very soon.

16

all spoilt

Cecillie removes her trainers and squashes her feet down into the cool layers of sand. She takes off all her clothes except her knickers and walks slowly to the sea. The beach is virtually deserted with only a few families around; further up, two small children squeal and giggle as they run in and out of the waves.

She breathes the air deep into her lungs. Her limbs still feel shaky. The journey here was a nightmare. Twice she nearly lost her balance when she made a mistake with the gears and the moped jumped and jerked, and most of the time she couldn't see properly because she was crying. She should have stopped but she needed to get right away.

The shallow water is warm. She carries on forward; she wants to be cold. The colder the better, it'll make her feel clean. When the sea is up to her thighs she dives in. The icy water smacks her skin but it's a fleeting sensation as her body soon acclimatizes. She swims for a couple of minutes then floats on her back, gently moving her arms in arcs. The sun is hot on her face and she closes her eyes and watches the colours swirl on her eyelids. Blue, green, orange, black. The salt burns her lips.

She licks them; the tang of the salt on her tongue is so familiar that it reminds her of Luc. They were going to do this together she remembers, and is jolted upright by the thought. She finds herself facing out to sea with nothing but blue water and blue sky in front of her. She and Luc were going to spend the afternoon here.

If he was beside her this minute she would drag him down, push his face into the sea, keep his head under until she let him surface, spluttering. She'd demand answers to her questions. What the fuck do you think you were playing at? What the fuck did you think you were doing? Wasn't making love with me enough?

She punches the water, kicks her legs furiously trying to fill her mind with the noise. One night, they all kept saying. One night that's all, things got out of hand, that's all. That's all, that's all. Well one night of things getting out of hand is too much.

'Too much,' she shouts into the air, her chest heaving with the effort. Her heart clenches, her fists clench in response. She kicks her legs harder but soon tires and floats again, calmer now. She remembers her old trick of turning in a circle, like a Catherine wheel. She has to concentrate on which direction to move her legs and her arms and gradually she begins to turn. She gathers speed. She focuses on the sun spinning like a yellow ball above her; blinks away drops of water that splash up when she misjudges her arm movements. She continues until she feels dizzy.

She unrolls her towel and lies down to dry off. The sun prickles the water on her skin and she shivers when a breeze blows across her but she soon warms up.

She can't sleep. Instead, Frédérique's words flood her mind.

'One night, that's all. It was a mistake.' And she sees Frédérique's smile which she hadn't understood at the time but which she now recognizes as the smile of victory. Cecillie tenses her body against the coming anger. The smug bitch, the sneaky, scheming bitch. Frédérique has always wanted Luc; she's always been after him, only Cecillie didn't realize how close she'd got.

She tries to recall anything horrible that Luc's ever said about Frédérique – a pain in the arse, a control freak, neurotic and – after Frédérique turned up at Cecillie's place – deluded and obsessive. But he's also spoken favourably about her; she's articulate and engaging and knows her stuff, and of course, at the party, in front of everyone he'd said that she was beautiful.

'Christ,' she thinks. 'Christ, Christ.' She digs her hands into the sand. She can't bear to think of Luc with someone else, she can't bear it. How could he have been so weak? It's the evidence of his weakness that shocks her the most. He was so perfect, now he seems cheap. It's all spoilt, she thinks and starts to cry.

Cecillie wakes up when clouds cover the sun and the breeze picks up. She dresses quickly. She feels light-headed, a headache lurks behind her eyes and her stomach feels empty. The thought of food makes her feel sick, but she knows that the only way to ease the nausea is to eat something.

In the town, the bleached wood and pastel-painted buildings look shabby in the gentle light. There are still plenty of holidaymakers around.

She spots a phone booth and parks in front of it. Rummaging around in her pockets she comes up with a heap of change. She dials her grandmother's number.

'Gran? It's Cecillie!'

She hears the raspy breath of her grandmother as if she's rushed to the phone.

'Darling. How are you?'

'I'm fine. I've only this minute come from the beach.'

'I got your letter, sweetheart and I've sent one back. You should get it soon.'

Cecillie freezes. It had slipped her mind that she'd written to her gran about the baby. 'Have I let you down?' she asks, cautiously.

'Not if you're happy, darling. Are you happy?'

These words open the floodgates. Cecillie tries her hardest to cry silently so that she doesn't upset her grandmother. She searches for a response to the question which won't give her gran the wrong idea about Luc; that would be a kind of betrayal, she thinks, when she hasn't even listened to what he has to say.

'Cecillie, sweetheart, are you crying?' Her gran's worried voice penetrates her thoughts. 'What is it? Has something happened?'

'Everything's OK,' she manages to say, swallowing repeatedly. 'I just feel like crying sometimes.'

'That's your hormones, dear,' her grandmother says chirpily. 'It was the same for me. I'd burst into tears at the drop of a hat and I've never got over it. I cry at all those dreadful movies, you know, that really aren't worth a fig.'

Cecillie giggles. 'I cry at stories in the newspaper.'

'There we are then. That's having babies for you.'

Cecillie sniffs loudly.

'So you're OK, love?'

'Yes, I am.'

'You'll ring me won't you, if you're frightened or worried about anything?'

'Yes.'

'Promise?'

'I promise.'

'It's hot there still is it?'

'Not as much.'

'Have you told your mum and dad yet?'

'No.'

'You must, Cecillie.'

'I don't know what to say to them,' Cecillie says, bleakly. 'They won't understand and Mum will get really upset.'

'I'll talk to her.'

The phone bleeps a warning that her money has almost run out.

'Oh Gran, my money's gone.'

'It was lovely to hear from you.'

'Got to go now.'

'Don't forget to write with your new address.'

'I won't. Bye.'

'Take care, sweetheart.'

Cecillie holds the phone in her hand for a moment before replacing it. She is lucky, Cecillie thinks, with a burst of pride, to have a grandmother like her.

'Are you hungry, baby?' she asks her stomach as she sits at a table in a café across the road. She orders an orange juice and a croque-monsieur. When it arrives, she takes big mouthfuls, ignoring the cheese burning her tongue. Since she sat down, she's been impatient to get going. She's homesick, not for

England, but for her apartment and for Luc. She has to get back to him.

She takes the same route through the flat farmland between the city proper and the beach town that she travelled earlier. In the evening light, the tall vines throw giant shadows across the road. The setting sun is huge, hovering above the end of the road. It seems so big, so close that she feels that she'll ride straight in, and it'll close around her like a warm orange blanket. She shivers. The drift towards autumn is more noticeable out in the country. The evening air can be quite sharp.

Cecillie feels strange. She must have overdone it in the sun – there's a tingling heat inside her body even though she feels cold on the outside. Her stomach churns on the greasy cheese, the sticky, oily bread that she stuffed down. She takes shallow, rapid breaths to relieve the queasiness.

She turns off the road, towards a building; she needs a drink of water. As she gets nearer she hears music. It's a farm disco; she's been to one like it before. The track is rutted and each bounce sends a spurt of nausea up her throat.

The barn is steaming inside. It's packed with people, loud and hot, hot, hot. Most of the blokes are stripped to the waist and a lot of the girls are in bras, or tiny crop tops. Cecillie feels overdressed in her T-shirt. She's dizzy and struggling to breathe. She finds a free chair in a corner. Her head is full of a high humming. The bass of the music vibrates through her.

When the dizziness eases, she pushes her way towards the bar. Everyone around her is smiling and laughing. Their happiness is infectious. She feels a surge of energy: her feet step and slide in perfect rhythm, not missing the beat once as she dances along. She strips off her T-shirt and ties it around her waist. She moves her hands across her bare stomach, feeling the hot, rounded skin. 'Hello, baby,' she says. 'Are you enjoying the dance?' People smile and say hello as she moves through them but when she next looks up over the heads of the crowd the bar seems to have disappeared. She slows her pace, twists round to try and orientate herself. Sour saliva squirts into her mouth as the nausea rushes up towards her throat.

'Hey!' someone shouts, leaning in front of her face. 'Are you OK?'

The first cramp hits her like she's been punched in the stomach. She gasps and doubles up, dropping to the floor where she crouches. Feet dance around her. Everything's revolving. A man is helping her up, she can see his mouth red and gaping, but she can't make out what he's saying. She clenches her teeth together. The pain is coming in waves now. He leads her to the toilets.

'Thanks,' she manages to say. 'I'll be OK now.'

'Are you sure?'

'Yeah.'

Both loos are occupied. She sinks down against the wall as pain shoots through her. She throws up. A cold sweat covers her body, and she can feel wetness in her knickers, a thick wetness, coming out of her. She wipes her mouth on her T-shirt before pulling it on.

A girl comes out of one cubicle and helps her inside.

'Do you want me to stay?' she asks but Cecillie says no, locking the door behind her. She wants to be on her own; she knows this is going to be bad. The toilet is filthy; the floor is covered with paper, with fag ends, the toilet pan is full, piled high with paper, with shit and piss.

Cecillie scrabbles to get her shorts and knickers down. She falls back onto the toilet. Blood pours out with each cramp. She rocks to and fro; concentrates on not closing her eyes, on not fainting, on staying upright. That's all she can do.

The pains subside. She pads her knickers with toilet paper and forces herself to stand up. She looks in the pan. There's blood, but not as much as she thought; amongst it is a small lump of dark and light matter, and in the centre a tiny mauve shape. She bites her hand to stop herself screaming. Is that her baby?

'Oh my god, oh my god,' she sobs, swaying from side to side, and, finally, hearing her own voice, she feels calmer.

It seems wrong to leave the baby lying amongst everyone's shit and piss. She attempts to flush the loo but it's broken. She finds a tissue in her pocket and, her stomach heaving, scoops out the lump. She wraps more toilet paper around it, without looking.

A short distance up the farm track there's a group of stunted trees that look silver in the evening light. Cecillie walks towards them. She kneels in front of one and digs a small hollow at its base. The soil is sandy and soft. She places the tissue package in the hole and covers it over. She stands up, brushes her hands off on her shorts and heads back to the bar for her moped. She's shivering badly but the cramps have receded to a dull ache. Like period pain, only ten times worse. She has to think straight, she tells herself, as she starts the engine, and take the quickest route back. Soon, she comforts herself, soon she'll be home.

* * *

Luc is lying on Cecillie's bed when he hears a commotion down in the hallway. Doors banging, people shouting, then Monsieur Bayard calls his name, urgently. 'Luc, Luc, Luc.'

He runs down the stairs and sees Bryony, and Monsieur Bayard trying to drag Cecillie through the front door into the building.

'She's fainted,' Bryony says, her eyes wide with shock.

'Jesus Christ.'

Luc hoists her up and holds her across his chest. She's very heavy, his arms feel like they're being pulled out of their sockets, his biceps twitch in protest but he refuses any help. He carries her slowly, carefully up the stairs. Cecillie's head lolls over his shoulder. He stops on the second flight, consumed by the fear that she's dead. All he's sure about is his own heart is thumping. But then she stirs, and he rushes on up to the apartment.

Behind him he can hear voices; he can sense faces peering from half-open doors.

'Go away,' he says in his mind, gritting his teeth.

He lowers Cecillie onto the bed. Bryony appears beside him.

'Monsieur B's phoned for a doctor.'

Luc smoothes Cecillie's hair away from her face. The skin appears yellow beneath a red flush. She's very, very hot. Her arms are covered in a red rash.

Bryony disappears and returns minutes later with a bowl of warm water, a flannel and a towel. Luc's already started to undress Cecillie. Her clothes feel damp. He has the crazy idea that she must have fallen into the sea until he realizes that it's sweat. He can smell it and vomit, and a strange, sweet, iron odour.

'Can I help?' Bryony asks.

'No.'

He wipes the flannel gently across Cecillie's face, arms and chest. He covers her top half with the towel, and starts to undo her shorts. It's then that he sees the red trickle of dried blood on her thigh, and the dark stain on the crotch of her shorts.

'Oh fuck, oh fuck. She's bleeding.' His hands fly away from her. He turns to Bryony. 'Where's the fucking doctor? Get the fucking doctor.' He hears her running down the stairs.

'Cecillie, my lovely,' he whispers. 'You're going to be OK.'

His hands tremble as he unzips her shorts and pulls them down. Blood-soaked tissues come with them.

'Jesus Christ,' he says. 'Jesus fucking Christ.'

Cecillie moans, and opens her eyes.

'Luc.'

'It's OK,' he tells her. 'Shush now, you'll be OK.'

'The baby,' she says.

He cleans her up as best he can and wraps a blanket over her, kissing her gently on the head.

Monsieur Bayard ushers a tall man into the apartment. 'It's the doctor,' he whispers and leaves the room.

The doctor sits down on the bed.

'Hello,' he says. 'I'd like to ask you a few questions.'

Cecillie licks her lips and the doctor sends Luc for a drink of water. From behind the kitchen screen he can hear fragments of the doctor's questions, but nothing of Cecillie's answers.

'. . . in pain?'

'. . . it start?'

The doctor appears in the kitchen, washes his hands at the sink and takes the glass from Luc.

'I need to examine her. If you could wait here a moment.'

Luc sits down at the table, his legs are trembling and his mouth is dry. He gulps some of the water from the bottle. Please, he thinks, please let her be OK.

The doctor returns some minutes later and washes his hands again.

'I've given her some strong painkillers,' he says. 'If she starts bleeding again, she'll need to go to hospital immediately. She'll have to go tomorrow anyway, for a check-up and an injection; I've explained all of this to her. For the time being, she should get some rest. I'll come first thing in the morning to see her.'

Luc almost chokes on his question. 'And the baby?'

'I'm sorry,' says the doctor, placing his hand on Luc's shoulder. 'She's lost the baby.'

Cecillie is asleep by the time he sees the doctor out. The flush of fever has faded and left her very pale. Luc turns off the light and carefully lies down beside her.

In the morning, the doctor tells Cecillie the time of the hospital appointment he's made for her. He reassures them both that Cecillie is OK but advises her to take things very, very easy for the next few days. He repeats this several times. Very, very easy. Luc is struck by the seriousness of the doctor.

'Don't underestimate what your body's been through,' he tells Cecillie and Cecillie just stares at him.

For a while after the doctor's gone, they remain in the same position, with Cecillie lying on one side of the bed, him sitting on the other. Neither of them speaks. It's as if the magnitude of what they've been through has rendered them both mute.

Inside Luc ricochets between a crashing, wonderful relief

that Cecillie is still alive – he had stayed awake all last night, watching every breath, terrified that he was going to lose her – and a terrible emptiness when he remembers that the baby's gone. All the plans, all their talk, all their time spent together over the last few weeks has been with the baby in mind. Their baby has been the centre of their happiness and excitement.

What, he thinks, can they possibly talk about now?

Later, in the evening, Luc stands on the balcony. He rubs his face. His jaw aches from the tension of seeing Blythe and Bryony, and Monsieur Bayard.

They were all in Monsieur Bayard's lounge and it was soon apparent that they knew about the baby. Bryony hugged him, Blythe and Monsieur B shook his hand. All of them said how sorry they were.

'I'm sorry, mate.'

'I'm so sorry, Luc. Give Cec a big hug from me.'

'It's a shock, my boy, I am very sorry for you both.'

It is a shock. It's like someone switched off his life – their lives – yesterday and said, OK, now start again. And that's exactly what they'll have to do, he knows. They can't continue to remain silent, to stare into the gap of their future that their baby has left. They will have to do something.

He decides to make a coffee. He's standing with the packet in his hand and is about to call and ask Cecillie if she wants one when he catches himself in time. Cecillie hasn't been drinking it because it made her feel ill – and now she's lost the baby it's like saying, well at least you can drink coffee now. He leaves the kitchen, defeated.

Cecillie is looking at him.

'Would you like a bath?' he asks her, then adds, 'I'll help you.'

He washes her hair first. Gently rubbing in the shampoo, massaging her scalp. He kisses her on the neck, her beautiful neck; thin and vulnerable. Thank god he still has her, he thinks, as he rinses the soap off her head.

Then he begins washing her. He does her back, feeling the bumps of her spine under the sponge and gently wipes her bony shoulders. He eases her backwards so that she's lying down in the water and soaps her feet, then her legs but when he touches her stomach, she flinches and struggles to sit up. He thinks he must have hurt her, imagining how tender everything must be.

'I'm sorry,' he says. 'I didn't mean . . .'

'No,' she says, shaking her head. 'No, no.'

He's horrified to think there will be more tears. 'Cecillie . . .'

'Our baby,' she says, sobbing.

He feels his throat tighten, his chest heave. He's crying too. He feels her touch his face, fleetingly as if she's brushing away his tears.

'Don't please,' she says quietly. 'Don't please, please don't.'

But he can't stop. He hangs uselessly over the edge of the bath, as tears and snot pour out of him, while Cecillie sits in the water, her head down, her hands gripping the sponge repeating, 'please don't, please don't.'

"Would you like change?" he asked. [illegible]

He waited [illegible]

[illegible] Thank [illegible]

[illegible]

[illegible]

[illegible]

[illegible]

[illegible]

17

packed up

Blythe lies quietly. The room is filled with the grey, cool light of early morning. Bryony is breathing softly beside him. The rest of the house is quiet, thank god. Although they are less intense, the house noises still haunt him; he can't escape them completely. It's worse at night when he's the only one awake. The sounds are amplified and the slamming doors, the creaking floorboards and beds, the flushing loos and rattling pipes assault his ears.

At night too, he sometimes hears Cecillie upstairs, crying. She doesn't wake up, Luc told him the other night when they were having a few beers together; she's crying in her sleep and she says she doesn't remember her dreams. Blythe gets a brief sniff of cigarette smoke through his open window as Luc lights up on the balcony, then sometimes, like last night, he hears Luc go out and not return until the morning.

When there's silence like now, all this night-time activity feels unreal to Blythe as if he's the one that's been dreaming.

In half an hour, he and Bryony will need to get up. His stomach begins the unmistakable sensation of needing a crap.

It's his nerves. He crapped non-stop all yesterday. One time when he was heading off to the loo again, Bryony had looked at him and said, 'If it worries you that much, I don't think you should go.' She was half-joking, half-serious. Sometimes, he knows, the changes in their relationship, and the speed of those changes, worry her, as they do him, but mostly when they talk it over they calm each other and smooth out their anxieties. He's noticed that they're finding it increasingly easy to maintain an excited confidence.

Everything's going their way. Blythe's uncle's come up with the goods; he's been promised a bar job, four nights, Saturday all day. They're going to rent a flat together; Bryony's parents will help them pay for it. Bryony talks constantly about them and the rest of her family and friends. He has the impression that her parents' house is huge and always full of people. You'll love them, she says all the time, you'll love Mum, you'll love my friend Julie, you'll love Grandpa, you'll love Pookie, you'll love Sasha and Stephen and Bridget and . . . The list of people goes on, with accompanying scraps of information. Grandpa is her mum's father, a musician; Sasha is the one who stood her fiancé up at the church, then married Stephen, a cousin. Stephen, the cousin, is bald at twenty-six (not surprisingly in Blythe's opinion being married to the unpredictable Sasha), Pookie's the twelve-year-old cat, Julie's Bryony's oldest friend; they met at infant school. He feels that he knows them already and is ready to like everybody. The one thing that sets his nerves going, and his bowels start complaining just thinking about it, is the breezy way Bryony says, 'They're all looking forward to meeting you.'

He's stopped asking, 'But will *they* love *me*? Will they even *like* me?' It sounds childish and stupid. After all, if Bryony loves him, why shouldn't the whole bloody lot of them think he's fantastic, consider him some fucking eighth wonder of the fucking world!

Bryony stirs a little. He studies her. Her lips are wobbling in her sleep, like she's trying to say something, but the rest of her face is expressionless. Now that he's accepted his love for Bryony, it's mushrooming daily. Little things about her send a rush of affection straight through his body, in a beeline to his dick, giving him an instant erection and making his balls ache. That's if they're not already aching from screwing. He's never screwed so much in his life. Each time Bryony reaches out and touches him, in the middle of a conversation or to get his attention, it fills him with desire.

He fingers some of her hair which has crept onto his pillow. He'd like to wake her up and screw while she's all warm and sleepy but he knows that he should leave her asleep for as long as possible. She was pretty tired yesterday. The strain of dealing with Cecillie is taking its toll.

Yesterday Bryony helped Cecillie with her packing, the day before she spent hours talking to her, while Luc and he went out drinking. He hates seeing his friends like this, he hates the way Cecillie sits, her eyes dead, not speaking, and he hates seeing Luc battering himself against the wall of Cecillie's hurt. Fucking useless. It was horrible when Luc appealed to him, 'Why won't she let me take care of her?' Nobody understands why.

Each day Blythe and Bryony compare notes. They feel wrong doing it, but they're constantly hoping to find ways to help their friends talk to each other, to close the gap that's grown between them. It was Bryony's suggestion that Cecillie return with them for a holiday, to try and give the two of them some time to heal. Blythe's still not convinced it's the best course of action, but like Bryony said, it was the first time in ages that Cecillie actually responded to a suggestion with interest, and made a decision. But he also knows Luc feels betrayed – as though they're helping Cecillie to run out on him.

It hasn't escaped Blythe's notice that the further apart Cecillie and Luc become, the closer he and Bryony get. Thank god this isn't happening to us, they say sometimes and then feel guilty that they should feel happiness within their friends' pain. He's never felt so easy with anyone and he's sure Bryony feels the same. They keep catching themselves, grinning stupidly at each other, for no reason.

Under the sheet, the tip of his finger makes contact with the warm skin on Bryony's stomach. The warmth startles him like an electric shock travelling up his arm. He runs his finger lazily up her body. Up, gently to the hollow of her neck and back down again, right down to the fuzz of her fanny. He feels the bump, bump of the ridges of the bones on her chest, then the softer swell of her stomach, the wiry fluffiness of her fanny hair. He tries to run a line straight down to her belly button and on, cutting her in half. When this works, he does it again. Each time it's the same and it seems incredible to him that her body should be so symmetrical, so perfect.

Bryony smiles and screws up her nose. She shifts over to lie against him. He puts his arm around her.

'What time is it?' she asks, muffled into his armpit.

He tells her.

'Oh god,' she moans. 'Already.'

Outside, in the hallway Monsieur Bayard's door opens.

'Why don't you go and buy something for breakfast?' Bryony suggests.

He stands looking at their bags and rucksacks and a suitcase of Bryony's. Last night he had to finish off Bryony's packing while she was upstairs helping Cecillie do hers. He'd found stuff of Bryony's he doesn't remember ever seeing before; some clothes he's sure – and hopes – she's never worn, a giant French dictionary, a terribly old-fashioned, grown-up looking pair of shoes. He had felt a bit furtive when he made these discoveries, and hasn't mentioned them to Bryony yet. The thought that soon he'll be on daily, intimate terms with Bryony and all her belongings, amazes him.

Outside it's warmer than he expected. Last night it had rained briefly and there's a damp, boiled smell coming from the pavements. There aren't many people about; a couple of dog walkers, a few city suits. Looming ahead is the spire of the cathedral. In all the time he's been in the city, he's never been to see it, never been inside. There's a lot he hasn't done, he thinks as he looks around him, but it's too late now and, frankly, he doesn't give a shit. He's not interested in a load of old buildings. That wasn't what he was ever here for.

He turns the corner and it's as if the city's come to life; there's traffic and people and the smell of sweet baking. There's a car nearby pumping out bass and he falls into step with the beat, thrashing his feet up and down, avoiding the people, avoiding the cars, dodging in between them, smiling and nodding and swinging his arms.

Frédérique is planning her day as she showers. She has two clients to see in the morning and after that she's going to make a dent in the paperwork that's accumulated over the last few weeks and about which Fernand's been giving heavy hints since Monday. She'll work through her lunchtime, nip out in the afternoon for some shopping and pick up her dry cleaning at the same time. She turns the heat up and lets the water soak her hair and stream down her shoulders which she hunches up and then drops, draws up and drops. Steam rises in the bathroom.

She'll ring Jacques first thing then, if he agrees, she'll go straight from work to see him. If not, she'll come back home, get changed, eat something and go over to the bar later. She wants to see him at some point today. Yesterday evening Frédérique's solicitor rang with news of progress with the gallery's negotiation of the long-term lease for Jacques's ballroom which she and Fernand intend to use for permanent exhibition space. She needs to talk to Jacques about it. She'd also like to find out if there have been any developments on Jacques's purchase of a tiny premises next to the gallery which he's going to design into a small bar to capture the thirsty, hungry gallery clients.

Frédérique and Jacques are excited about these plans. On a business level, they have great hopes for the success of both enterprises, but there's also a personal element which, though unspoken, drives them on. Jacques is pushing through paperwork at a great rate and Frédérique pities her own solicitor whom she's been hounding daily about the gallery's contract. But it's important to her, and she's sure it's the same for Jacques, that they secure these links to each other's future. Frédérique's encouraged by the way her world is becoming increasingly interwoven with Jacques's in all kinds of ways. She's delighted to see the new friendship between Fernand

and Jacques developing; they've even started going to a gym together. Probably, Frédérique thinks but hasn't said, because Fernand's remarrying in a couple of month's time to Bridgit – actually his second cousin – who's nine years younger than him, and pretty fit. Bridgit's an architect and she's the one that's drawing up plans for the two buildings. And a niece of Frédérique's has recently moved to the city and started working in Jacques's bar as a waitress. She's shaping up pretty well, Jacques has said, so much so that he's thinking about training her up to take on some extra responsibilities.

These connections between them lessen Frédérique's unease about the past difficulties her relationship with Jacques has suffered. They inspire her with a confidence that a future together will exist. She still hates to remember how close they came to going their separate ways.

Frédérique shampoos her hair, massaging her scalp hard.

She's been shocked to discover that she finds Jacques attractive now in a way she never did. Her body, she thinks as she holds herself still, a bottle in her hand, her body wants him. It seems that finally her body and mind are in sync; there's an internal voice, like her own mother, telling her that Jacques is a good catch, that she should keep hold of him. At first she felt a little ashamed of these feelings but they're real and she can't ignore them, so she's learning to enjoy them. Her body tingles whenever she's with him, pictures of him naked flash up in her mind constantly as she talks. She imagines the most intimate things he could do to her, has done to her before, all the time that she's chatting. Sometimes the pictures are so vivid, she's afraid Jacques will guess about them and she flushes with embarrassment.

She turns the shower off.

Her inconstancy is amazing. The thought of Luc's body no longer moves her, although she can admire Luc in the most objective sense, has even admitted to herself that his is the best-looking body she has ever been naked with. She understands now that she was rejected simply because she was the wrong woman. She wasn't Cecillie. The emotion, the passion she felt for Luc at the time, now eludes her. 'Frivolous,' she says as she rubs her hair dry. Her body heats with a new thought of Jacques. 'Frivolous, frivolous.'

One day she was pretending that she no longer felt anything for Luc, desperately trying to maintain some equilibrium in his presence and then suddenly it was the truth. She is tremendously sorry for him and for Cecillie, about their baby. She feels it deeper than they will ever understand, more than she understands herself. When she heard, not from Luc, but from Cecillie's friend, Bryony, it upset her terribly. That evening before going to see Jacques, she went into a church, for the first time in years, and lit a candle for them. But she can't help them; they wouldn't, naturally, want her involvement; and so they are no longer as much in her mind.

Instead she's worrying about Jacques. And she knows that for the time being this is the way it's going to be. It's not always easy, it's not always happy excitement between them. It would be stupid to think that it could be. There is, of course, sometimes tension, some awkward moments that afterwards weigh heavily on Frédérique's mind. She's surprised at the strength of her tenderness towards Jacques, surprised too at how much older he seems lately. It's like having a preview of him at sixty.

The thought of this makes her look at her reflection in the bathroom mirror. This summer has aged them both.

But she can do something about that, she tells herself, reaching for her face cream and smoothing it over her face. She squeezes eye drops in to soothe her eyes, rubs lotion from another blue glass jar into her neck and collects her make-up together. She concentrates on her forehead, cheeks, nose, lips, eyes; each by turn. Foundation, mascara, eye shadow and lipstick. She ruffles her hair dry with the towel, then pulls it into place with her fingers.

She feels ready to start the day.

Luc stands in his painting room and sees dust and dirt, grease and stickiness all around him. He's filled with the dull awareness that it's Cecillie's last day. On the table in front of him is her box. It's an ordinary cardboard box. The flaps on the top are folded closed. On the side is written in yellow pen, 'Cecillie's things'. It's Bryony's handwriting. Bryony helped Cecillie pack everything up but Cecillie brought it over on her own yesterday, the box strapped to the back of her moped. He carried it in and placed it where it now sits.

'Are you still sure about moving?' he asked afterwards, as they sat in the kitchen and added, hoping that he would be able to make the arrangements if necessary, 'I could probably cancel the new lease.'

The truth is he would rather have waited to move until Cecillie returned, and they could choose another apartment together. Cecillie had looked confused at first, but then said, very firmly. 'No, don't do that.'

He'd wanted to ask her 'Why? What does that mean? Will

you definitely be coming back then? Will you be living in it with me?' He wanted to have her promise, have her write it down. Get it guaranteed. But he let the moment pass.

The box, he thinks, as he runs a finger over one corner and then down the side, is a token of her intention to return. But it's only a token. It's not a guarantee.

He's worried about her returning to England. He's afraid that she'll plunge into mourning like her mother and never resurface. He expressed his concerns as subtly as he could but he still upset her.

'I'm not like my mother,' she told him, crying again. 'How can you even think that? And anyway, it's not her I'm going to be with, it's Gran.'

But he's suspicious of her background; it's in the genes after all, isn't it? And it would explain why she's taking the miscarriage so badly. He understands that it's sad, everybody knows that. But the nurses, some of his friends, Monsieur Bayard, even Bryony – everyone is shocked at how dramatically Cecillie's reacted.

'She's so mixed up at the moment,' Bryony said when he asked her whether Cecillie had talked to her. Bryony was as puzzled as he is. 'I can only think – you know what she's like – she goes into everything with her heart full on. The baby meant such a lot to her.'

'It meant a lot to me, too,' he said, angrily. And what about me? he wants to ask anyone who'll bother to listen. Sometimes it's on the tip of his tongue to say to Cecillie, do you care about how I'm feeling?

Luc sits on the table.

Last night he dreamt about the baby. He was in this room

and he could hear a muffled banging coming from Cecillie's box. He was so relieved because he knew immediately that it was the baby. The baby had been in the box all the time! But when he opened it, there was nothing there. The dream is hard to push out of his mind. What troubles him is that he half-believes that part of the dream may be true; that if he opens the box, it will be empty. And then he'll know that Cecillie isn't coming back.

Luc jumps down from the table and wrenches open the door of the big cupboard. Inside is the portrait of Cecillie. The old Cecillie. He tries to pull the painting out. It's unwieldy and a corner of the frame keeps catching on one of the hinges. He finally angles it out and props it up against the table. He brushes the dust off his hands onto his jeans, inspects a finger which he's cut. He's breathing heavily. He feels his chest going up and down, up and down. He needs to spit, to clear his throat and his mouth which is dry and stale.

He turns the painting first to face the door, then the window, to try and get the lighting right but it's no good. It isn't the Cecillie he wants to see. The Cecillie he wants is the Cecillie of his later sketches, the pinker, softer Cecillie.

'Jesus fucking Christ.'

He pulls the sketches from the box he's packed them into. His hands are shaking. But this isn't right either. He throws the papers in the air and they fly about the room, caught in the draught from the window. He expects to feel something but the most he can muster up is a short whimper, which makes him feel melodramatic and foolish.

He wanders down to the blue café and sits on the stone wall outside. A man is shovelling coal on the deck of one of the passing barges. He sees Luc and nods, touching his cap. Luc salutes back, shouts hello. It reminds him of Cecillie waving from her balcony, her big smile, her body striped with the black railings; of her calling out to tourists on the beach; of her turning round on her moped and giving him a cheery wave goodbye. A see-you-later wave. It's hard to imagine the city without her presence.

He lies on his back and looks up at the unblemished blue sky. It's hot. One of those last-ditch hot days before the autumn really takes hold. Motors rumble, water slaps against the brick bank below him.

He surfaces from a sleep which, though short, has been deep. He sits up and as he swings his legs to dangle them over the wall, he catches sight of the drop to the river below. His head swirls, his heart pounds. Would he have ever woken if he'd just rolled over the edge and gone tumbling down? Would he have opened his eyes, not to the blue sky but to the grey water rushing towards him, perhaps to the blur of brick patterning, to the frothy wake of a ship before he was sucked down, or chopped up by a propeller? Or would he simply have gone from sleep to deeper sleep, from dreams to a dream world? That he's still alive seems suddenly incredible, miraculous. His legs are shaking, his hands too, the whole of his body feels weak and yet laughter bubbles up inside him.

He wants to celebrate this moment with someone. With Cecillie. He was wrong to let himself get talked into Cecillie going away; he needs to keep her near. He needs to tell her that, although it's hard, although it's bloody terrible at the moment, they should stay together, not be apart. He gets up and starts to run.

* * *

Cecillie lies in bed. She looks at her watch. Someone bangs the bathroom door closed and decides to get up as soon as she hears them come out.

Her rucksack catches her eye; squat and round near the door. She took the rest of her belongings over to Luc's yesterday. One box among the rest of his boxes – all packed up and ready to go to their new apartment. In the afternoon, they came back here and after they'd eaten, they lay on the bed together. Cecillie at first pretended, then really did fall asleep. It was mean – her pretence – because it was their last evening together and she knew Luc badly wanted to talk; but she hadn't been able to face the same conversation they've had a thousand times before.

Cecillie props herself up on her pillow, so that the tops of the windows from the building opposite are visible.

She knows that Luc thinks the same as everyone else; that by simply knowing you can have another baby, you should feel all hunky-dory. They even told her at the hospital the day after to wait a couple of months before trying again as if she'd been about to hop into bed with Luc the minute she got home, as if being pregnant with one baby is the same as being pregnant with any other. But it isn't. The *idea* of a baby doesn't fill the gap that this one has left. This one was real: the way it snuck up on her made her feel like it already had a mind, a personality of its own. Any others are imaginary babies. Pretend babies. Yesterday when she said that to Luc, he looked hurt, so hurt, that she has to squeeze her eyes shut to erase the memory of his face from her mind.

They seem to take it in turns upsetting each other. Not deliberately, of course. It's just that one or other of them is constantly saying or doing the wrong thing. Like when Luc puts his arms around her; she freezes, not sure whether he's offering his body to her as comfort, or whether he's wanting more from her. She wants physical contact but not like that, not making love. The idea of sex fills her with horror, but how can she tell him that, when it used to be so nice? Instead she tries to avoid getting close in case there's a horrible misunderstanding and she has to say 'no' outright.

That's why she must get away. She has to start missing him, start wanting to be with him again. She's convinced that it's the only way to clear her mind of how it all was, before. When she comes back to the city Luc will be living in a different place; he'll be a different Luc to the one she first met, she'll be a different Cecillie. It will be easier then – not easy, she knows that – to start again. And physically too, she'll be able to cope. At the moment she's so tired that right now sitting in Grandma's front room watching crap TV, eating boiled eggs and soldiers and tinned rice pudding, seems like the most perfect way to live. She's tried telling Luc this, expressing it in the gentlest, most loving way that she can, but he doesn't understand. It's hardly surprising. After she's gone on so much about how she hates home, it must be a terrible shock to him for her to be running back there now. He seems to have got it into his head that she's connecting with her mother now on some morbid level. He's wrong. Cecillie doesn't even want to see her mum and she's made her grandmother promise not to tell her that Cecillie was ever pregnant. Cecillie can't prove these feelings to Luc. To do so means admitting to him the harsher truth, which is that his love is making her feel claustrophobic.

The bathroom door is unlocked and Monsieur Pasquet shuffles the short journey back into his apartment. She has to get up. Luc will soon be here to say goodbye. They've agreed to do this in private; he's not accompanying them to the airport. That's for the best. To say a quiet goodbye, alone.

Cecillie sits with her folded clothes on the bed. Bryony washed and ironed them perfectly and she can smell their washing-powder freshness.

Cecillie looks down at her naked body and her hand steals onto her stomach. Some mornings she wakes up and thinks the baby's still there and every time she's shocked to find that her stomach's flat. It feels disloyal, unfaithful for her body to have resumed its previous shape so quickly. She wants to cover herself in front of Luc and say, it's not my fault that my body is going back to normal, it's not how I feel inside. But it isn't Luc that cares, anyway, it's her. She presses her fists hard, hard into her flesh.

When she runs over that day in her mind, she can stop it at any point and change the story. She can stop it so she doesn't ride off without Luc, she can alter it so that she doesn't go swimming, but turns round up the road and goes home. She can stop it earlier on so that she never goes up to Frédérique's office so she doesn't hear about Frédérique and Luc, she can change it way back where Jacques doesn't go to see Luc and even further back in time where Frédérique doesn't turn up at Luc's place and she and Luc don't . . . Cecillie now knows everything about that night and it no longer seems important.

The only thing that matters now is that everything happened exactly as it did. She can re-imagine it in a million different ways but the reality stays the same. The baby's gone. She lost it.

A second ago, the front door slammed and now there's someone running up the stairs. She knows that it's Luc, she knows that and she isn't dressed yet. She looks at her knickers which she's holding and squeezes them tight in her hand. Her thumb hurts. She doesn't remember how she did it, but there's a lump on the joint and a small bruise has blossomed on the skin. It makes simple things, like getting dressed, difficult. She bends it slowly, testing for the source of the pain. How would she manage if it wasn't there at all? she wonders. It would be tricky. And without a hand, a leg, an arm, an eye, it would be more complicated still. It would be much harder to manage without any of those than it will ever be to manage without the baby. A baby isn't vital. A baby doesn't make your life easier. In fact, she's pretty sure that it makes life more demanding when you've got one. It's not the same thing at all. Her heart screws up tight telling her that of course it isn't the same, you can't even begin to compare. Losing her baby is much worse than anything she can possibly imagine, it's worse than any of these things.

She looks at the door, she looks at her knickers, still in her hand and feels her thumb throbbing. She tries to compose herself, but she's trembling. She must get dressed. She must be ready for Luc. She must be ready to leave. But she can't move. She stares at the door and holds her breath. He's here now and she's not ready. 'Oh god,' she says quietly. 'Oh god, oh god.'